# THAT SPECIAL SOMETHING

ERIN MCRAE AND RACHELINE MALTESE

AVIAN30
NEW YORK, NEW YORK
2024

Avian30
New York, New York
*That Special Something* by Erin McRae and Racheline Maltese

Copyright 2024
ISBN: 978-1-946192-17-2

www.Avian30.com



First Avian30 Printing: August 2024
Printed in the USA

# Authors' Note

This book is set in a fictional small town in Maine. The particularly observant amongst you may notice the longitude and latitude coordinates we offer for it throughout are actually in the Atlantic Ocean. This was an intentional choice to avoid burdening any actual towns on the Maine coast with this particular story.

Please note that Chapter 30 contains a character vividly recollecting an accident she had on a bicycle in New York City traffic, and Chapter 34 contains a discussion of, and pushback against, eating disorder culture and normalization in the entertainment industry. Additionally, while the subject of pregnancy becomes an essential topic, no one gets pregnant in the course of the story and no one who wants to be pregnant struggles with fertility in the course of this book.

Finally, this book was a particularly challenging one for us to write, not because of its contents but because of the contents of our lives outside of it. We hope that this novel offers hope, distraction, and hilarity to anyone else facing big changes they did not plan to sign up for.

# CHAPTER 1



THE LIME SUGAR GLAZE did not want to set.

"The humidity in this town," Callie muttered as she wiped her sticky hands on her apron.

Baking, even professionally, was a continual learning curve. She had hoped to master this particular issue before her opening day, but she wasn't as fast in the kitchen as she'd once been. Fortunately, the rest of the claws were on track to be done in time, because she was absolutely, positively not postponing her big debut.

*Hidden Cove*, the TV series that filmed down the road from her bakery in the tiny town of Fly-Debate, was re-starting shooting on location now that the worst of the winter's deep freeze was over. Everyone remotely involved in Callie's purchase of the shop had been insistent she be open when that particular circus came back to town. She'd also been warned the production kept odd hours, but running her own business in coastal Maine meant she too could keep whatever hours she wanted. Opening, closing, baking...her shop and her kitchen were hers alone.

At only twenty-six, it felt like a miracle. Callie owned Maine's Original Sweet Claws, the building it was in, some of the original proprietor's classic recipes, and the boat she lived on. In her shop, no one could yell at her about their philosophy of being a chef — or subject her to their accompanying sexist nonsense. She could experiment with the flavors she wanted and do work she loved. Not bad for a culinary school dropout, even if the money to do all that had come from a personal injury settlement. But Callie wasn't going to dwell on that right now. Not on the very first day of the rest of her doughnut empire life.

Her thoughts were interrupted when a man banged in through

the shop door, sending the little bell above it jingling.

"You're back!" he exclaimed, throwing out his arms in victorious welcome.

Despite the familiarity directed at her, Callie had no idea who he was. If she'd seen him before, she definitely would have remembered. He wore, like almost everyone in Maine in early spring, a flannel shirt and jeans under an unzipped parka. But while his clothes may have been unmemorable, he was not. He was tall and broad-shouldered, with salt-and-pepper hair that was pulled back into a short ponytail. His blue eyes sparkled at her above his scruff and a classically gorgeous jawline.

Callie couldn't think of a single thing to say. In the face of a face like that — at four thirty in the morning, no less! — her customer service patter was failing her.

"Well, you're new," he amended. "At least I think you are. But the doughnuts!"

"Claws, actually." Because of course she could find the words to be pedantic about baked goods to the most attractive person she'd ever seen. "But it's okay if you call them doughnuts. They're sort of like a subspecies. And yes they're back, and yes I'm new." She stuck out her hand across the counter. "Callie."

He grabbed it and offered a friendly flash of teeth. "Beckett."

As his fingers — warm and rough and big — touched hers, Callie choked back a gasp. He had dimples, because apparently his face wasn't attractive enough already, and there was both a confidence and a sweetness to the way he looked at her. She hadn't known someone's smile could be literally breathtaking in real life, but wow, it sure could be.

She wanted to reach out and touch so much more than his hand. Which she had definitely been holding too long.

Callie fluttered her fingers out of his grasp. The rough skin around his nails tugged, ever so briefly, on the wool of her wrist warmers. It was obvious he worked hard with those hands, and she had to tamp down on her desire in order to focus on what he was saying.

"It's good to have you, ma'am," he said. "We don't get many new people in town."

She tilted her head to one side. *Ma'am?* Was she old enough to be a ma'am? Sometimes that could sound like an insult, but right now it felt charming. Polite. Maybe a little absurd, but only in the best way. Callie really needed to find more words. And to stop staring at his mouth.

She asked the first thing she could think of.

"Are you with the show?" she asked. It came out slightly strangled as she tried, desperately, to stay cool.

"Yeah," he replied, but didn't elaborate.

He glanced down for a moment, presumably to see what was in the display case, but it had the effect of making him seem bashful. Callie took a deep breath. This was her shop, and she wasn't going to let herself be intimidated by unexpected hotness.

"If you're after claws, I have two kinds ready now but the rest won't be done for at least another twenty minutes. I didn't mean to be open yet."

"Oh, shit, I am so sorry," Beckett said, looking around, presumably for the cues he had missed. "I didn't mean to barge in on you when you were closed."

"It's fine," she assured him, a laugh bubbling out of her and taking at least some of the tension between them with it. "I had the door unlocked because I assumed I'd have everything done before anyone came by. But the pressure dropped again last night, and it's wreaking havoc with my ratios. And you production people keep hours even more freakishly early than I was warned about. I do have coffee though!"

"Ah...." For a moment he seemed to flounder, but then recovered himself. "Coffee would be brilliant. And —" He looked at his watch. "Damn. Hey, if I put in an order now, will you put some claws aside for me, and I'll send a PA down to pick them up at lunch or something?"

"No problem at all," she said as she poured coffee into a to-go cup, even though she wished he'd come back for the order himself. "Worried we're gonna sell out?"

Beckett laughed. It was unexpectedly high-pitched and slightly breathy, almost like a giggle. Which wasn't, somehow, what he was supposed to sound like. Callie thought he was all the more interesting for it.

"Small town, long hours," he said easily. "You've been missed." He glanced around the shop, taking it in. "Oh, I like the mural." He waved at the half-finished painting covering most of the back wall.

"Thanks, I hired this local girl to do it. She's been on vacation with her family, though, so she didn't have time to finish before we opened."

"Emma, right?" He asked.

Callie croggled. "Yeah," she said. "How do you know Emma?"

"Like I said, small town. You're not the first business around here to have some of her art."

"She's really talented! Now. Tell me what you want and I'll put it aside." Callie wasn't convinced the demand was going to be what he imagined, but she'd take the fantasy. "We'll have key lime pie, your basic chocolate cake, glazed vanilla, glazed strawberry, and the lobsters."

Callie had thought lobster claws were the kitschiest thing she'd ever heard of when she was first investigating purchasing the shop. They were the shop's signature product, a Maine-themed, bright orange, creamsicle-flavored version of the traditional bear claw. But both Helen, the shop's former owner, and Sydney, Helen's best friend's granddaughter and Callie's own best friend, had assured her it was a reliable hit. Time would tell.

"Six of each?" Beckett said. "Actually six of each, but a dozen of the lobsters. The folks in makeup are going to want those, and it's too early in the week for doughnut violence."

"That's a more exciting first order than I was expecting. You keep coming around, and I might just sell out regularly."

"You should count on it. Now what do I owe you?" he asked as he patted himself down in an obvious effort to remember which pocket he had shoved his wallet in.

Callie tried not to laugh in sympathy and shook her head. "Whoever you send can pay when they pick 'em up. And the coffee's on me. Wouldn't want you to drop a light or something on someone if you're not fully caffeinated."

## CHAPTER 2

44°30'41.8"N 67°20'49.7"W
Temp: 39.9°F
Pressure: 30.05 inHg
Wind: 3.45 mph, S
Visibility: 9.94 mi

Beckett sipped his coffee as he walked from his car to the makeup trailer. It was excellent, strong and dark, and he felt a slight pang of conscience that he'd let the claw girl — Callie — think he was crew. But there was no gracious way to correct that kind of misapprehension.

What was he supposed to have said? *I'm more likely to get lights dropped on me than the other way around?* Humorous, yes, but that would have unfairly maligned his crew and made his own situation both obvious and awkward. Most importantly, it was not the way to make a favorable impression on a charming and attractive woman willing to banter with him at a doughnut shop before sunrise. And Beckett did like to make good impressions.

Which was why, instead of stopping at his trailer first, he went directly to makeup. They would be glad both for his promptness and the news he came bearing.

"The doughnuts are back!" Beckett announced as he pushed the door open with perhaps a tad too much enthusiasm.

Marla, one of the makeup artists, looked up at him from where she was setting out her kit and bushes for the day. "Seriously?"

"No, I'm lying about the claw shop," Beckett laughed. "What the fuck? Of course they're back." Communication at this hour of the morning and on a set rife with practical jokers was often hard.

Marla pointed at him with a powder brush. "You're telling us this and you didn't bring any?"

"Not ready yet. I'm gonna have someone go grab them at lunch."

"That's the best news I've had in a while. By the way, you're early," she said sternly.

"I know, but by the time I do anything else, it'll be time for me to be here anyway."

Marla sighed. "Fine. Sit. I see you, making a whole career out of being happy to be told what to do."

"It's a feature, not a bug." Beckett shucked off his coat and obediently sat down. "And make sure you save one for Robert." Robert was his best friend, and also the director of photography for *Hidden Cove*. "Now, he asked. "How dirty am I going to get today?"

"Absolutely fucking filthy."

"Yesss." Beckett pulled out the elastic holding his hair back and ran his hands through it. "Bring it on."

Beckett meant it, too. Hours in the makeup chair and a shoot for which most actors were perpetually coated in both real and stylized grime was not everyone's idea of a good time, but he never minded. It was a relief to be transformed into someone else for a while, and he got to zone out while Marla did her thing. The process was almost meditative, and he had dozed off in the chair more than once over the years.

But he tried not to do things like that. Being first on the call sheet meant being the chief morale officer of the production. He couldn't fix every issue that arose; nothing could make sixteen-hour days or overnight shoots less miserable no matter how good the people were. But Beckett could at least be a perpetual source of good cheer. He figured he owed that debt, not just to the show that was finally making something of his career, but to everyone else stuck here in the mud making it happen for a lot less glory.

Today they were shooting with the fishing boats down at the beach, and not even an hour in, Beckett was soaked to the hips and had scraped his knuckles on a gunwale. Still, he whistled to himself as he splashed back to shore as the scene was reset. He never had so much fun as on days like this, when filming felt less like work and more like summer camp.

Darcy, his co-star and on-screen romantic interest, was waiting primly on the rocks, a ski jacket on over her full-skirted dress. The breeze tugged at her blonde ringlets artfully, and she raised a perfectly manicured eyebrow as he took off his boots and dumped seawater out of them.

"Having fun?" she asked.

"Always." Beckett grinned up at her, sincere down to his frozen bones. "Anything for the craft."

"Speak for yourself. My socks are heated and there's nothing wrong with my craft."

Beckett laughed. "Lucky you, I'm not allowed."

"Why not?" Darcy frowned prettily.

Beckett gestured at his feet. "I just dumped a gallon of water out of my boots."

"Ah." Darcy pondered that. "Electrocution risk?"

He nodded. "Electrocution risk."

"Did you know," Darcy said. "That platypuses have electroreceptors on their bills that help them locate food?"

"No." Beckett blinked. "How did you know that?" As far as he knew, trivia about Australian fauna wasn't in Darcy's wheelhouse, but Darcy's wheelhouse was uniquely and delightfully unpredictable. Which was just one of the reasons Beckett loved working with her. She took a little getting used to — She was flighty, sometimes sharp, and had absolutely no tact. But in the years they'd been working together Beckett had come to appreciate her as an excellent actor and someone he never tired of doting on.

"I did a social media campaign for the LA zoo a while back," Darcy explained. "I got to hold a koala! They aren't soft at all, you'd think they would be. Sharks have electroreceptors too. But platypuses are also venomous."

Beckett took a second to parse through that variety of information. "I didn't know any of that."

"Yeah, they've got spurs on their hind legs! Which I guess means platypuses could be more deadly than sharks?"

"Now there's a question I've never pondered before." Beckett grinned. This sort of odd pronouncement was one of the things that made being friends with Darcy so delightful. "Think anyone's ever done a study on it?"

"We don't have either of those here, so why worry?" she asked cheerily.

Beckett stared at her. It was never the trivia that was odd so much as her bid to make it relevant to their current circumstances.

❈

The doughnuts arrived at some point while they were trying to get a shot, so Beckett didn't even hear about it until he and Darcy were finished on the beach. Which was the correct, if disappointing, order of events for getting their jobs done.

While Beckett would have liked to have tried one (or several), the crew's enthusiasm for the quickly devoured pastries made him feel a bit like a hero and as if something secretly out of whack on set had been put to rights. It was — just as talking to Callie on her first day of business had been — a good feeling.

And now, he had a brilliant excuse to go back to the shop tomorrow.

# CHAPTER 3

44°32'30.1"N 67°29'45.7"W

Temp: 48.9°F
Pressure: 30.04 inHg
Wind: 10.4 mph, S
Visibility: ≥ 10.00 mi

Callie looked up from her tablet, where she'd been going over the day's receipts, to see Emma shouldering her way through the door with her case of painting supplies.

"How'd the first morning go?" Emma asked.

"Can't complain," Callie said. "We're all sold out."

"Well done, you." Emma pulled off her knit hat, her mop of curly hair — pink, this week — over close-shaved sides springing loose. She tossed her hat, coat and bag on one of the tables, revealing an outfit that consisted of scuffed combat boots, a vintage Ramones t-shirt and, despite the spring chill, fishnet tights under jean shorts.

Emma was one of the first friends Callie had made in Fly-Debate. She'd graduated high school last year, and was now taking odd jobs with the intention of going to art school at some point.

"People liked your mural." Callie straightened up and flipped her tablet case closed.

"Awesome. They'll like it better once it's actually done. Sorry about that whole family vacay thing."

"No worries. I'd spring for the warm weather too if it were me," Callie said.

"You would," Emma said and nodded at the wrist warmers Callie had pulled up over her fingers.

Whenever the weather was cold — which meant any time the temperature fell below sixty-five degrees Fahrenheit — the pins holding together the bones in her wrist and her femur ached. Callie's collection of fingerless gloves was extensive, to say nothing of her legwarmers and fleece-lined leggings.

"Yeah, fair," she admitted.

While Emma went to work on the mural, Callie cleaned up,

prepped for the next morning's bake, and — just in case — made a plan for how she could scale up production. She worked at a table in the seating area so she could have a better view of the street outside and the cars and people going past. For a town of eight hundred people, there was more traffic than she'd expected when she first moved here. Fly-Debate, with its wonderfully absurd Puritan name, was on the coastal road that ran from Bangor farther north to Portland farther south, and plenty of tourists were willing to take the winding scenic route that ran right past her door.

Callie had spent the winter cleaning and renovating the shop, and was now confident that anyone, tourist or local or production-related, would enjoy the spot. Her dad was an electrician and also generally handy, and the know-how she'd picked up from him had been vital to her ability to do the renovations herself. The building still had its original wood floors, which she'd refinished, and tin ceilings. The ceiling had been a lot of work; water damage had meant she'd needed to sand, finish, re-paint and finally re-hang a lot of the tiles, but the result was spectacular. As a final touch she'd added new seating and lighting to make the space a satisfying mix of modern farmhouse and mid-century diner.

The early afternoon sun spilled artfully through the windows onto her table, catching motes of dust and making the wood grain glow. Callie pulled out her phone to take a picture, making sure to catch Emma in the background perched halfway up a ladder with a paintbrush in her teeth and another in her hand. She posted it to the shop's social media accounts, which had about four followers each right now, but at least it was something to do.

> Opening day ended early...never thought we'd sell out so soon! See you again tomorrow morning, Fly-Debate!

Her phone pinged almost instantly with a reply from Sydney.

> **Sydney:** You sold out already??? Congrats!!!
> **Callie:** Thanks! The lobster claws were the first to go.
> **Sydney:** Told you!
> **Callie:** Also, some of those dudes in production are hot!
> **Sydney:** Hahahah. Big men lift heavy things.
> **Callie:** I am here for it!

And they, or at least Beckett, were here for the lobster claws. Callie went back to her planning document and added another note. *Food coloring.* If people were going to keep snapping up the lobster claws like they had today, she was going to need more orange.

Another bonus of selling out early was that Callie got to drive home in the daylight. Maine was often foggy, but this afternoon the sun sparkled off the waves as she turned down the road that ran along a rocky finger of land before dipping down toward the water. Not the open Atlantic, but a sheltered inlet between two fir-draped ridges. Here was a marina, populated by fishing craft, a couple of sailboats, and the outboard motorboats the locals used to navigate between bayside towns; The water route was often faster and more direct than going around by land. There were never more than a dozen boats there at any time, the most cheerful of which was the blue houseboat moored at the end of Dock Three.

Callie parked in the marina lot, waved hello to a couple of guys working on the motor of a beautiful red lobster boat, and made her way down the dock, her shoes clomping satisfyingly on the planks.

As proud as she was of her shop, Callie was equally proud of the *Lobster Taco.* She'd bought the boat from a lesbian artist couple who'd been living on it while on sabbatical from one of their university jobs. She still didn't know what had horrified her parents more: That she had moved to Maine, that she'd bought a doughnut shop in an ancient and at times crumbling building, or that she now lived on a houseboat with a somewhat dubious name.

The boat hadn't required renovation like the shop had, but weathering her first Maine winter on it had been a genuine struggle. Keeping the plumbing unfrozen, dealing with ice damage, doing emergency propane furnace maintenance in the middle of a nor'easter…. Callie hadn't been prepared. But she had loved every minute of it. And now she, and the *Lobster Taco*, were bonded forever.

On the exterior of the boat, next to the door, was a picture of a jauntily waving lobster in a taco shell, a sailor's hat perched on its head.

"Hello, girl," she said as he let herself in, patting the claw as she always did.

The boat rocked gently beneath her feet, which she liked to think was the *Lobster Taco's* way of saying hello back. The boat wasn't large — tiny galley, built-in bench and table, a bed built against the hull with storage cabinets underneath, and a stern deck only big enough for two folding chairs — but it was more space than she'd had in her New York apartment.

And it was quiet.

Callie had never minded the rush and noise of New York or the Boston of her childhood. But after her accident and recovery, during which she'd always been surrounded by other people, the lack of human noise out here on the water was a balm. There were no parents to watch her every move, no nurses always checking on her in the unsettled night, no one to worry or scold or judge when she struggled.

She set her bag on the bench and turned to the kitchen — about four square feet of countertop, a two-burner stove, and a narrow floor-to-ceiling cabinet — to make herself a pot of tea. When it was done brewing, she took her mug out to the deck and settled into one of the chairs to watch the water and the sky.

The bay was the glittering, fragile blue of early spring, and the wind coming over the waves had a bite to it. Despite the twinges of pain that flared up, the fresh air was bracing. Callie tipped her head back to look up at the sky; the vibrant sapphire dome filled all her vision. For that moment she was free.

# CHAPTER 4

44°35'38.3"N 67°21'54.6"W
Temp: 44.1°F
Pressure: 29.93 inHg
Wind: 3.36 mph, SW
Visibility: 10.00 mi

**B**Y THE TIME HE GOT HOME from work that night Beckett's hands were aching and swollen, thanks to all the saltwater that had gotten into his scrapes. Even getting his key in the lock and turned was painful.

He dropped his gear by the front door and made a beeline for the shower. The hot water was a welcome relief on his shoulders, though it made the fresh cuts on his hands sting more as he washed them out. Once he was clean and somewhat less sore, he pulled on jeans and an old sweatshirt, ran his fingers through his hair to comb it out, and went to see about dinner.

Beckett's apartment was the walkout basement level of an old house. It was far from the standard fare for TV stars on location, but there just wasn't that much here. His little place consisted of a kitchen, bedroom, and living room, and had come with a bare minimum of furniture that he hadn't bothered to add to. It was possibly better suited to a college student than a functional adult in their forties, but it was still one of Beckett's favorite places he'd lived. There was no endless commute or glaring LA sun waiting for him outside the door. He could open a window at night and hear nothing but crickets and peepers. The occasional sounds from the family who owned the house and lived above him were a comfort rather than a nuisance, a slice of the life he hoped to have himself one day.

In the kitchen Beckett threw together a grilled cheese. While that sizzled on the stove he scrolled through his phone notifications — most of which were from his family's group chat. Beckett had three younger siblings, two siblings-in-law, and parents who knew their way around a smartphone. Which meant that hardly a day went by without a minor inundation of kid pictures, gossip, and humorous griping.

**Thomas:** Got a call from Sophie's teacher. Guess who's teaching the other kids in class how to use four-letter words in a sentence.
**Christine:** Is she actually using them correctly?
**Thomas:** (Un)fortunately, yes.
**Christine:** Tell her I'm extremely proud of her.
**Mom:** Yes! She's clearly been learning! ;)
**Christine:** Meanwhile, this is why we can't have nice things.

Attached was a photo of her and her girlfriend's cat stuck halfway up a screen door.

**Dad:** Squirrels taunting him again?
**Taylor:** How could you tell.
**Knox:** Opening night got pushed back...again...UGH.

Nothing remarkable, just the thousand and one little matters that made up everyday life and which were always either funnier or less dreadful when shared. Sometimes it felt hard to contribute himself; his life was so strange, even though his job was, in theory, just a job like any other.

**Beckett:** They reset the "Beckett made himself bleed at work" clock today.

He sent along a picture of his scraped knuckles.

**Christine:** For a change.
**Beckett:** I'll have you know I made it three whole weeks last time.

Maybe, eventually, he'd also have a family life to chitchat with them about. But for now, his petty on-set injuries would have to do.

The next morning Beckett had another five a.m. call, which was typical, followed by a half-day, which was rare and exciting. When he was done on set, the weather was still sunny and mild. A westerly breeze was invigorating rather than chilling, and the buds on the trees were beginning to swell, giving the illusion of a pale green haze spreading across the hills. Beckett couldn't resist the lure of such a pleasant day. He would drive down the coast to try his luck at a Troppy sighting.

Troppy was one of the institutions along this part of the Maine coast. He was a red-billed tropicbird which, as its name implied, lived in the tropics — or should have been doing so. Instead, this one had appeared every summer for the last twenty years two thousand miles north of anywhere it was reasonable for him to be. Like most things in Maine, the Troppy situation was a little strange, but it was as good a diversion as any.

But such a mission required provisions. Which provided an excuse to stop in at the newly reopened Sweet Claws He could get coffee, the doughnuts he hadn't gotten to try the day before and — if he was lucky and she favored him with her attention — a few words with the delightful woman who ran it.

He saw her as soon as he pulled around the corner onto the town's main road. She was perched on a ladder outside the store, paintbrush in hand, filling in the letters she'd added below the shop's name: *By Callie.* She glanced over her shoulder as Beckett pulled his car into one of the parking spaces in front of the shop and climbed out.

"Hello there," she called down with a smile that made him stop in his tracks. She was so vibrant, as if all the warmth and brightness of the spring day emanated from her being. Her hair was pulled back in a chaotic ponytail, and the sun gleamed on the coppery curls.

"Beckett, right?" she said, setting the paintbrush down. "Is the ladder in the way?" .

"Yep, that's me. And no, not at all." Beckett was thrilled she'd remembered his name. "Do you need any help?"

Her smile didn't fade, but it did take on a sly edge. "Given that I just finished, no, I'm good."

"Sorry, I didn't mean to —" Beckett was somewhat mortified. His desire to be helpful sometimes came off as patronizing and he knew it. "Seemed rude not to offer. Didn't mean you're not capable."

"Good." Callie put a hand on her hip. "Because I am immensely capable."

"So I can see."

"Excellent. Now, with that established —" Callie started down the ladder. "Give me your hand."

"Yes, ma'am." Beckett held up his hand, and Callie grabbed it.

Beckett's nerves zinged with the touch. The tips of her fingers were cool, the wool of her gloves soft. She smiled at him and held his gaze as she made her way down the ladder, like some sort of perfectly disheveled doughnut princess.

When she was two rungs from the bottom, Beckett gave in to impulse. He put his hands on her waist and lifted her the rest of the way to the ground.

"That was unexpected." Callie blinked up at him, but didn't step back.

Beckett didn't drop his hands.

"I should be mad at you," she said. "But that was very impressive, so good thing you're charming."

"I do my best." Beckett said. It was one of his go-to ways of deflecting praise, but right now he really meant it.

Callie gave a thoughtful hum, and they remained stranded there together. Beckett thought he could get used to the feeling of it. The fabric of her sweatshirt was warm under his palms. Her eyes were brown, framed with fine lashes, and as Beckett watched, Callie's gaze dipped, briefly but unmistakably, to his mouth.

A bolt of heat shot straight through him. He'd succumbed to impulse, and now every part of him wanted to draw Callie closer, tip back her head, and find out what her smile felt like against his lips. Which was not a thing to do without asking to a girl he barely knew.

Beckett made himself release her and took a step back, but he did it slowly, his eyes on hers the whole time.

"So, um," Callie said, twining her own fingers together and clasping them in front of her. "How'd everyone like the claws?"

Beckett tamped down the urge to take her hands. She didn't need to fidget in front of him. He was plenty nervous for the both of them.

"They loved them," he said enthusiastically. "In fact, they finished them before I even got to try any."

"Aww, that's a shame."

"But I've got the afternoon off and was hoping to fill up on coffee and claws I don't have to share with anyone," he said. "If you haven't sold out already?" he added hopefully.

"You're in luck. I did bigger batches today, and they've managed to make it this long. But I also have samples!" She gestured to a little table by the shop door that Beckett hadn't noticed before. "Everything I had yesterday, plus raspberry-lemon."

"Branching out already?" Beckett was impressed. And hungry.

"I had to almost double how many claws I made, it would have been boring doing the same flavors for all of those."

"You are the best kind of workaholic. I'll try the lobster claw," Beckett decided. Marla had been emphatic on the excellence of those ones in particular.

Callie handed him the pastry, tucked in a little square of parchment paper.

"Not sure being a workaholic is a virtue," she said, "but I'll take the compliment."

He popped the pastry in his mouth. It melted on his tongue, flaky layers giving way to an orange filling that was the perfect mix of citrus and cream.

"Oh my God, that's better than sex," he blurted.

Callie stared at him, a blush spreading over her face, but she held his gaze steadily.

"Thank you," she said. "By the way, you are so awkward."

Beckett laughed. Not only was she right, it felt like strange praise he was more than happy to take.

# CHAPTER 5

44°32'30.1"N 67°29'45.7"W
Temp: 66.9°F
Pressure: 30.15 inHg
Wind: 13.9 mph, NW
Visibility:  9.94 mi

THE DOUGHNUTS SOLD OUT all that first week. Then they sold out all the next. Callie had to adjust her game plan. She worked longer hours and made bigger batches. She closed during the afternoon lull to do a second bake and have a nap on the cot she'd put in her little office in the back of the shop. That way she could be ready when the production team got off work in the evenings.

Beckett was back at least a few times a week, with his soulful blue eyes and his knee-weakening smile. Every time he came in he stayed longer, not just to flirt — at which he was delightful — but to talk. They chatted about the weather — smalltalk, yes, but serious smalltalk when living so close to the ocean — Callie's experiments in claw flavors, the books they were reading.

He took a thoughtful interest in the things she expressed an interest in and seemed like he had a full internal life of his own. It was a low bar, but after some of the men she had dated when she lived in New York, a necessary one.

Beckett came into the shop one day while Callie was listening to an audiobook about shipbuilding in Maine. He returned the next day with a well-thumbed copy of a different book on the same subject, bursting with photographs and illustrations.

"In case you're interested," he said, sliding it onto the counter almost shyly.

Callie pounced, eagerly flipping through the pages and glad there was no one else in the shop who needed attending to. She'd tried to get her hands on this title before, but it had been out of print for years.

"This so cool! Where did you get this?"

He shrugged, diffident, though he seemed delighted to have pleased her.

"The show's about people and ships on the coast, late-nineteenth century. We do a lot of research. You hang onto it," he said, when she tried to give it back along with his claws and cup of coffee. "I've read it at least a dozen times."

Beckett was definitely her favorite amongst customers. Some of that was the sizable orders he often made. The gentle encouragement and ongoing enthusiasm didn't hurt either. Neither did his good looks — *his arms, oh my god his arms.* Callie didn't know how she was supposed to look at his biceps and not want to bite them. But there was also the gentle flirting. Not over the line and not with intent. It made her feel special, but it also made her feel safe.

As high as the demand for the claws were, people also appreciated eggs, bacon, sandwiches, fresh fruit, and more coffee than Callie would have thought any town could consume.

She wasn't running a restaurant. Not really. But sometimes she faked it a bit. The bizarre hours the production kept meant people were hungry and tired at times it was hard to find anything open, so she often served up whatever food she fancied making well into the night ... or morning, depending how you looked at it.

Callie was at the shop one morning long before even the early dawn of late spring when the bell over the door jingled. She emerged from the kitchen wiping her hands on her apron to find four of her regulars, Beckett included. From the volume of their chatter and laughter she suspected they were on their way out of the bar down the street rather than on their way into work.

Potentially drunk customers were never anyone's favorite, but they seemed jovial enough and Beckett's presence meant she didn't feel particularly on guard. He was so persistently determined to be a gentleman, even to the point of absurdity, that she had to assume that would carry over to his friends and their state of inebriation.

"What can I get for you boys?" she asked, putting a hand on her hip and letting her amusement at their state show.

"D'you have any coffee?" Beckett asked very seriously as he

leaned against the counter. His smile was a little slower to come and a little wider than usual, and it was possible that the counter was actively holding him up.

Callie didn't mind. She let herself bask for a moment in his gaze. He had a way of looking at her that made her feel like the only girl in the whole wide world. Somehow, even drunk at an obscene hour of the morning, that power remained.

She liked it.

"Not yet, but I can put some on," she offered.

"That would be amaaaaaaazing." Beckett seemed to drag the word on forever, possibly due to enthusiasm. Possibly because he was forgetting that words, as a general rule, needed to end.

Callie laughed. "Coffee it is."

Beckett smiled at her again. In his current state his face was softer than it usually was. Suddenly she was interested not just in his charm and how he looked whenever he appeared in her shop, but in whatever the rest of his life was like. Who was Beckett when he was at home and was he even more beautiful?

She shook her head — at him, at herself, at this whole ridiculous situation, and went to start the coffeemaker.

"What else can I get you?" she asked as she measured out grounds.

"If there's food currently ready...we would be indebted," Beckett said.

"I can do you some eggs and bacon, some fruit if you want, and if you loiter long enough, claws will happen. Although you all look like you need your sleep more," she said mock-sternly.

The men settled down on stools by Beckett at the counter and chatted amongst themselves as she threw food together and shoved water at them. Callie was on her way back into the kitchen to keep an eye on the doughnuts when one of the men called to her.

"Hey, honey, where you going?" His tone was that of all men hitting on service staff everywhere, at once too friendly, condescending and entirely infuriating.

Callie bristled, but kept her tone light as she replied. "You all want claws, someone's got to keep making them."

Next to his terrible friend, Beckett seemed to be trying to catch her eye, but she was focused on the problem at hand.

"Nooo, there's no rush, stay out here a while," the same guy cajoled. Another one of the dudes tried to shush him, but he ignored him. "Breakfast is better with a view. Chat with us."

Callie took a breath, ready to put the fear of God into the heart of this man who had made the very poor decision to make her life hard tonight.

"Matt, shut the fuck up." Beckett was still on his stool — and still holding a fork — but his shoulders had stiffened and his brow was furrowed in a positively fearsome glare.

The problem customer, Matt apparently, held up his hands. "Hey, Becks, I was just —"

"Do not finish that sentence." Beckett's voice was low, almost a growl, and while she didn't need him to defend her, Callie definitely appreciated both the concept and the execution. After all, being a good dude required action in moments such as these. Aside from her immediate problems, she was glad Beckett knew this.

Beckett's friend, on the other hand, did not know when to stop talking.

"Oh come on, you know you wanna know if the carpet matches the drapes," he pressed.

"That escalated quickly," Callie muttered to herself.

"I told you to stop and you should have listened to me before you got ugly on top of disrespectful." Beckett was still holding the fork.

The two other men in the party echoed Beckett's displeasure, but were also busy telling Beckett to calm down, like this was some sort of both-sides thing. Which it really wasn't. Callie wished she'd felt like she could expect better from people, but she didn't. Which did, at least, stave off disappointment.

"I just wanted to talk to her. You made it a thing, so I made it a thing," Matt protested.

Beckett let the fork clatter onto his plate. Callie was, honestly, a touch relieved.

"Yeah, you have a problem with me, you address that to me. She doesn't owe you conversation, and then you had to go and demonstrate why. Your behavior reflects on all of us, and all of us reflect on the production, which this town so very generously puts up with." His glare softened as he darted a glance at Callie. "I'm sorry about him, Callie. Would you like me to throw him out and if so, with or without a takeout container?"

Callie laughed at that. She reached under the counter and tossed a to-go container at Beckett, who turned to the offender.

"Food, container, now. And then you can wait for us, and the car, outside. Got it?"

"Beckssssssss. I'm just drunk," Matt whined.

"I'm drunk too, and I'm not saying shit like that to a lady who did us a favor. You can apologize before you go."

"'M sorry," Matt muttered, not meeting anyone's eyes as he slunk out.

"Thank you," Callie said crisply to the closing door. "And thank you," she said to Beckett, sincerely, "but you do keep shitty company."

He nodded, his eyes fixed on her. "It's no good when sets choose our friends. I won't let that happen again." He turned to the other two members of his party. "Next time, worry less about what I'm going to do and worry more about stopping the problem, yeah?"

There were some grumbles at that, and Callie wondered what the situation between the four of them was going to look like when and if they decided to sort it out sober.

"You all right?" Beckett asked her.

Callie shrugged. "I've dealt with worse. New York food culture definitely introduced me to more than one random drunk dude thinking he's clever."

Beckett nodded seriously, like he was, as usual, taking her words in and giving them weight.

"Doesn't mean it feels good," he said.

"No it does not."

Beckett held her gaze another moment before glancing away, that almost-shy look on his face again. "These other two are mostly harmless. We'll eat and be outta here as quick as we can."

"Okay," she said, unsure of how to extricate herself from the moment they were now in together. "I'm... gonna go... doughnut. Holler if any of you all actually need anything." She escaped into the kitchen, feeling extremely tired by things people thought it was okay to say to women in general and to redheads in particular.

"Also," Callie muttered to herself. "'Doughnut' is not a verb. What is even wrong with you?"

# CHAPTER 6



ECKETT'S ROUTE TO HIS FRIEND Robert's house the next afternoon took him right past Sweet Claws. Given how late Callie had been working, he was surprised to see the lights on. Did she ever take a day off?

Beckett pulled into one of the parking spots in front of the shop without thinking. She was surely fine after the events of the preceding night, but checking in with her would be a decent thing to do. And he could grab doughnuts for the cookout at Robert's while he was at it.

The bell over the door rang as he pushed it open, but there were no other customers and no one appeared from the kitchen. For a moment he worried he'd once more barged in when the shop wasn't open. *Because that's exactly what she needs right now.*

After a moment he caught the faint drone of audio coming from somewhere in the back of the shop. But before he could figure out what it was, he noticed a new column on the big chalkboard on which Callie wrote the menu.

*Sweet Claws Ban List,* it said, underlined twice. Beneath that it just said *Matt.*

Beckett laughed aloud.

"Oh, shit!" There was a clang and clatter from the back and Callie emerged poking at her phone with flour-covered hands. "Oh my gosh, I'm so sorry — there." The audio stopped, and she slapped the phone down on the counter. "Hi. What can I — oh, it's you. You're awake?" She sounded surprised.

"It's three in the afternoon, I don't think I get any points for that," he said, knowing he probably looked rough.

"Hungover?" Her tone was both judgmental and amused.

"Slight headache," he admitted. "Otherwise fine."

"Water will help with that. And coffee."

"I will happily take either or both. If you're offering."

"Water and coffee, coming up." Callie winked at him and turned away toward the coffee machine.

The wink was, as far as Beckett was concerned, playing dirty.

He slid onto one of the stools. "Don't stop whatever you were listening to on my account."

"Nah, it's all good." Callie was wearing bright purple wrist warmers this morning. "I just had that on to keep the other half of my brain awake so I didn't fall asleep in the middle of a batch."

"How late were you here last night? Beckett asked, before he thought better of it. "Sorry," he added quickly. "That's not actually any of my business."

"I just gave you shit about your hangover, I hereby give you permission to make small talk about my schedule." Callie gave him a bright smile over her shoulder, and for a moment Beckett couldn't breathe. "That was actually the start of my day. I'm still here!"

Beckett tamped down on the urge to give her advice or urge her to rest. He knew nothing about running a business, but the whole of his life existed in its current form because of all the years he had pushed too hard and past all good sense. If this was her mountain, he wasn't going to tell her to climb it more gently.

"Do you need anything else?" she asked, sliding a cup of coffee and a glass of water across the counter at him. "Or did you just come in to bask in my company?"

Beckett was caught out. He should have been grateful for the opportunity to admit that yes, he liked spending time around this woman he barely knew, but instead, his overwhelming urge was to hide. He stumbled over his words trying to find a suitable answer.

"Yes, I mean no. I mean, I promised my buddy I'd stop for something if you were open." A plausible lie.

Callie raised both eyebrows but didn't acknowledge the chaos words tumbling from his lips. *Thank God.*

"Better buddy than last night I hope," she said. It wasn't a question. More a giant signpost, rightfully demanding he proceed with caution.

"Yes! Yeah. Totally great. He and his wife and their kids live up the road." He nodded vaguely in the direction of Robert's house. "We're doing a cookout tonight."

"Oh, nice. Is he from *Hidden Cove* too?"

"Yeah, the director of photography. But I've known him since forever," Beckett added, feeling the need to emphasize he had friends of choice, not circumstance, who were not assholes. "We went to college together."

"Holding on to long-term connections, I approve."

"I try." His job didn't make it easy. But what were people for if not the deep web of meaning between them? Being able to make his way through art and life with the people he adored made all the hard stuff worth it, and he had a long habit of encouraging productions to hire his many absurdly talented friends whenever possible.

Not that he felt like confessing any of that. For one thing, Callie still thought he was crew, and getting into the details about his best friend or his own philosophy of making entertainment for a living was a sure way to get caught. Still, he didn't want even this casual relationship with Callie to be built entirely on lies of omission. He needed to fess up about *something*.

He hesitated only a moment before he said, "Actually that was a lie."

Callie looked confused. Which was fair. Beckett knew he was being confusing.

"You don't work with him? Your buddy?" she asked.

"Robert," he supplied. "And no, I do work with him. Sorry, I'm being weird. But about why I came in today.... I didn't promise him I'd get doughnuts. Although I do intend to bring doughnuts with me. But I stopped by because I wanted to check in with you once I was, you know, capable of having a complete and sober conversation. But I felt shy about it, so I lied, and now we're here in this mess of a conversation."

Callie, somehow, miraculously was still smiling at him. But whether the expression on her face was fond wonder or incredulity, he wasn't entirely sure.

When she said nothing, he spoke again.

"You're okay?" he asked.

"That's actually kind of sweet of you." Callie said with a quizzical laugh.

Beckett let out a relieved breath.

"I'm fine. Thanks for asking." She pointed at the chalkboard. "I started a ban list."

"I see that. I expect it'll keep everyone in line."

"I hope so."

Beckett rubbed his thumbs against the rim of his coffee cup. "This will sound weird, but anyone fucks with you, tell them you're my friend. They'll stop."

She looked him up and down. Possibly dubiously. Which felt disappointing in a way he would examine later.

"Why?" she asked. "What are you? The set's bouncer?"

Beckett shrugged. He knew his body was both fit and bulky and if he wanted to use it to intimidate, he certainly could, although that was never his first choice for solving a problem. But if something was awry, it was his job to deal with it, one way or another. On set, that meant he made sure the right people heard about problems. Callie didn't need to know that worked because he happened to be the show's star.

He cleared his throat. "Not really, but I'm more than happy to make life hard for someone messing with one of the institutions that take life around here from fantastic to sublime."

Callie laughed and put her hands on her hips. It was quite clear that he didn't intimidate her in the least, and oh, Beckett was glad of it. "I'm an institution now, am I?"

"The claws are. You probably gotta last a year out here before you count as one," he said. "Although last night surely counts as double time. You didn't have to cook for us either; you're appreciated."

She quirked her mouth and narrowed her eyes at him. "Why thank you. While unnecessary, it's always nice to be liked."

Boy, was it ever. Beckett felt his breath catch at her playfulness. And her confidence. And that hint of delighting in a challenge he could increasingly see she brought to everything she did.

By the time Beckett climbed out of his car at Robert's house, he had a list of topics he knew he needed to run by his ever-sensible best friend. But first, he was going to enjoy his visit to someone else's fairytale life.

Robert and his family lived outside of town on a few acres of land that were mostly evergreen forest, their house tucked under the eaves of the woods. Beckett took a deep breath of the pine-scented air, smiled to himself at the shouts of Dominic and

Grayson playing in the yard...and narrowly missed getting hit in the head with a frisbee.

He ducked with an undignified yelp, and the frisbee smacked harmlessly off a nearby tree.

"Grayson!" Robert yelled from the deck at his child.

"Sorry!" Grayson yelled back.

Beckett laughed. He picked up the frisbee and tossed it back across the yard. Zoe, their Labrador retriever, pelted after it eagerly.

"You okay?" Robert asked as Beckett jogged up the steps to the deck. He had a baseball cap from a decades-old project on over his dark brown hair, and he wore one of his apparently infinite collection of black hoodies.

Beckett nodded. "Didn't even clip me. And you know I take a lot worse filming."

"I do, and I worry about it," Robert said.

"That's a you problem," Beckett said genially as he knocked the side of his hand against the deck's wooden rail. It was an old argument about Beckett's propensity for risk and his not-always-stellar relationship with his body.

"Mmm," Robert said, his judgment evident. "Anyway. Julie and Dahlia are napping. Come help me with the grill."

"Can I bounce something off you?" Beckett asked once he'd helped carry all the food from the kitchen out to the deck, leaning against the deck railing while Robert flipped strips of zucchini.He and Robert could say anything to each other, but this was Beckett's way of prefacing that the conversation was important to him, involved emotions, and that he was — in one way or another — slightly embarrassed about it. Ultimately, he wasn't getting Robert's permission to bring up the issue, so much as his own.

"Go for it."

Beckett took a deep breath to sustain himself before he rushed in. "How bad of an idea is it to ask out Callie?"

"Who?" Robert looked blank.

"The girl at the doughnut shop."

Robert looked at him wearily. "I thought you'd decided not to do this anymore."

Beckett narrowed his eyes at his friend. "Define 'this.'"

"Fucking around in a tiny company town because you fall in love extremely easily and want to nest with everyone you fuck while they just want to have a good time with the handsome guy with good manners."

Beckett rocked back on his heels, feeling a little stung. He knew exactly what Robert was talking about. It just wasn't an accurate portrayal of recent or current events. That was the problem with old friends; sometimes they didn't notice you were finally growing up.

"One, I haven't fucked, or fucked around with, anyone in this town or crew," Beckett said, unable to hide that he was ruffled. In the past he'd certainly fallen too fast, too hard, and with too many expectations. But he hadn't had a relationship that was more than casual in almost a decade, and hadn't dated at all since he'd moved to Maine.  "And two, even if I had, I'm not clear how any of that makes me the bad guy."

Robert shrugged. "It doesn't. I'm just saying the blast radius on your choices — even your sweet, well-considered choices — tends to be really fucking big. Fly-Debate does not need that. Do you even know how old she is?"

"Oh, come on, that's not fair. I fuck up in all sorts of ways, but it is never that one."

Robert cut him off. "I'm not asking if it's legal, I'm asking if it's ill-advised."

"Why are you being so negative about this? She went to culinary school and owns her own business, so —"

"Because, Beckett, there's no one alive who wouldn't sleep with you if asked."

"You shot me down," Beckett pointed out. It was not a fact he remotely cared about at this point in his life except for when it was occasionally useful in arguments that featured his looks or charm.

Robert mock-glared at him. "We were nineteen, I am apparently heterosexual in the face of even your considerable charm, and, most importantly, I have been immune to your bullshit from the moment I met you. Because, dear Lord, someone has to be."

"Look," Beckett said. "I'm forty-four. All the rest of our friends and relatives are married and have kids or happily *aren't* married or happily *don't* have kids."

"Not Knox," Robert pointed out. "Who is, last you told me, living a glorious life of dissatisfaction and drama in New York, or did that change?"

"No, that did not change." Beckett shuddered. "He's not even thirty, so that does not count right now."

"You were married by twenty-five."

"And divorced by twenty-eight. Now I'm out here in the middle of nowhere in a tiny town and with a close-knit crew it would be a terrible choice to date within. Except now there's someone new, and I am fascinated and maybe want to give this a try?"

Whatever Robert was about to say in reply was interrupted by the door to the house sliding open. Robert's wife stepped out holding a sleepy-eyed, rosy-cheeked baby on her hip.

"Hi Julie. Hi Dahlia." Beckett smiled at the baby. He held out his hands. "Can I hold you?"

Dahlia, all of ten months old, leaned towards him, arms outstretched and a giant baby smile on her face. Beckett's heart melted as he took her from Julie, her little warm weight settling perfectly on his hip.

"Good luck with her," Julie said dryly. "She's in the middle of another 'leap.' Growth spurt, sleep regression, the works. Plus she hates everyone right now and she kicks. Also, her nails are really sharp. Assume she will injure you."

"What? Nooo. Not my tiniest sack of potatoes." Beckett bounced Dahlia in his arms, delighted by her giggle. Nothing in the way of fame or money or awards could equal the satisfaction of making a baby laugh.

Then, in the mystifying way of such small creatures, Dahlia suddenly shifted her weight to let him know that she was done and to put her down *right now*. She wasn't walking yet, but she could bobble around with someone holding her hands, and she made it very clear with grunts and grabbing at Beckett's fingers that she expected him to do just that.

"There's one more thing," Beckett said, as Dahlia steered him, hunched over to reach her little hands, around the deck. "And Julie, I want your read on this, too."

"Beckett wants to ask out the doughnut girl," Robert explained to her.

Julie's eyebrows shot up. "Callie?"

"You know her?" Beckett asked, hopeful. He wanted his

friends' advice, but he also wanted to talk about Callie to someone who had actually seen her and what had entranced him so thoroughly.

"We've chatted a few times," Julie said. "Dahlia and I stop in most days when we take a walk in town. She's a pistol."

"She is that." Beckett chuckled. "So last night, me and a couple of the guys went out for drinks and then ended up at Sweet Claws...." He briefly relayed what had happened, both what Matt had done and how he himself had responded. "And I don't want it to be like...I 'rescued' her and am now asking her out. Even though I'm pretty sure she was at least potentially interested before — I don't want her to think I've got any leverage over her for that. Also, I'm pretty sure she has no idea who I am."

"Jesus, Beckett." Robert laughed. "Where to even start with you."

"Oh! One more question."

"I shudder to inquire," Robert said dryly.

"Do I tell production what Matt did?"

"That's a good one." Robert looked thoughtful.

"What do you think?" Julie asked.

"I think yes, because that kind of behavior isn't acceptable, but I also think telling them to fire him because he hassled the woman I'm into is a bad look."

"It's not a great one," Julie acknowledged. "But you can give them the data, which is the right thing to do, and then they can choose what to do with that data. Knowing them, they will also make the right choice."

"True," Beckett acknowledged. "But what about Callie?"

"I imagine you'd have to talk to Callie about that," Robert said. "Use those big blue eyes of yours."

"I'll do my best," Beckett said. "If I can ever manage to run into her when she's not actively working."

On top of everything else, he was not going to ask anyone out while they were standing behind their own counter.

# Chapter 7



ONE OF CALLIE'S TWO STAND MIXERS stopped working right in the middle of her prep for the day. As far as she could tell once she'd asked the internet, it was something with the mixer's unappetizingly named worm gear. But she couldn't be sure.

With only one mixer working, the rest of the prep was a pain in the ass. She could, and did, mix some of the extra dough by hand, but that was slow going. Emma came in partway through the morning to work on the mural but abandoned her paintbrushes to pitch in. But even with her help, kneading took forever and was also murder on Callie's hands.

Despite her preoccupation with baking-related problems, Callie kept looking for the flash of graying ponytail that would presage the arrival of Beckett, but he never appeared. That was probably for the best; it wasn't like she'd have any time to actually talk to him.

Once the few claws they managed to put together sold out, Callie scribbled a sign and put it on the door: *Sorry, pastry sold out due to unforeseen stand mixer gremlins.*

She left Emma to her painting and the peace of an empty shop and headed for the nearest big box hardware store. Which, because Fly-Debate was barely a speck along the coastline, was forty-five minutes away.

When she arrived, she was not expecting an entire wall of worm gears. Several of which seemed to almost match what she wanted and none of which were the same — possibly proprietary — model as the one she was replacing. That wasn't necessarily a problem. Sometimes the internet was wrong. Sometimes manufacturers wanted nothing so much as for you to send the machine back to them for an overpriced repair. But however this got solved, Callie needed to solve it today.

She was ten minutes into alternately staring at the gears, examining their teeth, and checking the sizes against the instructions she had open on her phone when someone called her name. Softly.

She glanced up to see none other than Beckett, who was holding a tube of caulk in one hand and a box of ant traps in the other.

That, Callie thought, looked like an entirely bad day. Her heart thumped. He, as ever, looked like a dream. A messy, slightly disheveled dream, who also thought her doughnuts were better than sex.

"Hi!" she chirped, failing to make her voice as normal as possible against the nervous desire he provoked in her. She cleared her throat.

Beckett tilted his head curiously at her. His gray-streaked hair, not pulled back for once, brushed the top of his shoulders. It was tousled — not even artfully, it was just a mess, like he'd just come in from dealing with wind and waves.

The slightly disheveled look was devastatingly attractive on him.

"Hi," she said again, in what she hoped, desperately, a more normal tone. "Yes, I do exist outside of Sweet Claws."

"I was beginning to wonder," he said. His voice was low, intimate almost, as he offered her the smile that continued to unhinge her every time he used it.

*Goddammit*, Callie thought in general frustration at every facet of his being.

"I mean, barely," she made herself say, nodding towards the shelves in front of her. "I'm trying to repair one of my mixers."

"D'you need any help?"

Callie narrowed her eyes at him, her instinctive self-sufficiency and general competence at war with the fact that she liked him, and, well, his fucking smile. "I'm going to take that the right way, but no, unless you have a sudden expertise in worm gears. In which case I would not be above accepting help." She hesitated. She was a little desperate. "Do you?"

He laughed, all dimples and sparkling blue eyes. "I know there aren't actual worms involved, but that sounds unappealing," he said.

"I had the same thought myself."

"And sadly no, though if I did I would be at your service."

His voice dropped ever so slightly on the word *service*, and between that and his earnest desire to be useful in her time of need something fluttered low in Callie's stomach.

She wanted to say something, anything, in reply, but she was terrified she might blurt something absurd and far too revelatory. Like, *you can be at my service anytime you damn well want.*

Callie cleared her throat again, hoping her burning cheeks didn't mean she was blushing visibly. "What are you in for?" she asked.

Beckett held up the caulk, either oblivious to her internal struggle or just gracious. "Ants." Then he held up the ant traps. "Ants that need to die."

Callie grimaced, as if she hadn't already deduced that was the problem. But small talk with beautiful men had basic requirements.

"Oh, that's a pain," she said. "Can't you just call whoever you're renting from?"

He sighed and glanced off to the side. "Production says I'm not supposed to, which, fine, but it's weird since they live upstairs and it's not that big of a deal. But I also don't want to just knock on the door. They've got young kids and don't need to spend time scrambling to deal with something I can do myself."

Callie was touched by his consideration. "Fair. There's a reason I've been running the shop all by my lonesome. Last week it was a short in a light switch. This week it's the mixer. Next week, it'll surely be something else. If it's not, I'll finally redo the shelves in the back so they actually make sense."

If she was going to babble, at least it was about construction projects and not the way she wanted to put her hands in his hair and see what he did when she pulled on it. Because she was having suspicions.

"That's a lot of work all by yourself. I'm impressed."

"You should be," she said, regaining her footing. He was gorgeous and charming but this was where she was comfortable. "I'm very impressive. Also my dad's an electrician; you pick stuff up."

Beckett opened his mouth as if to say something, hesitated, then closed it again. She was reminded of the time he'd lied about why he'd come to the shop only to confess to it half a second later.

"Spit it out," she prodded.

Beckett blinked at her, evidently startled that whatever was going on in his head was obvious on his face.

"Do you want to go out sometime?" he blurted.

"What?" Callie was sure her lust-addled brain had misheard.

"I just — sorry if I'm presuming." Beckett glanced down at the things in his hands and then back up to her. Callie wasn't sure if he was taking in the absurdity of the moment or being bashful, but he gave her a look from under his eyelashes that would, she was sure, fell anyone.

He took a deep breath. "What I mean is… would you want to go out with me? We could get drinks or coffee somewhere. Eat food that you didn't have to make. Have a conversation where I wasn't interrupting you trying to get something done."

"I'm usually trying to get something done," she said, slowly, to buy herself time. Had he just asked her out? Or was this all just that trick her post-accident brain sometimes pulled, where it refused to move at the same speed as whatever was happening around her? Too fast, too slow, and definitely in its own, sometimes faulty, world.

Sure, he was hot, they had a great flirtation going on, and she had been wanting to sample some of that for a while. But that had been a fantasy. One that didn't involve having to navigate another person in the midst of her own hard-won independence. Did she really want to close the gap between how much she wanted to put her hands on him and how much being vulnerable, physically or emotionally, just hadn't been her thing in a long time?

Beckett shifted slightly from foot to foot as he fidgeted with the edge of the box containing the ant traps. However quietly, he seemed on the verge of unraveling, which was fascinating.

"You mean like a date?" she asked, needing, somehow, to confirm the obvious.

"Yeah."

Callie wanted to devour him and his silver fox disaster energy, but none of her hesitation was ebbing as the awkward seconds ticked by between them. She liked Beckett; she didn't want him to turn out to be disappointing, and she definitely didn't want to have to be mad at him later. A date could lead to both of those things… and a lot of awkwardness in the small town in which they both lived.

"Can I get back to you?" she asked slowly. "Because I am not averse to the idea and we both know you're cute, but it has been a hot minute since I dated anybody. And honestly I haven't been thinking about dating at all."

<pre>
44°35'38.3"N 67°21'54.6"W
           Temp: 75.9°F
   Pressure: 29.89 inHg
       Wind: 9.17 mph, S
     Visibility: 9.94 mi
</pre>

"**I** have done an asinine thing, my soon-to-be-dead, six-legged non-friends."

Beckett crouched on the floor of his living room, carefully piping caulk along the crack in the paneling by the sliding glass door through which the ants were making their way.

He had a vast number of tasks he needed to be attending to in his limited free time that were not dealing with the ants that had, over the last few weeks, progressed from occasional emissaries from the outside world to full-fledged columns of miniature thieving soldiers. The ants, however, were not sensitive to the demands of his life — from learning his lines, which were proving particularly vexing this week, to fretting about the impulse that had caused him to ask Callie out. He'd been gracious, he hoped, and so had she, but *maybe* was the worst of all possible answers. Now they were set in a mutual and peculiar limbo.

Normally, Beckett would complain to Robert about this sort of thing, but Robert had his own responsibilities on a day off and had also made his opinion on the situation quite clear. Beckett's siblings, were he to call or text one of them, would just tease him mercilessly. Which meant, as far as complaining and advice went, the ants were all that was left.

"I was going to ask out the extremely attractive, very funny, smarter-than-me woman who runs the doughnut shop," he explained to them. "At some point. After I'd been open about what my job is. In a careful, considered, well-planned moment that respected her time and her boundaries and most of all, *her*. Because I really try not to be the dick who asks waiters or baristas for their numbers."

The ants, scurrying about in eager confusion, made no reply.

"But you know what I did instead?" Beckett continued. "I asked her out in the middle of a hardware store. Where she was just trying to get parts to fix something. And instead of laughing in my face, which I would have deserved, or saying no, which would have been fine and ended all our mutual suffering, she asked to think about it."

Beckett wondered what Callie was doing right now. She was probably back at the shop fixing that mixer. He could imagine her frown of concentration, see the way her forehead crinkled as she focused on the task in front of her. It was an appealing picture. And, as he now lived in dread of ever going back to Sweet Claws, one that he was appalled at himself for dwelling on.

"If I don't it will be weird," he muttered. "And if I do it will also be weird, but at least won't look like I'm ignoring her or freaking out. Even though I am definitely freaking out."

His phone, all the way on the other side of the apartment, rang as if in reply. He startled, and his heart sped up before he remembered that Callie didn't even have his number. Whatever this was, it wasn't her. Beckett swore, set down the caulk and pushed himself to his feet to retrieve it.

His agent's name was on the screen. Despite his career being in a very comfortable — and thoroughly booked — place, he answered with a trepidation born of too many years waiting for the phone calls that would make or break his career.

"Beckett," his agent said cheerily. "How are you this fine afternoon?"

"Dealing with an ant infestation," Beckett said. "What's up?"

"I wanted to check in with you. And put a bug in your ear. No pun intended."

Beckett laughed awkwardly. One of the best things about having had a steady gig these last few years had been talking to his agent as little as possible. "Oh?"

"Have you thought about what you want to do next?" The question was obviously leading. But it also made no sense.

"Next?" Beckett repeated blankly. "After what?"

His agent chuckled, as if Beckett had been making a joke. "After *Hidden Cove*."

"But we're still going." Beckett felt like he was missing something. "We're in the middle of a season, the ratings are entirely solid, the network likes us... hell, the network trusts us! What could be better than that? This isn't ending anytime soon."

"You always want to be prepared, and a man should always plan his future at the height of his power," his agent said patiently. "Look, just consider these check-in calls me earning my percentage."

Beckett gave a nervous laugh. He didn't want to deal with this, but that was fair. The guy made a good chunk of change off him every year by doing essentially nothing at this point. He couldn't fault him for trying to be useful.

"Plus, you'll be back here sooner or later."

Beckett felt himself physically pull back from his phone. By *here* his agent meant LA, and while he had said it casually, it felt ominous. Like a threat. Beckett's heart plummeted at the very idea even though, with any luck, that prospect was still years away. LA was bad for him and both could not be a part of his career going forward and was, eventually, going to be an unavoidable part of his career going forward.

But that was a set of feelings he was not going to share with his agent, not now, not today. He began to pace back and forth across his apartment. "Let's worry about later, later, yeah?"

His agent sighed. "One day, later is going to be now, and no one wants to scramble. I know this show is exhausting and you need your shooting hiatus downtime. But we need to start thinking about life beyond this show, build your brand as something other than a grungy historical boat guy with a secret. So this is me telling you that it's time to think about what new and juicy and different thing you want to do next so we can start making it happen."

Beckett was somewhat offended at the implied slight on his work ethic. Last year, over the break between seasons, he'd done a play in New York. The year before that, he'd done an independent movie that had been neither a commercial nor a critical success, but had been fun and let him stretch his acting muscles beyond a character he knew so well.

"I always work during our big shooting breaks." He didn't even try to keep his tone friendly.

"I know," his agent said. "But you haven't been doing anything that's gonna actually lead anywhere."

*Because I don't need it to,* Beckett thought viciously. He felt secure. Both in his now and in the belief that jobs would come knocking whenever he was finally, regretfully, freed up from *Hidden Cove.*

But his agent went on. "To that end, I've set up some meetings in New York for you. It's in a couple of weeks, and it shouldn't mess with your shooting schedule."

"I don't —"

"Beckett. Just to talk to people. You could maybe do some theater, some TV guest star stuff.... There's a lot of options that even involve me being sensitive to your feelings about the left coast; you can get over that next month. But I know you have friends and family in the city, so just go down for a few days, and we can all feel like we've done what we've needed to do."

As much as Beckett didn't want to admit it — this whole conversation was still giving him a bad feeling — the logic he was being presented with was sound.

"Yeah, I guess we can make that happen," he said, dragging a hand through his hair. He didn't want to argue lest it prolong this call.

"Good," his agent said, evidently satisfied but clearly not pleased. "I'll leave you to your scintillating evening. Good luck with the ants."

Beckett ended the call and leaned back against the counter. He felt stumped. What had just happened? And why? Obviously, no project lasted forever, but until this moment Beckett had felt like they were still on the upswing with *Hidden Cove*, closer to the beginning than the end. And he still very much hoped that was so. But something about that call was just wrong, and he was suddenly acutely aware of what he just didn't know. It filled him with dread; the last thing he wanted to do was to leave Maine.

"I'll give you this," he said out loud to the ants, as he pushed himself upright and went back to caulking. "You're better than living in LA."

# CHAPTER 9

44°32'30.1"N  67°29'45.7"W
Temp: 71.1°F
Pressure: 29.90 inHg
Wind: 4.60 mph, SE
Visibility: ≥ 10.00 mi

FIXING A STAND MIXER WAS unexpectedly disgusting. Callie had done enough work on the shop and her boat — and learned enough from her dad — that she knew that plenty of renovation and repair work was, by its nature, vile. But she'd had no idea there would be a pint of grease built up around the damaged gear or that, despite her best efforts, it would get all over her. Her t-shirt and jeans were ruined, and her handwarmers were an absolute disaster.

This was all Beckett's fault. She would have been able to concentrate if he hadn't asked her out in the middle of a hardware store.

"This bullshit had better work," she muttered as she plugged the machine back in and hit the on switch.

The mixer made an irritable and oddly thoughtful sound. Callie held her breath as the paddle slowly began to turn. After a moment the odd sound wound down as the machine finally decided to fully cooperate, the paddle spinning merrily.

"Thank you!" Callie slumped back onto her stool. If she had to decide how to respond to Beckett's offer, at least she didn't have to face that decision without an adequate claw supply for her customers.

She leaned forward again and flipped off the mixer, which came to an obedient stop with a minimum of terrible sound effects. Satisfied, she picked up her phone. There was one easy way out of having to make a decision about dating someone before she felt emotionally ready, and that was finding some objectionable piece of information about them online.

*Beckett*, she typed into the search bar, before realizing she didn't know his last name. *Callie, there's a reason to say no right there, you don't even know this guy.* But she sighed, and in the spirit of due diligence added *Hidden Cove* to her search in case that actually helped something useful turn up.

Did it ever.

Callie stared at her phone in disbelief, then shook her head in something like horror. "What the fuck," she said aloud. And then, again, because that didn't quite serve to express her feelings, *"What! The! Fuck!"*

She'd been assuming Beckett was crew. Somewhat senior, surely, based on his age, confidence, and easy way with people. She had referred to him as crew. To his face, more than once, and he'd never disabused her of the idea or even given a flicker of protest.

But he wasn't crew. Of course he wasn't. Looking the way he did, she should have known.

The first hit on Google was the headline *Beckett Brown at Emmys - red carpet photos*. Followed by a lot of stills from the goddamn show they were filming down the goddamn street and that she still hadn't watched because TV made her sad and restless.

Callie hastily clicked on them. There was no mistaking that face. That hair. That smile. Or the fact that, in several stills from the show, he was shirtless and just as stunningly fit as she had suspected. Actually, more so. There was a whole lot of man hiding under all that Maine flannel.

And there were so many pictures. From publicity photos to fan-made image sets. Because Beckett didn't just work on *Hidden Cove*.

He was the star.

"Fuck!" Callie shouted to the empty kitchen.

This changed everything. Which would have been a marginally more helpful sentiment if she'd had any idea how she felt about this mess before this moment.

She looked back at her phone and that soft, slightly smug smile of his.

"Why the fuck didn't you tell me?" Callie asked quietly.

One scenario, probably the best, was that there was no good way to casually drop that information, and he was either going to tell her on the date or was relying on her googling and freaking out exactly like she was now.

"Okay. Deep breath, Callie. You have to at least read his bio."

She remained half in hope of finding something terrible about him, which would make her decision easier. But it quickly became apparent that there was nothing to find. A steady series of appearances of greater or lesser importance in a string of TV shows and movies she hadn't seen and sometimes hadn't even heard of. A handful of stage performances. No major dating drama. An ex-wife; she and Beckett had divorced about the same time Callie had started high school. No kids, from the marriage or otherwise. He was from Seattle, which explained why he had the Maine vibe without the Maine accent, but didn't explain why he sometimes called her *ma'am*. Callie definitely thought of that as a Southern thing, but maybe he did it simply because he was old.

*Is forty-four old?*

Beckett was eighteen years older than her. Which, on its own, wasn't necessarily a problem, but combined with the fact that he was a celebrity, might not be great. If he was the kind of guy who made a habit of using his position to date women nearly two decades younger than him, that was something Callie wanted nothing to do with. If he wasn't.... then the age difference was just one more thing about this that was awkward and messy. Which wasn't necessarily bad. Sometimes, life was just like that.

But she did need to know which one it was before she got in too deep. Or at all. The internet had no definitive information, which left her with two choices. The first, to ask Beckett himself, wasn't necessarily going to give her reliable data.

The second was to ask Sydney. Her family was from Fly-Debate. She was familiar with the *Hidden Cove* production from long before Callie had ever arrived in Maine. More than that, Callie's friendship with her had been one of the few that had survived both her accident and her departure from culinary school. Callie trusted her read on things and her willingness to say and deal with unpleasant things.

She glanced at the clock; it was early evening. Sydney might be in the middle of a shift at the restaurant she worked at, but there was a chance this was a day off. Regardless, Callie had to at least try. What if Beckett came in for coffee and a claw tomorrow morning and she had nothing resembling an answer, just an ongoing case of shock?

She grabbed her phone off the counter and scrolled through her contacts to make the call with near violence.

"Question for you," Callie said as soon as her friend picked up. "Have you got a minute?"

"Yeah? Is everything okay?" Sydney sounded concerned.

"It's fine," Callie said. And for a moment that steadied her. This situation was ridiculous, but it wasn't life or death. "But somebody asked me out and I need to know if you've got any dirt on them."

"That's a good problem to have at least. But why would I know?"

"Because this is the tiniest of towns and your family knows everyone."

"True. Which makes this kind of concerning," Sydney pointed out. "I can't think of anyone there I'd recommend as a dating option. Who is it?"

"A customer." Callie knew it sounded terrible. Dudes who hit on waitstaff were the worst and usually on a power trip.

"Ew," Sydney said. "At least I assume that's ew?"

"Could be. Hell, should be. But it doesn't feel gross? He's lovely, actually,"

Callie was more than aware that she still wasn't giving Sydney the information she needed to offer any sort of useful insight. But she also knew that once she uttered this aloud, there'd be no taking it back. The situation with Beckett would be real and subject to the whims and opinions of a world outside her own head. And that world would care — a lot. Fame kind of had that effect; she'd seen it with the cults of personality around celebrity chefs.

"So what's the problem?" Sydney asked.

Callie tucked the phone between her shoulder and her ear and began gathering the tools she'd been using to repair the mixer. She had far too much nervous energy to be able to sit still.

"For one, I haven't been on a date since before the accident."

"All the more reason to get back on the horse now. If that's what you want to do and this person doesn't suck.

"Yeah. Well. Also. He's a lot older than me," Callie said, wondering when her tongue was going to find its courage.

"How much older?"

Callie tore off a piece of shop towel to wipe the grease off her screwdriver. "He's forty-four."

There was a pause on the other end of the line. "That's not quite within the half-plus-seven rule."

"Believe me, I know." *Also not the biggest red flag here.*

"You're twenty-six. If the government thinks you're an adult, and you think you're an adult, and he thinks you're an adult — what-the-fuck-ever? If you're comfortable, nobody gets to judge. Is he cute? He's not a gold-digger, is he? Like, after your doughnut fortune."

Callie wanted to laugh at that, but was wound too tightly for the sound to actually escape her body. Instead, she balled up the greasy paper towel and threw it into the garbage.

"I do not have a doughnut fortune, and he likely neither wants it, nor needs it," she said. Her mind flashed to the smile Beckett always had for her; he would, she hoped, laugh at this conversation. "More like... he's successful in his career and absolutely, devastatingly good looking?"

"Nothing you're saying here sounds like a problem," Sydney said. "Although it's Fly-Debate and if someone by that description existed, I'd know it."

Callie could hear the frown in her friend's voice and knew that now was the time to share the whole truth if she was ever going to share it at all.

"We're getting to that. You know the thing where seventy-five percent of the shop's customer base works for *Hidden Cove*?"

"Ohhhhhhh," Sydney said.

"He works on the show."

"Cast or crew?"

Callie gave a panicky laugh. "See, that, that question right there, that's the question I should have asked the first day he told me he was with the production."

"You didn't ask?"

"No. Why would I have asked? That's a weird question to ask a total stranger!" Callie gestured wildly; It didn't matter that Sydney couldn't see her. "I don't watch the show, I don't know anything about TV, and like, I am here for claws, not — whatever is going on down at the beach."

"So he's an actor," Sydney said slowly.

Callie pressed her hand to her forehead and considered a full-on swoon. This conversation definitely called for dramatics.

"Yes, Sydney. Yes, he's an actor, which I only realized last night when I googled him because he asked me out in a hardware store. I told him I would think about it because I had exactly zero plans to date anyone out here!"

"Who the fuck is it?" Sydney demanded.

*Deep breaths, Callie.* "Beckett Brown."

There was a long pause on the other end of the line. Finally, Sydney spoke. Her voice sounded slightly strangled. "You are shitting me."

"I am not."

"This is some vengeful prank for encouraging you to buy a doughnut shop in the ass middle of nowhere."

Callie gave a choked laugh that was possibly teetering on a sob. "Not a prank."

"Beckett Brown asked you out?"

"Uh huh."

"And you thought he was crew?!"

"Crew can be hot too! I don't know." Callie couldn't help but be defensive about how long it had taken her to realize the shape of the situation she was in. "He wears a lot of flannel and his hair is always a disaster. I thought he was just, like, a guy, coming in for claws before work like everybody else!"

"This is beyond fucked up." Sydney sounded awed by the prospect.

"You think? This is why I need dirt." Callie desperately needed Sydney to have dirt. She did not feel capable of being able to make a decision otherwise.

"I'm afraid I can't help you there." Callie could practically hear Sydney shaking her head.

"Why not?" she demanded.

"There is no dirt to be had. Beckett Brown is a perfect angel and a beautiful specimen of a man."

Callie scoffed. "I'll give you that second part, but nobody is an angel."

"Maybe. But a whole lot of the internet calls him Saint Beckett of Hollywood."

"Noooooooooo." Callie gave a disbelieving laugh. He always seemed lovely, but she had always assumed there was a catch lurking somewhere. There was no way he was just...that good. Was there? "That's so awkward. Also why?"

"Apparently he's a dream on set. Anyone who joined the crew on *Hidden Cove* after the first season is like 'yeah I only moved to Maine to work on this project because Beckett was involved and he's great.' He is legendarily gracious to fans and went to bat, very publicly, to make sure his female costar was making as much as he was. He is so good, he is basically unattainable. Except for, it would seem, the thing where he's asked you out."

Callie stared at the counter in front of her without seeing it. She felt, again, like the world was slightly out of whack. When Beckett had first asked her out the only problem she'd had was whether she wanted to dip her feet back in the dating pool. But now the question was whether she wanted to date someone considerably older, with a high-profile job, and who a lot of people had a lot of expectations of.

Except when it came to doughnuts, other people's expectations were not exactly Callie's thing.

# CHAPTER 10

44°32'30.1"N 67°29'45.7"W
Temp: 48.0°F
Pressure: 30.32 inHg
Wind: 5.75 mph, SE
Visibility: ≥ 10.00 mi

B ECKETT DECIDED TO WAIT a couple of days before he went back to Sweet Claws. The suspense was threatening to kill him, but Callie deserved time to make up her mind and the last thing he wanted was for her to feel like he was pressuring her. But he also didn't want to look cold or like he was ghosting her. So today was the day. Even if he didn't quite know what they'd say to each other if she didn't volunteer an answer.

"You, Beckett, have fucked this up before it's even started," he muttered to himself as he parked in front of the shop.

The bell over the door jingled as he pushed it open. The place was empty of other customers, at least for the moment. Hopefully that meant they wouldn't have to navigate around having an audience. A glance at the ban board told him his name wasn't on it. Which didn't mean Callie was going to say yes, but hopefully at least meant she didn't hate him.

Beckett waited by the counter and tried not to fidget. After a moment, Callie stepped out from the shop's backroom, carrying a tray of fresh lobster claws. Her hair, while tied up, was working hard to escape its confines. Beckett could relate. And while he was sure it was annoying to her, she looked beautiful.

Her eyes, sparkling and amused, snapped immediately to his.

"Why, good morning, Saint Beckett." Her tone of voice suggested the idea of a murder might have crossed her mind over the past few days. Beckett didn't blame her at all. There was nothing on this earth he could say to that terrible nickname, nor did he have an excuse for not telling her what she now so obviously knew.

"Ah?" he said weakly.

Callie set the tray on the counter. "Hell of a thing to spring on a girl."

47

"Technically I didn't spring it on you because I didn't tell you." Beckett bit his lip apologetically.

"Really?" She put a hand on her hip and stared at him hard. "That's your defense?"

"No?" he squeaked.

Callie started moving the lobster claws onto their rack in the display case without breaking eye contact. "I assumed you were crew. To your face. More than once. And you did not correct me."

"There was no way to do that without looking like a jackass." Beckett hadn't walked into the store feeling particularly confident and he definitely wasn't getting more so now. Still, he wanted to defend his honor at least a little

"And letting me find out on my own doesn't have the same result?" Callie challenged. "Did you think I wasn't going to google?"

"No, I didn't," he admitted. "Although maybe I hoped. Maybe you don't like the internet."

Callie kept stacking doughnuts in the display case. "Only a man twenty years older than me could possibly say that with a straight face."

"Is it twenty?" Beckett twisted his hands together. This was distressing. "I was hoping it wouldn't be that much."

"Congrats, it's only eighteen, but that's another thing," she said as she placed the last claw and slid the case closed.

"Yeah." He waited to see if she would articulate further objection to the legitimately not-fantastic age difference, but it was clear she hadn't quite found words for that aspect of the mess he had created. Maybe she didn't need to. He could definitely imagine what she was thinking.

*Might as well cut to the chase.* "So how much of a dealbreaker am I?"

"Haven't decided yet," Callie told him bluntly. "How old are the women you usually date?"

That she was even asking felt like a miracle. "Youngest was around your age but that was about six years ago —"

"Yeah, so not as bad," she pointed out.

"At least I'm aware?" he offered. "I told myself that you own your own business. You're obviously an adult and a very competent one at that."

Callie blew right past his attempt to explain his logic. "And the oldest?" she prompted.

Beckett tried not to smile in relief. At least he'd get an A on this one. "Almost fifty. When I was thirty."

She blinked at him.

"Yeah. He hoped he didn't sound too defensive. "Not the answer you were expecting."

"No," she said quizzically. "What was up with that?"

"Nothing." Beckett shrugged. "Why should the age gap in one direction be unpleasantly expected and in the other, shocking?"

Callie sighed. "Because we live in the world and the world is terrible?"

"Can I acknowledge your point without endorsing it?" Beckett asked before returning to her question. "Great chemistry. We laughed a lot. It was the right thing at the right time. We're still friends, and she's one of my go-tos for advice when my life feels like a bucket of chaos."

"Huh." Callie looked like she wanted to hear the whole story, and with that, Beckett wanted her to say yes, more than ever. To be with someone who wanted all of him — public and private — that was the dream, wasn't it?

It was time for one last roll of the die.

"Look," he said. "I may be the opposite of anything you're looking for, but I'm not whatever cliché you're expecting. Like I said the other day, I will cheerfully accept a no, I'm a big boy. But I feel like we both might enjoy you letting me fail on my own terms?"

"What if I don't say no?" Callie asked slyly.

Beckett reminded himself to keep breathing. "Then we go for dinner and, I don't know, maybe a movie, and I drop you off at your front porch?"

Callie narrowed her eyes slightly. "I don't have a porch. The nearest movie theater is over an hour away, and this town doesn't even have a restaurant."

"I can figure out a restaurant," Beckett assured her. *I can figure out anything you want. Even how to be less of a disaster.*

"Nothing fancy. Something that doesn't involve lobster and does involve actual spices."

Beckett tried not to smile too broadly, and was delighted to see an answering blush spread across Callie's cheeks.

"So is that a yes?" he asked.

She slumped dramatically. "Apparently." Callie dragged the word out. "Don't make me regret it, okay?"

Beckett pressed his hand to his heart. "On my honor," he said. He meant it, too.

"That," Callie said, "is slightly dramatic."

"Do you like it?" Beckett hoped she liked it. Or at least liked laughing at him. There were not, in light of his current professional success, nearly enough people who gave him shit.

She glanced pointedly at the clock on the wall. "Don't you have somewhere to be?"

Beckett followed her gaze and cursed. He was going to be late if he didn't leave right now — and leaving was the last thing he wanted to do. He wanted to stay here and bask in Callie's smile and her wit and her demands for his honesty. He also wanted to pull out his phone and find her a restaurant she would enjoy.

"I'll see you later?" he asked.

"You'd better," she shot back, with a smile that verged on the edge of wicked and made it even harder to leave. "First, though." She pushed her phone across the counter at him. "Give me your number."

He picked up the phone. She'd already made a contact entry for him: It said *Saint Beckett*.

# CHAPTER 11

44°16'43.7"N 68°09'10.7"W
Temp: 69.1°F
Pressure: 29.81 inHg
Wind: 13.8 mph, S
Visibility: ≥ 10.00 mi

Callie hadn't been on a date in years, not since before the accident. Even those dates had been with people her own age who weren't as attractive or successful as Beckett. On paper, that made her feel like she needed to step up her game, but in her gut, she knew that was silly. She had, without even trying, already captured his attention. She just had to be exactly who she already was. After all, he may have had to audition for his life here in Maine, but she hadn't, and she wasn't about to start now.

That said, she still wanted to wear something cute, because she liked looking cute. There was minimal storage space on the *Lobster Taco* for anything she didn't need on a daily basis, but she finally found, at the bottom of her storage trunk, a couple of dresses that didn't have any baking or repair-related stains on them.

On date day she brought the green daisy-splashed dress and her favorite boots that made her walk like she was queen of the universe with her to the shop...along with, of course, fleece-lined leggings and a sweater. To keep avoiding stains she waited to change until after she'd closed down in the late afternoon. When she emerged from changing in the back room, she found that Emma had let herself into the shop with her keys and was spreading her painting supplies out on one of the tables.

"Oh hey, I like the boots," Emma said, glancing over at her. "I should be able to finish today, assuming the last coat dried like it was supposed to."

"Awesome!" Callie was excited for the mural to be complete, but also felt a slight pang. She would miss Emma's company in the shop. "Let me know if you need anything."

Callie went to work doing a last tidy behind the counter. Beckett had offered to pick her up at her house, but she was not ready to introduce him to the boat yet. She didn't want him to react to it the way nearly everyone else in her life had — with a mix of bafflement and concern.

She had just finished sweeping out the seating area when Beckett appeared at the door, his hand raised to knock at the glass. Callie went to let him in.

"Sorry, sir." She leaned on her broom. "We're closed for the day."

"Well shit," he said. "There go my evening plans."

As Callie laughed, Emma, perched on a ladder painting the very top corner of the mural, glanced over her shoulder. "Hey, Beckett."

Beckett greeted her with similar low-key familiarity. "Hey Emma. How's it going?"

"Can't complain. How's Darcy?"

"Still bizarre, still heterosexual, and still too old for you," Beckett said fondly.

Callie watched, baffled, as they continued to banter back and forth about whoever Darcy was.

"One day," Emma sighed. "I will accidentally fall into an alternate universe where two of those things are not true. She can keep the bizarre."

Callie must have looked as confused as she felt, because Emma said, "Darcy's his costar. On *Hidden Cove*?"

"Emma has a crush," Beckett added.

Callie stared at her, then at Beckett, then back at Emma in consternation. "Am I the only person in town who didn't know who he was?"

"Um, going to go with yes," Emma said.

Callie caught Beckett's eye and they shared a mutually abashed smile. Despite her initial hesitance, she was struck by how happy this turn of events had made her. She got to go on a date with that face, which to her still wasn't famous, just special.

The rest of him wasn't bad either. His shirt sleeves were pushed up to his elbows, showing off his forearms, and his jeans, which had the distressed look that came from wear, not a factory, cupped his... everything... perfectly. His hair, half-pulled back, was freshly combed and slightly damp. *Just out of the shower*, Callie's brain supplied oh-so-helpfully, before she clamped down firmly on that train of thought.

He still didn't look like those red-carpet photos she had found, and for that she was relieved. But he had put in effort, and the distance was smaller. If he had always appeared to her like this, she might have suspected he was an actor sooner. But Beckett in the flesh was all texture and nerves, and that was far more attractive than the obviously planned faux casualness of those photos.

As Beckett's eyes flicked over her in turn, it took Callie a second to realize she hadn't been caught staring; he was checking her out just as much as she had him. She felt her cheeks go pink.

"You look lovely," he said.

"Thank you. So do you." Was that an odd thing to say to a man? Callie decided she didn't care. She liked the word and she liked it for him. "Now give me two seconds to reset the chairs."

"Can I help?" Beckett asked eagerly.

Callie grabbed a chair off one of the tables and set it back on the floor. "Are you trying to make a good impression?"

"Maybe. Is it working?"

"Too early to say. But do keep up the good job."

Callie stepped past him to grab another chair, and as she did she caught a glimpse of his face as he turned his head to follow her. He was glowing with delight.

*I did that*, she thought. *I made him look that way.*

Callie didn't usually bother driving all the way to Bar Harbor or Bangor; most of what she needed, she could either get in Fly-Debate or down the road in Sealport. So this drive, out towards Bar Harbor for Korean food, felt like an adventure, and that was before she considered the man doing the driving.

They fell into pleasant conversation as easily as they'd done in the shop, except now she didn't have to keep one eye on the door or the mixers or the oven. They could just talk without interruptions or commerce. All she had to watch was Beckett's face as he talked and his hands — immense and somewhat battered — as he drove.

Once they reached the town, Beckett navigated with familiar ease and parked on a side street. From there they walked to the restaurant, which turned out to be a delightful hole-in-the-wall serving all sorts of Korean dishes Callie hadn't had since leaving New York.

They got pajeon — hers with beef and his with pork and kimchi — and took their food outside to eat at one of the picnic tables behind the restaurant. They had a spectacular view over the ocean, white wisps of mist dancing like ghosts over the blue summer waves. The breeze tugged at their hair and seagulls stalked nearby, clearly waiting for their moment.

"So I'm curious," Beckett asked as he tore off another section of his pancake. "How'd you end up in Maine? You're not from around here."

"What makes you so sure about that?" Callie was curious.

"Accent. The way you walk. The pace at which you do everything."

Callie tilted her head at him. It should have been weird, but it wasn't. She was fascinated to have been so observed and it must have shown on her face.

"It's my job," he said with a shrug.

"Paying attention to people?" She was surprised. To the extent she'd thought about it at all, Callie had assumed acting was about appearing to be someone other than oneself.

"Yup." Beckett nodded. "How they do things, why they do things, that whole show. So." His focus on her was like a tractor beam; entire and compelling. "What's your story?"

"Do you want the short version or the long version?"

"Long," Beckett said immediately. "Obviously."

Callie fidgeted with her chopsticks. She hadn't actually told this story before. Anyone who might have been interested in it had lived through it with her. "I'm from Boston originally."

"Boston, Boston or like random Boston suburbs?" Beckett asked.

"Boston, Boston. The North End. Picture the whole loud Italian-Greek, a million relatives, everyone yells at each other because it's fun thing," she said, even though she had never found it fun at all.

"Got it. And Callie is short for...?"

She blushed, feeling almost as if she should have revealed it sooner. "Calliope."

"And you'll kill me if I call you that?"

Callie wasn't actually sure. But she'd never let anyone outside her family use it and felt no reason to start now.

"Yeah. Probably. Anyway, I did community college for a bit while I tried to figure out what I wanted to do with my life and that turned out to be going to culinary school in New York. I was going to be the most famous chef," she said. "Or at least, have a trendy place somewhere in Brooklyn. You know, the kind of place that has board games and fries everything in duck fat?"

"Those are good places," Beckett concurred.

"I know. But, um." Callie picked up her bubble tea, took a sip, put it back down, and braced herself. "Middle of my junior year, I was in a car accident."

Beckett made a concerned sound but didn't interrupt, for which she was grateful.

"It was pretty bad. I mean, obviously I was fine, because I'm sitting right here. But it messed me up for a while."

She rubbed her thumb over the logo on her cup, not quite able to look at Beckett, who was most definitely looking at her, his face gentle and open. Listening to her as if her story, not his reaction to it, were the most important thing happening right now. And maybe — maybe she could tell him the whole story. Someday. But not now. No matter how kind and attentive he was, she wasn't ready for how she felt sure it would make him look at her differently. Like she wasn't capable of doing all the things she already had with her life. Besides, it really wasn't first date material.

But she had to say something. "I had to go back to live with my folks for a bit. And my parents...hovered. Like a lot. Because, again, Italian. Greek. That's what we do. I was so excited to get back to New York once everything was sorted, but when I did, and I got back to class, I just —" She stopped, frustrated, unable to find words that were both true and palatable to an outside audience.

"Go on."

"I hated it," she admitted. "All the bullshit just seemed so stupid, you know, after the whole accident thing. So, I took some time off and to do that I moved back home again. Which sucked. Again." Callie gave him a self-effacing smile.

"That can't have been easy," Beckett said. Which was a platitude, but he was so clearly sincere about it Callie didn't mind.

"It was not," she said emphatically. "This must sound terrible to you. Like, I assume your life is your dream and you've worked so hard for it, and I just suddenly walked away from mine."

Beckett tipped his head, his gaze still focused on her. "Why would I think that?"

"Because that's what people think," Callie said. She felt paralyzed. "That's what my parents think. At least, I think that's what they think. For people who communicate intensely, they don't always communicate clearly. At least with me."

Beckett smiled gently. "You haven't even gotten to the end of telling me how you wound up in Maine with a successful store where you cook every day. If it makes you happy, how on earth could I think you've given up on anything? How could anyone?"

"Let's get to that, then." Callie tried to put the fact that she'd just shown off way too many insecurities for a first date out of her head. "Okay. So. I'm home with my parents. And Sydney, my best friend from school, is from up here, and that summer she invited me to visit so I could get a break. I'd never packed so fast in my life, and if I told you my parents were practically running down the road chasing my car like dogs in a cartoon, I'd only be exaggerating a little bit."

Beckett huffed a laugh. "What type of dogs?"

That was not the question she'd been expecting. "Like a little white poodle that needs its eyes cleaned," she said after a moment's consideration.

Becket laughed and suddenly all her embarrassment about her history ebbed, at least for a moment.

"Anyway, it was just good to be somewhere else," Callie said. "The air was clean, and the views were great, and there's that whole Maine stereotype of people keeping to themselves and being a bit odd and just making a go at life on their own terms. It was the right moment for me to really fall for that."

"How'd you end up with Sweet Claws?" Beckett prompted.

"Sydney's grandma is best friends with the former shop owner. She was ready to retire and move somewhere warmer, and she wanted someone who could take over the shop and maintain its legacy. I needed something to do, and I had money from the accident settlement. So I bought a doughnut shop and...here I am."

She made herself look up and meet his eyes, still intent on her. Which was, honestly, a lot.

"So to recap," he said, rolling his chopsticks back and forth between his fingers. "You ditched school, up and moved to a new town in the middle of nowhere in Maine, became an entrepreneur without any sort of business degree, and have been running your own shop, extremely successfully, ever since?"

"Um, yeah." It sounded different, when he put it like that.

"That's a hell of a story. You didn't give up on a dream, you're living it."

"What about you?" Callie asked, eager to direct the attention away from herself. It was wonderful, but also so much, and she needed mental space from it for a moment to acclimate. "Tell me how your dream led to the wonders of Fly-Debate."

"What, you didn't read my Wikipedia page while you were googling?"

"You asshole," Callie scoffed. "I skimmed the whole thing, but it didn't answer my questions at all."

Beckett giggled, the sound as unexpectedly high-pitched and immensely charming to Callie's ear as ever.

"I grew up in Seattle," he said when he had subsided. "My parents are still there. One brother and his family are in Portland — Oregon, not Maine — and one's in New York City. My sister and her girlfriend are in Vancouver."

"Are you the oldest or the youngest?" Callie asked.

"Why couldn't I be one of the ones in the middle?"

Callie shook her head. "Nope, not possible. You're a lot. I just can't tell if you're the eldest with leader and independence vibes or the youngest who has a very special relationship with attention."

Beckett tossed his head back and laughed. "Why do I feel like you have my number?"

"So," Beckett said, leaning back on the picnic bench. They'd finished eating ages ago, but they'd been absorbed in conversation and neither of them had yet made a move to leave. "I was thinking, I don't know if you have to get back home, but if you want to stay out a bit longer...there's an axe-throwing place down the street."

Callie blinked at him. She was thrilled that the date was going to continue, but whatever proposition she had expected during the first half of his query had not involved axes. Or weaponry of any sort.

"Axe throwing?" she repeated.

"Yeah. Too much?"

"Oh no." Callie slapped her hands down on the table and pushed herself to her feet. "Needed a moment to take the concept in, but exactly the right amount." An active challenge, and someone not assuming she was too weak or not recovered enough to handle it? She was so on board. Sure, Beckett called her *ma'am* occasionally and held doors for her, but it didn't feel condescending when he did. More like he was, somehow, in awe of her instead.

The axe-throwing parlor was, like most things in Bar Harbor, a short walk away. The kid behind the desk gave them a very serious safety spiel and then led them to their lane, which had a target at the far end and was surrounded by a chain-link fence that reached the ceiling, presumably to stop wild throws from causing serious injuries to innocent bystanders.

"Have you ever done this before?" Callie watched as Beckett hefted one of the axes and eyed the target. She wanted to know if she was about to get trounced...and wondered if this was his go-to date activity here.

"Never in my life."

"Oh good!" That was both delightful and intriguing. "I am going to wipe the floor with you."

"Oh yeah?"

"Absolutely." Callie couldn't help pushing, and was gratified to see Beckett's face light up. She wondered if, in his circumstances, people tended to humor him far more than they should.

"We'll see about that." He gave her a sly look as if he suspected she would, in fact, make good on her threat.

Beckett lifted the axe over his head and threw it. It hit the wall handle first and clunked to the ground.

Callie cackled. "Well done."

"Shush, you." But Beckett was laughing too as he retrieved his axe. He seemed totally unconcerned about being made a fool of in a physical activity, and Callie felt fond of him for it. How many other men would have done the same?

"Okay, my turn." Callie stepped up to the throwing line, lifted her axe, and threw. It didn't make the target, but it did, at least, stick in the wall. "HAH!" She pumped her fist in the air.

Beckett grinned. "All right, now it's on."

Neither of them were any good, but Beckett persisted in being not weird about it. He was so eager for at least one of them to succeed at this assignment even if mutual, delighted incompetence seemed as if it would rule the day. They laughed so much that Callie's abs grew sore.

Finally, one of Beckett's throws actually hit somewhere within the circle, and he yelled in triumph. His eyes were sparkling, his cheeks were flushed, and Callie, having already entered into whatever pool of absurdity Beckett was going to be in her life, knew she needed to kiss him then and there. And better that she make the first move, if the age difference and his apparent celebrity status weren't going to be weird.

She put a hand on his chest. Even through the shirt she could tell he was the ridiculously fit man she had seen on the internet. She caught a glimpse of his face, surprised and delighted, right before she pressed her mouth to his.

It was a good thing Callie didn't close her eyes, or else she would have missed Beckett closing his own as he hooked his fingers through the chain link of the cage behind him. She had intended for the kiss to be chaste, but with that reaction she had to tug, just slightly, at his lower lip.

Beckett groaned and sagged back into the fence he was holding onto. She followed and the arm that wasn't holding onto the fence came to rest around her waist.

She pulled her mouth away, but nothing else.

"Do you like that?" she asked. "Me running the show?"

His arm tightened around her waist. "I like everything," he said, letting go of the fence to touch her face ever so delicately.

Callie sucked in a breath. She had not been prepared for this hint of submissiveness without a hint of passivity. Hell, she hadn't been prepared for the way he looked at her with a sort of hungry reverence.

"I think," she said carefully, "that you are going to be a menace."

"You don't even know," he murmured. He nudged her away from him slightly, which was disappointing until he took one of her hands in both of his, fiddled with the edge of her wrist warmer, then looked into her eyes. "May I?"

She suddenly didn't trust herself to speak, but she nodded. He peeled the warmer back to press his lips to the center of her palm. It was, somehow, not chaste. Not at all.

Callie concentrated on her knees continuing to work, but wasn't sure she was acing it. Her struggle must have been obvious, because Beckett gave the softest of laughs.

"It's okay," he said. "I'm very, very good at this."

She laughed and snatched her hand away in mock outrage. "And very, very arrogant!"

"Only sometimes, but it is a flaw," he conceded. "Hopefully, you'll be willing to overlook it."

"And if I'm not?" she asked, stepping back with the most challenging smile she could muster.

"Well, then," he said with a smile. "I hope you'll put me in my place."

After a few more rounds of throwing and at least as many of flirting, they finally stepped out of the axe parlor. The night air was cool and tinged with salt. Beckett paused for a moment, presumably to appreciate the sea air, and Callie seized on the moment. She didn't think Beckett was ready for the date to end, and she also didn't need to wait for him to ask first.

"Want to take a walk?" she said.

He nodded "Come on, I know a path."

"Do you, now?" Callie folded her fingers through his. Beckett's hands were big. And warm. And as deliciously rough as they looked.

Beckett gave a breathy laugh. "Don't make it scandalous before we've even gotten scandalous."

She thought about protesting. They had been a bit scandalous, at least by axe-throwing standards. But she kept that thought to herself, focusing instead on his hand in her own. She could imagine all too easily what those massive, blunt fingers would feel like elsewhere on her body.

Callie tried to focus. The night was lovely, and Beckett was lovely, but she had questions. The chemistry between them had already been clearly established, which made it even more important to talk before this went any further. In any situation that wasn't bizarre in all the ways this situation clearly was, she'd be angling to go home with this man tonight. And she'd succeed. But they had an age gap, his celebrity status, and her personal history to contend with.

Beckett led them down a street a ways, then down a sidewalk that cut between buildings. The sound of the waves was much louder and then suddenly before them was the ocean, the rising moon painting a silver trail across the water.

"It's beautiful." Callie sighed.

"Yeah." Beckett tightened his hand in hers. "Come on, it's this way."

He led them to a wooden stairway that brought them down amongst seaside boulders. Here the crash of the surf was all-encompassing, and the lights of the town suddenly seemed very far away. She let herself take one moment to truly enjoy the moment for what it was, unconnected to anything else. For all the mess and pain of the road that had led her here, Maine was beautiful and would always have her heart.

Callie inhaled the salt-tanged air and pulled her hand gently from Beckett's. "I'm going to sit on this rock," she said, "and you are going to sit on that one, over there, where I can't touch you, even though I really want to, so if this has been your long-standing secret makeout spot, sorry about that."

She couldn't see much of his face in the dark, but Beckett shook his head with a soft laugh and did as he was told.

Callie arranged herself on her rock, rough to the touch but still warm from the sun of the day now gone.

"This has been extremely nice," she said. "And I have a lot more questions."

Beckett, his arms looped loosely around his knees, nodded. The breeze tugged at his hair. "Shoot," he said, as good-natured as ever. Callie wondered if all her carefulness about him just made her seem young and foolish and not up to the peculiarities of his life.

"First, *is* this your long-standing secret makeout spot?"

"I'm sorry?"

"Just, one wonders why you know this whole path here in this town that's an hour away from where you actually live. Is this where you take all your dates?"

"Oh. No. I don't actually date that much." Beckett shook his head. "Troppy's had a den around here the last couple of summers,

I came down to try to get a look at him."

"What the fuck is a Troppy?" Callie was baffled.

"That random bird from somewhere way warmer that keeps coming up here in the summer to bang lobster buoys?"

"How does Maine keep getting more odd?" Callie shook her head. "What with the shop and all, birding has not been a pursuit I've had time for although I keep meaning to. But we're getting off-topic. Because what I really need to know is — Why are you single?" Callie was suddenly too frustrated with everything from her want to the peculiarity of the situation to ask questions that were measured or nice.

Beckett looked at her thoughtfully for a moment before he responded. "I work with a tight-knit crew in a small town. The risk of disaster is just too high."

"Then why pick me?" Callie asked.

"I didn't pick you. I wasn't looking. But then there you were. You're gorgeous. You're smart. You have your own thing going on and great boundaries. You talk to me like I'm a person. The claws are great. Your smile lives rent-free in my head. And that laundry list isn't even the point. I just...every time I see you, it's like I exhale. Tonight — even with the grilling —"

"The grilling is necessary," Callie said firmly.

"It is, and even with it, that hasn't changed."

"Well." Callie looked down at her hands, hoping her flaming cheeks weren't showing in the dark. Her self-esteem was as healthy as anyone's, but even so, such a speech, from this man she was so entranced by, was overwhelming. "That's funny, because every time I see you, you take my breath away."

"Occupational hazard," Beckett said lightly, like he wanted to brush the compliment aside.

"No, I don't think it is." Callie glanced sideways to meet Beckett's eyes, and lost any hope the dark had hidden her flushed cheeks. Beckett's were on fire.

He held her gaze for a long moment, and it didn't matter that they weren't touching; Callie felt like the air between them was crackling.

Finally, Beckett cleared his throat. "Does that mean there's a second date in here somewhere for us?"

"I sure as hell hope so."

Beckett huffed a laugh that sounded relieved. "Next week I

have to go down to New York for some meetings, but maybe the week after that? We could come back here, if you want. Try for a Troppy sighting?"

Callie finally reached across the distance between them; Beckett caught her hand. "I'll pencil you in."

# CHAPTER 12

<pre>
40.7128° N, 74.0060° W
          Temp: 78.1°F
  Pressure: 30.02 inHg
     Wind: 12.8 mph, SW
  Visibility: 10.00 mi
</pre>

SWITCHING GEARS FROM the daily adventures of *Hidden Cove* and his very promising first date with Callie to heading down to New York to entertain ideas for future projects was not Beckett's idea of a good time. While he could turn on a dime emotionally as an actor, he was not wired that way as a person.

The flight from Bangor to LaGuardia was less than two hours, but the mental space between the tranquility of Fly-Debate and the rush of the city made it seem like it should have been much longer. Beckett didn't hate New York, but he wasn't quite made for it either. He spent the journey going over his schedule and trying to get into the right mental space for playing the part of gregarious actor instead of who he got to be in Maine which was, simply, himself.

He thought about Callie as he took the subway from meeting to meeting. What part of the city had she lived in? He hadn't asked, which was silly of him. They could have compared notes.

*You could text her*, part of his brain told him, but the other part of him, the sensible part he had spent a lot of time training and nurturing, reminded him that they'd only been on one date, and her story about leaving the city had been complicated. As much as he wanted to see New York through her eyes, that conversation could wait until the next time he saw her in person.

The meetings, in Beckett's professional opinion, were bland and went no better nor worse than he had expected. He was merely doing what his job required of him, and the discussions were so exploratory there wasn't even anything rude in how intensely non-committal he felt. A theatrical revival, an indie film with a script that had been getting some buzz. It was all work he could do, but none of it felt like the right fit for the person he was right now. Instead of hating his agent for wasting his time — which he did a little — he tried to be grateful for the opportunities this trip was actually providing.

Once his professional obligations were complete, Beckett headed to his youngest brother's apartment, a walkup in a pre-war building in Brooklyn that had seen better days.

"I've got a question," Knox said in lieu of an actual hello, as he let him in.

"Yeah?" Beckett dropped his bag by the door and flopped down gracelessly on the couch, grateful he finally got to turn off for the day.

"How many times can someone audition to be dead on *Law & Order* and not have that pan out?"

"Bad day?" Beckett asked. Navigating his younger brother's acting career had always been tricky. He often found himself struggling to strike the right balance between realism and encouragement, acknowledging his own success but doing everything he could not to emphasize it.

"I walked into the audition and one of the people behind the table stared at me and said, 'You. Again.'"

Beckett tried not to laugh, but the story was, if not good, at least genuinely funny. "Hey, at least they remembered you."

"And better that than 'oh hey you're so-and-so's brother, right? You look just like him!'" Knox shook his head in irritation. "You ready for food?"

"I just got here," Beckett said, which was true. The exhaustion of the day, this trip, his entire life, had a habit of sinking into his bones when he broke with routine.

"Which means everyone wants to see you," Knox said.

"Yeah. All right." Beckett repressed the urge to grouse. It was unbecoming to someone as lucky as he was.

Because he and Knox were siblings who worked in the same business, sometimes in the same city, and also liked each other's company, they had an overlapping circle of friends. Nearly as importantly, they had a favorite gastropub a block and a half from Knox's apartment. As they approached it, Beckett — once again — thought of Callie, and her one-time plan to run a place like it. *I wonder if she'd approve of their duck fat fries.*

He followed Knox inside to find some of their usual crowd gathered in a predictable corner. Before he'd had a chance to do more than say hello and exchange a few hugs and handshakes, one figure detached itself from the group and tugged him back toward the door.

Antonia, his one-time girlfriend and long-time very good friend, looked back at him over her shoulder with a playful grin. "I need some fresh air."

"Hello." Beckett said, both puzzled and entertained, as he was towed. "Was it something I said?"

Every word out of Antonia's mouth had always suggested the hint of an adventure where nothing could possibly go wrong. Beckett adored her and was grateful that they made even better friends than they had lovers. She was, quite simply, one of his favorite people and all they ever wanted was the absolute best for each other.

Outside, Antonia leaned against a concrete planter where a clutch of pansies bloomed.

"I have news," she announced.

"Bad or good?" Beckett braced himself. He was getting to that age where friends were sometimes on the receiving end of serious health diagnoses, and Antonia had almost two decades on him.

"Good for me. Presumably neutral for you, but you still get to hear it first."

"...Ah?"

"I'm getting married," she said.

"You're kidding," he said, breathless, amused, and something else, which he couldn't name and was a bit unsettling. Which wasn't the most polite answer, but he meant no ill by it. Of the moments that haunted him about his wayward youth, the one where he had clumsily sort-of tried to propose to Antonia — and then had to figure out how to cope with her very gentle refusal — was high on the list.

"I am not," she said primly.

"Fuck me." Beckett was glad she seemed entertained by whatever his face was doing.

"Not anymore, darling."

Beckett stared at her a moment, then threw back his head and laughed. It was too much. Strange, unexpected, delightful — and also bittersweet.

"I thought you were over marriage," he teased when he had recovered himself.

"I was," she said. "But then I met someone I wanted to try it with. And I wanted to tell you about it in person before you heard it from anyone else."

If asked, hypothetically, he would have said the special advance warning wasn't necessary, but here in this moment he was glad to have had it.

Beckett pulled her into a tight hug. "I'm extremely happy for you."

"Good. You should be." Antonia pulled back, clasping her hands around his upper arms and lifting her chin to look him in the eye. "Are you going to be having any issues? You know none of this has anything to do with you."

Beckett shook his head. Mixed as his feelings might have been, he was both a grownup and self-aware.

"I do know. I'm envious, but of you, not of them." And that was the truth of it. He didn't want to be the one Antonia had finally chosen. He just wanted that type of happily ever after of his own.

He considered, for a moment, telling Antonia about Callie. But now was not the time. It was too new, too uncertain. More importantly, he'd have rather died than let Antonia think he was trying to upstage her news. Yet something in his chosen and sensible silence nagged at him, as if he were committing a sin of omission against a future he desperately wanted.

# CHAPTER 13



CALLIE HATED THAT BECKETT was out of town; she was also grateful that he was out of town. Their date had been perfect — hot, respectful, silly. And if he weren't so entirely out of reach for the next few days, she might have been inclined to exercise an appalling lack of self-restraint that she was pretty sure would be reciprocated. Even if she wasn't exactly ready for where that would obviously lead.

She did, however, still have a business to run. One that desperately needed an employee other than her. Callie knew she was a control freak, and while the idea of leaving the shop in someone else's hands for even a few hours stressed her out, it was going to become necessary and soon.

Today's goals were to make a help wanted sign and create some sort of social media presence. Filming a short video introducing herself and the shop had seemed like a good — and easy — idea when she had first thought of it. But Callie was quickly realizing that she had no idea what she was doing.

Engaging chitchat with customers, she could do. Highly detailed explanations of baking science, she could also do. But quick, funny, informative, well-planned but casual videos that were going to make her shop a regional destination and might be a launch point for a mail order business down the road? Slightly harder. Especially since as soon as she had her phone on and pointed at herself, she lost all ability to speak like the cogent and, frankly, extremely charming person she knew herself to be.

*Beckett might have some advice,* she mused as she sat on her stool behind the counter and watched her latest attempt back. He did, after all, say words in front of cameras for a living. But asking felt presumptuous after just one date...and more than that, Callie had figured out more difficult things than this on her own. She wasn't going to start needing help now.

"Let's give this another go," she said aloud, but that take was quickly ruined as the door of the shop banged open.

In strode Emma, today wearing a Nirvana t-shirt, ripped jeans with fishnet tights visible through the holes, and thrifted designer boots. "My dad wants to see if you have any of the crème brûlée claws — oh. Am I interrupting something?"

"Yes to the claws, no to the interrupting. Just me failing to make a fool of myself on social media." Callie slid her phone onto the counter and turned to pick up a box for the requested claws. "Every time I try to record, I lose my train of thought, think I look weird, and generally am just super boring."

Emma hummed and gave her a considering look. "Are you just trying to babble at your phone?"

"Basically."

Emma stared at her. "That is not how you do that."

"Is this going to be a thing where you tell me you have like ten thousand followers or something?"

"Seventeen thousand, three hundred and one as of this morning, actually. On my mural account. You gotta write a script. Chaos only works as an illusion or a hair choice," she said pointing to her own mop of curls, which today were a vivid teal-and-blue.

"Are you saying that you have an expertise in social media?" Callie tore off a sheet of parchment paper to line the box with. "How many claws?"

"Four of the crème brûlée. And two of the almond, but those are just for me. I'm not like, a professional expert on social media, but I am nineteen. Instead of being old. Like you."

Emma was joking. But Callie still tried not to laugh. Now that she'd gone on a first date with a dude who was forty-four, she definitely needed people to call her old as often as possible; it levelled the playing field.

"Can I pay you to help me with my social media?" she asked, packing the requested claws neatly into the box.

"It's not like I've got anything else going on this week."

Suddenly Callie was struck by another idea. "Do you have anything going on next week?"

"Do you need time to psych yourself up to pandering to strangers on the internet?" Emma sounded unreasonably entertained by the possibility.

"No, but I desperately need to hire someone to work in this shop other than me. You know the town, you're gregarious, you have a good work ethic, and we've already established some level of trust — hourly wage over minimum, claws, and I'd pay you a separate fee for this socials thing."

"Flexible schedule so I can keep doing this painting thing?"

"Obviously," Callie said. "Just give me some notice."

Emma clapped her hands together and then pointed at Callie. "Put it on paper and you've got yourself a claw girl."

As she and Emma hashed out a plan that was only slightly more robust than the back of the pastry box they were writing it on, Callie's phone pinged. She glanced at it.

**Sydney:** Wanna do a call? I need to hear about your daaaaaaaaaaate.

**Callie:** I've got Emma here right now.

She set her phone back on the counter, where it immediately buzzed with an incoming call. The suggestion that she might be busy in the face of potential gossip clearly hadn't deterred Sydney in the least. Which she should have expected.

"Sorry about whatever this is going to be," Callie said to Emma as she accepted the call.

Emma leaned against the counter and shrugged as Sydney's voice came through the tinny speaker of the phone.

"All right, you are going to have to tell me *everything*," her friend demanded.

"Sydney!" Callie said with a laugh. "You're on speaker and I have people here."

"People other than Emma?" Sydney asked.

"No, but, surely, *surely* you have something going on in your life as well. We can do this later."

"You went on a date with Beckett Brown," Sydney said. "No, we cannot do this later."

"Oh yeah," Emma said with an exaggeratedly flat affect. "How'd that go?"

Callie shot her an amused look. "We went axe throwing," she said, for Sydney's benefit.

"You what?!" Sydney's outraged voice made the phone skitter

slightly along the counter. At some point Callie was going to have to take a serious look at how not-quite-level that was.

"Axe throwing," Callie repeated. "Like, sharp objects, at a wall?"

"These are not the details I called for," Sydney said.

"I'm not going to kiss and tell about the weird celebrity I went on a date with," Callie protested. "And it was two days ago. I don't get why you're throwing all this urgency at me now."

"I was busy," Sydney snapped without explanation. "Wait. How is he weird?! Oh my God, please tell me he's kinky. This is going to be amazing."

Callie stared at the phone in disbelief. When she'd first found out who Beckett was, her initial reaction had been horror at what that might say about him. Now, her horror was about the sorts of things his celebrity status made other people say. In the end, it was Emma who came to her rescue.

"No, no it's not," Emma interjected, throwing her hands up as if she could ward Sydney off, despite the fact that Sydney was down in New York. "Because I am also here and don't care and don't want to hear about any of this." She picked up the box Callie had packed for her. "No, I'm going to go and take my claws, and you can text me a work schedule later. Because I don't think your friend is going to be dissuaded, and this is going to less painful for everyone if I'm not here."

"I will absolutely do that," Callie said. "Thank you for understanding."

"No worries," Emma said, "but the price is any hot goss you get about Darcy, deal?"

"Deal," Callie said. Mainly because she didn't think that would be happening any time soon.

# CHAPTER 14

44°33'47.1"N 67°30'33.7"W
Temp: 66.0°F
Pressure: 29.96 inHg
Wind: 11.5 mph, SW
Visibility: 6.00 mi

A S BECKETT DROVE THE FAMILIAR road from the airport to his apartment, relief at being back in Maine settled into Beckett's bones. Sometimes he wondered why, exactly, he had so much affection for the place. On a project like *Hidden Cove* it was easy to get caught up in the idea that he was made for some rugged and difficult life out here at the edge of the Atlantic. He was not. He'd never been a Boy Scout, had no particular outdoor skills, and was neither in his interests nor his abilities any sort of manly man, whatever that meant. Some days, he was barely made for the relatively tame rigors of shooting scenes where he pretended to be such, as Robert was only too happy to remind him.

But there was barely any traffic on the highway here and the landscape was green with the coming summer. Beckett rolled down the windows and let the salt air roll over him. He fit in here, not because he had — or needed — any particularly extreme skills, but because he was an oddball who enjoyed nature, small towns, and empty spaces as much as he enjoyed people who were stridently committed to doing their own thing, no matter what that might be.

He hoped Callie was down for who he actually was, rather than whatever she thought his life looked like.

In the week after he returned from New York, Beckett's shooting schedule meant that he was only able to see Callie briefly in her shop in the mornings before he was due on set. Even with those time limitations, there was no shortage of flirting — accompanied, often as not, by Emma's sarcastic commentary. He did his best not to let too much of his frustration with his schedule show. It was the nature of his job, and there were better ways to express his enthusiasm for Callie than to complain about everything else.

As soon as a break in his filming schedule appeared Beckett made a point to set a date with her. There was nothing else he was more interested in doing with his free time. Maybe that was a bit schoolboy-crush of him, but he didn't care. New relationship energy was a good time.

When the occasion finally arrived, he grinned to himself as he pushed open the shop door. The bells above it jingled merrily. Callie was behind the counter with Emma. They were wearing matching aprons spattered with flour and looked as grimly determined as two people could when staring down a tray of doughnuts.

Callie looked up at him and her face lit up. Beckett felt himself glow. Being better than doughnuts felt good, and her smile stopped Beckett in his tracks.

"Hello, stranger," she said in a voice somewhere between a purr and a drawl but tinged with humor at the absurdity of the moment.

Beside her Emma, still regarding the claws, merely grunted. Beckett wasn't sure if it was a greeting or a judgment on him and Callie.

"We're learning about different types of glazes today," Callie explained with a pointed glance at her assistant.

"This is definitely more chemistry than I was expecting," Emma said. She finally looked up. "Not in the good way."

"It's like art, but you get to eat it," Beckett said encouragingly.

Emma shifted her gaze back to the claws and glared. "You come over here and say that."

Callie took off her apron and hung it on the row of pegs behind the counter. "Maybe some other day," she said. "Beckett and I have a date, and I'm done torturing you with baking science. For now. You sure you're okay holding down the shop on your own?"

"I absolutely am."

Calle, however, wasn't done fretting. "The production has the day off, so I doubt you'll have any sort of real rush," she ran on. "There's plenty of claws in the back if you need to restock the case.

If you do run out of anything —"

Emma rolled her eyes. "If I run out of anything, I'll update the menu. If I run out of everything, I'll make people coffee and tell them to come back tomorrow."

"If you have any questions you can always text, or call, or —"

"She's got this, Callie," Beckett interjected fondly. Callie ran her business with a degree of care and efficiency that would have made her an asset on any film set. And while her concern for both her employee and her shop was touching, she had made a good choice in her assistant.

"Fine, fine," Callie sang. "Beckett's right. You have got this, Emma."

"I know that," Emma said. "Now, stop worrying and go enjoy your date with, I suppose, the second-most attractive cast member of *Hidden Cove*."

"Second?!" Beckett put a hand to his heart, feigning dismay; Emma's crush on Darcy was probably visible from space, and never failed to entertain him.

Callie playfully pushed at his chest. "Take what you can get, Beckett. Now can we get out of here and go find that damn bird?"

This time Callie was the one to drive them to Bar Harbor. She had a modest-sized pickup truck, far from new but well-maintained. Beckett enjoyed watching her drive with the same degree of focus she brought to her shop. Her fingers, emerging today from neon-blue fingerless gloves, tapped a lively rhythm on the steering wheel as they talked about everything and nothing. Fog drifted in from the ocean, as it so often did, but it was interspersed with more patches of sunlit sky than he usually allowed himself to expect.

Once they'd reached Bar Harbor and parked Beckett led the way to the same rocky beach they'd ended their first date on.

"No promises," he said as they walked along the rocks to the path. He was faintly aware that he was on the edge of babbling because he liked Callie so much. "This is where Troppy's den was last year, but I haven't heard anything about where he's settled this year. Or if he's even back yet."

Judging from the look on Callie's face, she was also more than aware of his nerves. Beckett mentally tried to calm himself. He was charming on and off screen, just in very different ways. He knew that and had to trust it. More importantly, he had to trust Callie.

"So that we're clear," she said. "Troppy was not actually the main attraction of this outing for me."

That was reassuring, not surprising, and definitely flirtatious. Still, he shrugged.

"Just wanted to be upfront," he said. "Don't want to promise you a bird and have there not be a bird."

"You're a very strange man, aren't you?"

Beckett looked up at the sky and thought about it for a moment. "Nah. Just a little bit more honest and awkward than is generally a good fit in my profession." He looked back down towards Callie and gave her a half-bashful smile.

"Beckett?"

"Yeah?"

"You know how you told me to worry less before?"

"Yeah?"

"Worry less," Callie said firmly, and oh, turnabout was fair play.

The path that wove its way around the rocky headland was slippery with sea spray. The clouds scudded low overhead, trailing away from the coast in streaks of white and gray. The wind tugged at Beckett's hair and made Callie's curls dance around her shoulders as they walked.

They hiked for the better part of an hour, and Beckett enjoyed the easy exertion as they climbed around boulders and navigated gravelly slopes. Callie held her own, but once or twice where the rocks had become particularly slippery or a small slope seemed dubiously stable, he saw nervousness flicker over her face, just for a second. He offered a hand every time, and eventually, when he didn't push and insist, she began to take it, less out of need, he suspected, than out of joy.

As they walked, they talked. About their own past birding expeditions, about Beckett's recent adventures in New York, about Callie's latest experiments in seasonal claw recipes (lemon and blueberry for the coming summer).

"Okay, worst college disaster," Beckett prompted.

Callie pinned him with a sharp look he possibly shouldn't have enjoyed as much as he did. "I'm not sure if I'm more afraid of your story or mine," she said.

Beckett chuckled. "Don't keep me in suspense!'

"All right. Does culinary school count?"

"Sure does."

"So. There's a restaurant at the school where we work in all the different roles — front of house, kitchen, all that — just so we really understand how the whole business works."

"No wonder you're so good at running the shop," Beckett said.

"It's terrifying every day, but thank you." Callie paused her narration to navigate a particularly sloped patch of the path. "Anyway, having a real restaurant means having real paying customers. And it's actually quite expensive. A bargain for what it is, but people consider it a nice night out. It's hard to get reservations."

Beckett looked at her earnestly. "Did you drop plates on people?"

Callie groaned. "No, I confused the sugar and the salt. In a series of desserts that cost more than movie tickets."

"You could have killed someone if they were off their blood-pressure meds," Beckett joked.

Callie, thankfully, took that the right way. "Yes indeed. Assuming anyone would have done more than taste that first bite. Which I assure you was not an issue. But I'm telling you right now, you need to top my shame on this."

Beckett laughed. "Oh, I've got you." And he did. The sheer number of disaster stories he had from college were legion. Unfortunately, as was probably typical of men his age who had joined fraternities in college, far too many of them involved alcohol. And those stories, by and large, weren't funny to anyone who hadn't been there and also reflected poorly on the participants. The situation with the goat, however....

Beckett tested the stability of a rock with his foot before putting his full weight on it. "So this is super cliché, but stick with me. I was in a frat in college."

"Oh no."

"And we stole a rival school's mascot."

"Aren't there movies about this sort of thing?" Callie sounded delightedly horrified already.

"Yes, and I have never been in one. Before I continue…. How much do you know about goats?"

"Only culinary things, and I am going to assume you neither ate nor milked the goat." Callie pushed a loose strand of hair behind her ear, and Beckett briefly became distracted imagining what her curls might feel like wrapped around his fingers.

"Okay," he said, shaking himself out of his reverie. "Goats will eat anything. Absolutely anything. And I don't know this in any official way, but I think in general they are super big fans of fabric."

"Does this story involve nudity?" Callie asked suspiciously.

"No, but it is the story about how I got blackballed from my fraternity."

"Go on…."

"So we stole this goat."

"How?" Callie demanded with a laugh.

Beckett waved his hand. "Not actually the interesting part of the story. Because it turns out it's incredibly easy to walk up to a goat and put it in a truck if you have stuff a goat wants."

"Which is to say, anything?"

"Bingo. Although I didn't realize that at the time. So when we got it back to our frat house, I said we should put it in the parlor."

"You had a parlor?"

Beckett ducked to dodge an overhanging branch, dripping with mist. "We only used it for formal events."

"Ohhhkay."

"So we put down a bunch of newspaper so it wouldn't shit everywhere, and took out all the breakable objects, and it all seemed like a great plan right up until the goat ate an antique wall hanging that had been embroidered by the mothers of our original founders in the 1870s."

Callie cackled. "Whooops."

"Yep. Hence the blackballing."

"You might have wound up the better for it." Callie's smile was gentler than he deserved.

"Almost certainly," Beckett admitted. "I auditioned for a school show 'cause I didn't know how to meet people after they kicked me out, and now here I am."

"Was the goat okay?"

Beckett chuckled, though he was touched by the question. "The goat was fine. He was duly returned to his university home, having presumably enjoyed the embroidered treat."

"It's here," Beckett said as they crested a last rise. The granite cliffs fell away down to the long, rolling waves below, and the wind was sharper here than ever.

Callie came to stand beside him. Beckett wrapped an arm around her, and she leaned against him, as comfortable as if they'd been doing this for years. A particularly strong gust of wind buffeted them, and she laughed, the sound vibrant and musical. When she turned to look up at him, her smile was luminous as the sun appearing through a rent in the clouds.

She returned her gaze to the vista before them and stepped forward, out of his grasp — but then she reached back towards him as if he was an anchor against the whole wide world.

"This is amazing," she called into the wind, her hand tight around his. Beckett felt a smile spread across his face; her joy was infectious.

"I think Troppy's den is over there." He pointed to a low shelf, maybe halfway down the cliff.

Callie dropped his hand to lift her binoculars to her eyes. "Nothing going on for now, at least."

"We've got ages before we have to start heading back. Want to get comfy and see if we get lucky?"

Callie looked at him, her eyebrows raised. "Really?"

"You know what I meant."

Beckett tried not to blush. He hadn't meant anything by it, but now he felt pinned by an accidental, clumsy, and frankly clichéd bit of flirting.

"Pretty sure I don't. Good thing I'm on board either way." Callie nudged his shoulder with hers as she unshouldered her backpack and dropped down to sit on a fallen tree beside the path. Beckett settled in next to her. For a while they sat in companionable silence, watching the waves roll in and crash on the rocks. Birds swooped above and below, none of them the red tropicbird, but plenty of terns, gulls and kestrels.

Callie took a deep breath and let it out, and Beckett could feel the calm that settled around her reaching out to pull him into its protective aura. He wanted to bask in the feeling forever.

"This is perfect," she said.

"Yeah."

"There aren't a lot of people I get to be quiet with." She said it like a confession.

Beckett desperately wanted to know the story that fit around that. He strongly suspected it had to do with her family, but now wasn't the time to ask.

"No need to talk on my account. Though if you want to — you should also feel free," Beckett added hastily. "Whatever you want."

"Is the thing where you're profoundly considerate part of the early Beckett-does-dating package or is that just...you?"

"It's been a while since I've been in the early dating phase," he admitted, "but I do try."

"Like you try to be good at making out?"

Beckett wanted her and as easy as it would have been to reel her in for a kiss then and there, he knew it wouldn't be enough to satisfy the heat that her joy, her body, and increasingly her soul, stirred in him. He reminded himself to enjoy the simple pleasure that was just raw and, for now, unsatisfied want.

"That," he said, "is the result of both good intentions and hard work."

They sat there like that until the weather, as it did often and regularly on the coast, began to shift. The clear sky out over the ocean grew pale. Fog rolled in, first in long ribbons and then thick, opaque waves that quickly coated everything around them in a fine haze of water droplets.

Beside Beckett, Callie shivered.

"You want to head back?" he asked.

"No," she said, her voice mournful. She glanced at her watch. "But the sun's going to set soon, and I guess we don't want to deal with the dark and the fog."

"Probably," Beckett agreed regretfully. Navigating the path in the dark was one thing, but the fog was going to make it harder to see and everything slippery.

Callie levered herself to her feet, wincing as she did so.

"You okay?" Beckett asked. As far as he was concerned, Callie did an impossible amount every day in a way that wasn't dissimilar from the burdens of his own work. Beckett knew the toll that took on his own body. He rarely gave himself the breaks he needed, and he knew that was no good. Worrying at the sight of someone else possibly doing the same felt unavoidable.

"Just sat too long and got stiff." Callie brushed dirt off the back of her pants. "That boulder was no good for my ass."

Beckett huffed a laugh. "I feel you."

"Do you now?" Callie peered at him and held her hand out to him.

He took it, and she pulled him to his feet. It felt like a statement on his entire being. And, he hoped, his future.

Sound traveled strangely in the fog: Sometimes the waves, dozens of feet below them as they hiked back to the car, sounded like they were about to crash over the path. The calls of birds far out to sea echoed as if they were right beside them. Beckett wondered if any of those cries were Troppy, having evaded being spotted during the day and now hunting for food or settling into his den for the night.

Back in Callie's truck, she put her key in the ignition but didn't turn it, instead shifting in her seat to face him.

"So I think we should go get dinner," she said. "But first I would very much like to make out with you again. If that's okay."

Beckett laughed, startled but delighted in the matter-of-fact nature of her desire. "You will get zero complaints from me."

"Excellent." Callie reached for him, but instead of reeling him in immediately for a kiss, she touched his face. Her fingers were gentle, exploratory, as they traced his cheekbone, the line of his jaw, brushed a loose strand of hair back against his forehead. Beckett was frozen to the spot. He was not used to anyone being so careful of him. Her touches were so gentle, so simple, but they made heat flare in his core. Or maybe that was Callie's gaze, brown-eyed, warm, and so attentive.

Her eyes flickered over his face, following the press of her fingers. Whatever she was seeing...Beckett was sure it was him, Beckett the nerd who liked to go birdwatching and once blew up all his college friendships by not quite knowing what to do with a stolen goat. Her gaze wasn't for Beckett the actor or whatever she thought a celebrity was like. And if she wanted to do nothing more than sit here and stare at him for the rest of the day, that was more than okay.

It was so nice to be real.

When she did, finally, press her mouth to his, Beckett made a sound that was close to a whimper. But he felt no embarrassment, only gratitude. When Callie dug her fingers into his hair and pulled, he stopped caring about anything else whatsoever.

"I'd like to see you again," Beckett said much later, while Callie drove them back to Fly-Debate through a landscape gone blue with dusk.

"I'd certainly hope." Callie shot him a sly sideways glance.

"Tuesday and Wednesday are my usual days off," he said. "So we could do next Wednesday, or...we could do Tuesday and hang out for longer than we can on a school night."

He wasn't suggesting an overnight, at least not necessarily. Continuing to take things slowly was a good way to respect both whatever boundaries Callie had and all the ways the circumstances of their individual lives might prove to be messily incompatible.

Callie nodded. "Tuesday sounds good."

"Do you want to come to my place? I could make us dinner."

Callie gave him a brief but devastating side-eye before returning her gaze to the road. "You're offering to cook for me, who spent three years at culinary school?"

"I know my way around a kitchen, and I don't totally suck at it," Beckett said. "And I'm definitely not going to make you cook on your day off."

"I appreciate the thought. Really," Callie said. "And I'm sure you're a perfectly fine cook. But I'm better, so how about I boss you around your kitchen instead?"

"Am I that obvious?" Beckett asked before he could think better of it.

"Little bit," Callie said through that wry, playful smile that had been plaguing his dreams since the moment he met her. "But to be clear, I'm into it."

# CHAPTER 15

44°35'38.3"N 67°21'54.6"W
Temp: 80.1°F
Pressure: 29.82 inHg
Wind: 3.45 mph, E
Visibility: ≥ 10.00 mi

D ESPITE HER BOLDNESS IN accepting — and altering — Beckett's offer to cook for her, Callie spent the week agonizing over what to make for dinner at his house. Her problem wasn't that she didn't have any good ideas; it was that she had approximately eight hundred ideas, all of which had their own merits in terms of cuisine type, ease of preparation, and degree of impressiveness.

In the end she decided on uovo in raviolo, which looked impressive but was not actually difficult — at least for her. Culinary school had drilled the necessary gentleness into her, the ingredients were all available on her regular grocery run, and no fancy kitchen implements were needed. Sure, Beckett probably didn't have pastry bags or a rolling pin, but those were easy enough to bring over herself.

Her plan had been to go grocery shopping on Tuesday evening before heading to Beckett's apartment, but that afternoon, as she was in the middle of glazing a batch of claws, her phone chirped with a text from him.

**Beckett**: Got let out early. Tell me what to pick up?

"Prepared and considerate," Callie muttered to herself before giving him a list.

Beckett's house was further from town than her boat was, all the way on the other side of the bay, and the drive was as scenic as any Callie had taken. She found the turn into the driveway without any trouble, thanks to a cluster of lobster buoys attached to the mailbox, and soon was parking in front of a modest ranch-style house nearly overshadowed by trees.

Going over to someone's house was another part of the dating dance she hadn't done in years. And she'd certainly never been over to a celebrity's home, although, to her relief, she'd been warned not to expect much. Which was good, as she didn't want to expect anything at all. Her stomach fluttered with nerves as she got out of her truck. A moss-grown stone path led from the driveway to the door of the walk-out basement, and banks of tiger lilies glowed in the afternoon light.

Before she could knock on the door it opened, and there stood Beckett. He wore jeans and a tight blue henley that highlighted the definition in his arms and shoulders. His hair was obviously wet, although no longer curling and *oh, he's just gotten out of the shower again*. She liked this pre-date habit.

"Hey," he said, pushing his damp hair out of his face. He stepped back to let her in, his eyes on her, his smile bright as if nothing delighted him more than her existence.

Callie was frozen in her tracks. *How is he so very attractive? And so very real? And so very normal?*

"Hi, you." She finally found her voice and leaned up to kiss him, like they'd been doing this forever. His beard scratched softly against her face, and she tugged gently against his lips before she pulled back again.

He looked slightly dazed as he waved her inside. "Come on in. I'd show you around, but you can pretty much see the whole thing from here."

He wasn't lying. The apartment itself was like something Callie expected a college student to be living in rather than anything she might have associated with a television star. Then again, this was a small town in Maine, and this was Beckett's work apartment, not his forever home.

The kitchen comprised a wall of cabinets and appliances with a short counter space, and was divided from the living room by a dining table and two mismatched wooden chairs. The living room furniture consisted of a loveseat she'd seen at Ikea, a coffee table that looked like it was straight from the 1950s, and a wicker rocking chair. Tying it all together, or at least trying to, was an orange-and-green area rug. To one side was a door, slightly ajar, that Callie assumed led to his bedroom.

She had to physically turn away from that and focus on the

kitchen because suddenly she wanted to know how many pillows Beckett slept with and what color his sheets were and what he looked like spread out against them. She had no plans to sleep with Beckett tonight — there was still so much about this situation she was learning to trust — but she definitely wanted to the moment she felt sure it wouldn't end in heartbreak.

"So. Food," she said, and if it was a little awkward, she almost didn't care. He had to know why, and there was no harm in that.

"Right." Beckett swallowed, and she realized it was more than possible that he was just as distracted by her as she was by him. Which was a heady thought. "So what are we making?"

*Focus, Callie. Focus.* "Uovo in raviolo. It's so good, but it takes too much effort to make when it's just me."

"I got everything you asked for." Beckett gestured at the kitchen counter.

"Awesome. And I brought some more stuff we're gonna need." Callie set her bag on the counter next to the groceries. "Have you ever made pasta before?"

She expected a no, but Beckett looked thoughtful. "My buddy Robert and I tried it once. I guess it went...okay?"

She tilted her head at that and felt a mix of emotions from mild surprise to gentle hope, right on up through morbid curiosity. That little question in his voice suggested it hadn't gone okay at all. Probably hadn't been as bad as the goat situation, though.

"This is going to be a great opportunity to refine your technique. We're gonna start with flour and eggs...."

Callie walked him through measuring out flour, making a well out of it, and breaking the eggs into its center to begin making the dough. He did it, without ceremony or pretense, but Callie was still transfixed as he cracked the eggs with one hand.

"You seem vaguely competent in the kitchen."

"I live alone, I have to be. I've just never had time to put any consistent effort into it."

"Fair enough," she said as she began to mix the ingredients together. Once it was slightly under control she grabbed his hands and placed them into the forming dough. "Now, knead. Until it's smooth and well-mixed."

Callie watched as Beckett sank his hands into the dough and proceeded to do as she'd said with methodical concentration. She had not realized how much of a problem his hands were going to present. She was transfixed by their size and their strength and she wanted those thick fingers gripping her flesh.... Or slipped up inside her.

*Or both, you really mean both,* she told herself before she finally managed to tear her eyes away and look at his face again. At which point, he proceeded to wink at her.

She laughed. "You absolute bastard."

"You were thinking loudly," he said.

"Mmmmm. No objections I hope?"

"Nope," he said as he continued to work.

"Good. You know, when I'm not just thinking it, I'll tell you right?"

"Figured. That's why I'm over here, just being good and doing the anticipation thing."

"And making sure we remember to eat." Callie added. She marveled at him and all his flirty attentiveness. He never pushed, but he was always right there, offering to if she wanted.

"So am I getting some of your culinary school knowledge here?" he asked.

Callie noted the deft change of topic. "Oh no." She laughed, maybe a little too bitterly. "This is all too casual and imprecise for that. This is from my grandma."

"Is that how you learned to cook? Originally? Your grandmother?"

"One of my many teachers. Greek-Italian family, remember? There was literally no escaping being competent in a kitchen."

"That sounds kind of amazing."

"Honestly, it kind of was." Which it had been, when relatives hadn't been badgering her to get married or not be hit by cars, or, more typically, both.

Getting the whole egg yolks into the raviolo proved to be where Beckett's kitchen proficiency fell down. He was all right at separating the yolks, but once it was time to close up the dough... egg everywhere. But this was fine, and low stakes. Much like the axe throwing, he brought a joy to failing, and Callie let him try and retry his approach until they were running low enough on eggs she had to take over if they were ever going to eat dinner.

Once the raviolo had been crafted, Callie turned their attention to dessert, which was comparatively easy: A pan of pistachio and rose-flavored claws she'd been experimenting with and was fully willing to test on Beckett. They just needed to be baked first.

She straightened up from sliding the claws into the oven and wiped the back of her hand across her sweaty forehead. "Once these are done, we'll pop the raviolo in some boiling water and dinner will be served."

"Sorry it's so hot in here," Beckett said. His own face was glistening, and his flyaways were a riot. Callie wanted nothing more than to press her mouth to the juncture of throat and collarbone and taste the salt of him there.

"I'm not. The hot and sweaty look is fantastic on you."

Beckett's cheeks flushed above his beard. "Thank you," he said with a small huff of laughter, which was a much more self-conscious reaction than she had expected.

"Bashful is also a good look on you, but surely you know what you look like," Callie added.

Beckett rubbed his hand along his jaw. "There's actually kinda a long answer to that?" he said. "Which I'm happy to give you whenever you want it, but I feel like I'm potentially killing a vibe here I don't really want to kill."

*That's interesting.* "I'll ask again later," she decided. "Because the vibe right now is great."

With that, she put her hands on his chest, the heat bleeding through his shirt, and tipped her face up to kiss him.

Beckett grabbed her face and kissed her back, swift and hard. Callie whimpered into his mouth, heat coursing through her. Then he bit her bottom lip, and Callie's brain shorted out.

She may have made a sound; she wasn't sure. Her ability to think was gone. There was only Beckett, the heat and strength and size of him enveloping her, and the bright sting of pain when he nipped at her mouth again.

"Holy shit." Callie pushed her hands against his chest. All it took was that gentlest of nudges for Beckett to pull back, his eyes glassy with desire but his smile smug. *How is he so* good? she wondered, not just about the kissing.

"You all right?" he asked, at once self-satisfied and concerned.

"You, sir, are a lot." Callie could still feel her heartbeat pounding all the way to her fingertips.

"Too much?" He was more concerned than smug now.

"No. Yes. A little," she confessed. Her nerves were on fire, it had been two years since she'd slept with anyone, and she needed a moment to collect herself. "I literally cannot think when you kiss me like that, are you always so bitey?"

Beckett laughed softly. "Do you like it?"

"Duh!" was the extent of Callie's ability to articulate. She pressed her forehead to his chest for a moment and closed her eyes. Despite the heat still zinging to the core of her, she felt safe here. Sheltered. Protected from the rest of the world and everything that had ever happened not in this room.

"Do you have an oven timer?" she asked.

"What?"

Callie picked her head up to look up at Beckett, who looked baffled. She, however, had a plan. "You know, oven timer. Thing you twist around like a clock and goes ding."

"So articulate."

"You try being kissed by you."

Beckett gave her a dimpled smile. "Yeah, I think so."

"You should find that," she said seriously. "I don't trust phone timers."

Beckett stepped away. Even that felt like a loss.

"Why don't you trust phone timers?" he asked curiously as he dug through a drawer.

Callie let a hint of mischief show through in her smile. "Because we've all gotten very good at ignoring our phones when we don't want to be interrupted."

Beckett finally found the timer and made a triumphant noise as he presented it to her. Callie set it for ten minutes.

"We need to check on that," she said, pointing at the oven, "when this goes off." She put the timer to the side on the counter and levered herself up to sit next to it. "And until then, we should make out."

She kicked a foot out to him, beckoning him to close the space between them. He wasted no time in stepping between her thighs. She whimpered against him as he kissed her. He was just as eager, his mouth firm and searching, his hands heavy on her thighs over the fabric of her jeans. Callie wrapped her legs around his and hooked her ankles together to pull him closer and let her hands roam all the muscled angles of him. As in the moment as she was, she was definitely planning ahead, albeit in an incoherent, porny torrent of images: Bodies twining together between cool summer sheets. Beckett's weight against her. Skin sliding on skin.

Hardness and heat. That damn self-satisfied smile of his...and knowing she'd be able to take him apart.

The images faded into glorious reality when Beckett slid his hands up between her legs. He took his time, watching her intently. Callie might have felt self-conscious at the attention — no one had ever looked at her like that, not even when she'd actually been having sex with them — but all her energy was focused on the trailing heat Beckett's touch left.

He traced his thumb along the inseam of her jeans, pressing as he went, until he finally got to her clit. Callie gasped sharply.

"This okay?" he asked, pressing again, blue eyes on her.

She nodded, and he twisted his hand to settle his fingers over the core of her. She was hot and damp and thrumming and god, she wanted him.

"You're so wet," he murmured into her skin.

"You can't just say stuff like that," Callie protested, or tried to. The words came out more like a garbled moan.

"Question."

"Why are you talking instead of kissing me?"

She could feel his smile against her throat. "It'll be worth it, I promise."

"Fiiiiine."

Beckett stopped kissing her throat, which suddenly made it seem like a very serious question was incoming.

"Can I make you come without taking your clothes off?" he asked, his blue eyes locked on hers.

"*Can you* as in will I let you try or *can you* as in you seem to think you have that skill?"

"Oh I can," Beckett repeated. "But since we're doing grammar pedantry, may I?"

"Oh, you can try," she said even as heat flooded her body at the very idea.

Beckett dropped another kiss on her lips. "Challenge accepted."

If Callie had thought she'd been overwhelmed by Beckett before, that had nothing on this moment, right now. Beckett kept kissing her — long, languid kisses that both set her at ease and left her lost. He worked methodically — a tug of her hair, a scrape of teeth over the shell of her ear, his tongue darting out to touch her open lips — until he found the thing that caused goosebumps to break out over her entire body.

He made a small sound of victory at that, and then kept doing it, while pressing the back of his knuckles between her legs and against her clit, for her to ride any way she wanted.

She had no idea why she had even bothered to doubt him. This was easy and perfect and just barely out of her grasp. At least right until he whispered in her ear.

"Time to let go."

She cried out in surprise as the first wave of her orgasm hit her, and then it kept going, and going. He shifted his fingers to touch her more gently, and that was all well and good but —

"Don't you dare move that hand, Beckett."

He froze at that, and then, carefully, gently pressed against her with those impossible fingers, an ebb and flow her body could answer as it came down and finally, finally, decided it was done.

Callie slumped against Beckett's chest, breathing hard. She wanted to lie down and let Beckett wrap her up in his arms and cuddle her through the afterglow. But to do that, she'd have to move, and that was definitely not going to happen just yet.

Belatedly, she realized her fingers were still digging into his arms. "Sorry," she said, loosening her grip.

"Don't be." Beckett pressed a kiss to her temple. He looked dazed. His cheeks were flushed, his eyes were wide, and his gaze was hazy. And he hadn't even gotten off.

Before she could offer to do something about that, Beckett straightened up from where they were slumped together. He crossed to the sink to turn on the tap. As Callie watched, baffled, he splashed a double handful of water on his face.

"Okay," he said, running wet hands through his hair. Stray drops of water ran down his temples and he wiped them off with the back of his hand. "Okay," he said again. "I'm okay. Now. Where were we?"

Before Callie could say anything, the oven timer went off.

# CHAPTER 16

<pre>
44°36'29.6"N 67°8'22.9"W
           Temp: 73.0°F
    Pressure: 29.75 inHg
        Wind: 9.17 mph, E
    Visibility:  10.00 mi
</pre>

BECKETT HAD THE WINDOWS down as he drove to Sweet Claws to pick Callie up for dinner at Robert's. He was eager; they hadn't seen each other since the night they'd cooked together at his apartment.

A week had passed and Beckett still found himself living in the delicious frustration of it. After dinner they'd made out on his couch for ages while the light outside the windows had faded from the glow of sunset to the deep velvet black of a summer night.

And that had been that. Callie had gone home and Beckett had reminded himself that desire was its own form of joy — even unsatisfied. That he wasn't even lying to himself was one of the benefits of getting older. The food, the company, the fooling around ... all of it had been great, and all of it had been a talisman that had gotten him through an unusually annoying week.

Matt, the crew member who had hassled Callie at Sweet Claws and who Beckett had duly reported to the production, had returned to LA. The official line was that he hadn't been a good fit for the show, which Beckett interpreted to mean he'd been fired. He didn't triumph in having cost someone their job — Matt was merely facing the consequences of his own actions — but Beckett was glad the *Hidden Cove* brass hadn't taken the incident lightly.

But any thoughts of Matt or indeed anything else vanished as he pulled up in front of Sweet Claws. Callie was already at the door locking up. She looked like a dream of summer in a yellow-flowered sundress, her coppery curls twisted into a braid and sunglasses perched on top of her head. When she turned around and saw him her smile was like the sun coming up over the hills.

*I am so gone*, Beckett admitted to himself.

Callie had brought a box full of claws with her to gift to their hosts, and her fingers tapped restlessly against it as Beckett turned his car into Robert's driveway, gravel crunching under the tires.

"Nervous?" he asked.

Callie looked over at him. "Should I be?"

"Nah," he said easily. "I'm just checking in. Robert and Julie are good people, and you're excellent. It's going to be fine."

"I appreciate the vote of confidence. Because I definitely feel like this is the get-approval-of-friends date and that's a little intimidating."

"Maybe, I'm getting your approval of my friends," Beckett suggested. After all, they did have a track record on that score.

As he and Callie climbed out of the car Robert waved from the open garage. He did not look ready for company, considering he was wearing earmuffs and safety glasses and holding an electric sander. Beckett did not feel one single iota of surprise at the sight of such ridiculousness, but was at least relieved when his friend put the sander down and began to divest himself of his safety gear.

"I was worried we were gonna have shop class instead of dinner," Beckett said when they reached Robert and his project.

Next to him, Callie shrugged. "I dunno," she said, "I could do shop class."

Beckett had never had any real concerns about her fitting in, or making a good impression, but if he had, they would've all vanished at that. Robert, he could tell, agreed.

"So you're Callie the doughnut girl," he said, warmly.

"That's me," Callie said brightly as she peered into the garage, where a half-built hull was overturned on a pair of sawhorses. "Am I seeing what I think I'm seeing?"

Robert's face lit up at her question. "My pet project. It's a peapod, at least it's supposed to be. C'mon, let me show you." *Hidden Cove* had made everyone working on it a little crazy over the years, each in their own ways. For Robert, it had been deciding to build a boat.

Beckett settled himself comfortably against a tool chest and proceeded to watch his best friend and his girlfriend bond over a shared passion for carpentry and, apparently, watercraft. He shrugged to himself. Stranger things had happened, but rarely better ones.

"What kind of finish are you going to use?" Callie asked curiously, running a fingertip along the grain of the planking.

"I was thinking tung oil," Robert said.

Callie hummed thoughtfully, her forehead creasing adorably. "Do you want my opinion?" she asked.

Robert tilted his head. "Sure."

"Oil gives you a gorgeous finish, but the work isn't worth it. You have to put on like twelve coats and then a bunch of UV protective finish, and it's an absolute pain to maintain."

Robert nodded seriously, but Beckett had questions. And not about oil finishes.

"Where did you learn so much about boats?" he asked. The woodworking know-how made sense with all the work she'd put into Sweet Claws, but the question of marine wood finishing was another matter.

"We live in Maine. Everyone knows boats," Callie said breezily.

Beckett added another tally mark to his mental column of possible Callie secrets. This one, when he got the story, was going to be good. He was sure of it.

"And on that note," Robert said, with a glance at his watch. "Unless we really want to swap shop class for dinner, I should get in to the house. C'mon, you two."

# CHAPTER 17

44°36'29.6"N 67°8'22.9"W
Temp: 71.1°F
Pressure: 29.77 inHg
Wind: 5.82 mph, SE
Visibility: 10.00 mi

ROBERT AND JULIE'S HOUSE was like a picture out of Callie's fantasies of an idyllic childhood. The windows were open to let in the soft summer breeze, the couches were untidy and clearly lived on, and the floor was an absolute mess of half-built lego constructions, baby toys, and children's footwear.

"I'd apologize for the mess," Robert said as everyone toed off their own shoes. "But that might make you think it ever doesn't look like this, which would be a lie."

"I love it," Callie said honestly. Her childhood had been chaotic and noisy, but that had been more the product of older family members and their adult drama and enthusiasms, not siblings or playmates.

"There you are! I was starting to wonder if the bears had gotten you." Robert's wife looked up from where she was sitting on the floor with a baby in her lap, a board book open in one hand. "Hi, Callie. Good to see you."

Callie waved to her. "You too! How are you?"

"Oh, you know. Living the dream," Julie said, with a soft smile of contentment that Callie envied.

"We were showing Callie the peapod," Robert said. "She has feelings about the finish."

"Oh God," Julie said. "She's one of y'all. Whyyyyyyyyyyy."

"Julie judges my seafaring ambitions," Robert said, going to the sink to wash his hands.

"No, Julie judges you taking up that much space in the garage for something that's not your car," Julie said. "But I do appreciate your seafaring ambitions more than the time you wanted to build a motorbike."

"Spoiler alert," Beckett put in, drily. "Robert was not allowed to build a motorbike."

"Julie is a smart woman," Callie said. Even as she enjoyed everyone's banter about it, Julie was right. It was too easy to get seriously hurt on one. And that was coming from her.

"And don't I know it." Robert leaned down to drop a kiss on Julie's cheek.

Beckett caught Callie's eye, and they exchanged smiles at the cuteness of the moment.

"Want me to start the grill?" Robert asked.

"If you would. But first, can you take her?" Julie nodded to the baby. "I have to pee."

"Can I?" Beckett offered.

"By all means. But she needs a change, which is why I was gonna make Robert do that."

"Oh that's no problem. Let's go get you cleaned up — wow, you do stink, little miss." Beckett laughed as he picked up the little girl, who giggled at him.

Callie already had a lot of evidence that Beckett was thoughtful and eager to help. Still, she was a little floored when he carried Dahlia over to the corner of the room where there was a stack of diapers and packs of wipes and just — changed the baby's diaper as if that was a thing men did as a matter of course. Which, in Callie's admittedly limited experience, was not at all the case.

Her musings on that point were interrupted by the two boys, aged about seven and five, barging into the house through the sliding door that led to the deck.

"Miss Doughnut Lady!" Grayson, the older of the two, called. "Want to watch me climb the tree?"

The younger boy, Dominic, held back a little, and returned Callie's smile shyly. She didn't see them in the shop as often as she did Julie and the baby, but they were still familiar faces.

"I would be happy to," she said. "Assuming it's all right with your folks?" She glanced over her shoulder.

Robert waved them on. "Go on, they've done more dangerous stuff than that."

"These kids are living *my* dream," Callie said as she and Beckett followed the boys outside, along with Julie and Dahlia. They were joined by a Labrador retriever, who sniffed happily all over Callie's hands and shoes, tail wagging ferociously, before dashing off after the boys.

"Yeah?" Beckett leaned back against the deck railing, which

was a pose that showed off his arms and chest to great advantage.

"Yeah." Callie resisted the urge to wrap her hands around his biceps. "Built-in playmates *and* being allowed to take managed risks?"

"Built-in playmates and managed risks was pretty much my entire life as a kid. Sometimes unmanaged risks," he added.

"Beckett, you are old, there is no way any of those risks were managed. Did you even have seatbelts when you were little?" Callie tugged her braid over her shoulder and twisted it around her fingers to keep herself from reaching out to touch him. Here, in his friends' backyard, was neither the time nor the place.

Beckett's mouth quirked with a smile, but his eyes strayed to her hands. "I'm not that old. Yes, we had them. Just...wearing them was still optional."

They were interrupted by a shout from the backyard. "Uncle Beckett! Miss Doughnut Lady! Watch us!!!"

Beckett turned around. "We're watching!"

Once the boys had gone up the tree and come down again, they demanded at least one of the grownups join them to play frisbee. Beckett gamely volunteered and Callie settled down on the deck next to Julie and Dahlia, who were stacking brightly colored blocks. Robert tended the grill.

"So, question for you," Callie said, beginning a block construction of her own.

"Mmm?" Julie asked.

"Is Beckett out there being awesome with your kids to give you the opportunity to tell me why he's terrible or is that, in fact, the extent of the message right there?"

Robert and Julie glanced at each other and had some sort of wordless conversation.

"Yes." Robert finally said.

"Interesting."

"Not what you expected?" Robert asked.

"Honestly? I don't know." Callie turned a block around in her hands. "We're having a great time. He's lovely. And unexpected. I keep waiting for the catch."

Julie nodded. "You're looking at it."

Callie started arranging blocks in rainbow order, only to have Dahlia pick up and chew on each one after she set it down. "Why is he single?" She'd asked Beckett that before, but she wanted his best friend's take.

"He doesn't seem single right now," Robert said.

Callie shook her head. Contemplating how serious of a relationship she and Beckett were in was a little too much for the present moment.

"I mean, why isn't he married with a bunch of kids?"

Robert seemed to ponder that. "He's a good guy. And my best friend — I love him like a brother. But you know the thing where sometimes you'll be talking to someone about a given topic and they say something totally random except it's not totally random? Like, there were a series of steps that got them there but they forgot to tell you what those steps were or that they happened?"

"Yeah?"

"That's what he does to people he dates. He falls too hard and too fast and makes leaps without checking in. And if it hasn't happened yet, it will. Your mission, if you choose to accept it, is to not kill him when he is inevitably exactly who he is."

Callie was surprised to feel something like — was it disappointment? That wasn't reasonable. She and Beckett had only been on three dates, not counting this family dinner with his friends. Callie hadn't been looking for a partner or even particularly looking toward the future. They weren't at all serious. But if what Robert and Julie were telling her was true, there wasn't anything particular about Beckett's interest in her. That he was dating her came down to what he himself had said at first: She wasn't a part of *Hidden Cove*, nor really an established part of the Fly-Debate community. If and when their relationship came to an end, the blast radius would be limited. He wanted to date someone; he just happened to be dating her. Callie could have been anyone.

But with that disappointment — if nothing else, her ego was stung — came relief. If Beckett wasn't serious about Callie in particular, the stakes of her relationship with him were a lot lower. Maybe that was the thing that Callie needed to finally take Sydney's advice, relax, and just enjoy being with him.

They ate out on the deck, which was exactly as chaotic as Callie would have expected of any meal involving three kids under the age of ten, plus one very good dog, Daisy, who deployed deadly puppy eyes in her ongoing quest for people food.

"Oh my God, she's worse than you are," Callie exclaimed to Beckett as Daisy sat on the floor next to her, watching beseechingly as they handed around a platter of hamburgers.

"I strongly doubt that," said Robert. "You've never seen Beckett at a meeting with the studio bigwigs. All he has to do is look at them and he gets what he wants."

"That is the product of a lot of experience and extremely calculated charm," Beckett protested. It sounded like an old, fond argument.

"I mean maybe, but it's mostly your eyes."

Callie felt a warmth bubble up in her chest. Such a comment between women wouldn't have been notable, but in her experience, men were too rarely affectionate and complimentary with each other in that way. Confidence, and non-toxic masculinity, was such a goddamn turn on.

"Speaking of things Beckett wants and gets," Julie put in. "How's the prep for the premiere going?"

Beckett groaned. "Nothing going on there is anything I want."

Robert cackled. "Only because you're allergic to LA."

"So are you," Beckett retorted.

"Yeah, but nobody needs my face at red carpet events."

"There is no reason the premiere has to be in LA," Beckett complained. "Literally everyone involved in the show is right here. Making us all fly back for seventy-two hours is nonsensical."

"What's wrong with LA? Or premieres or whatever?" Callie was curious. "A work trip to Los Angeles sounds awesome."

"There is nothing wrong with Los Angeles," Beckett said. "But basically, it's like...." He gestured, evidently looking for words. "The cast has to get photographed going to a party to celebrate the release of the show, which happens in a way completely unconnected to us having a party or watching the thing ourselves. So it's just this big manufactured thing followed by a couple of media days that involves like thirty interviews featuring the exact same questions every fifteen minutes from different journalists who are hoping I'll finally be tired enough to say something interesting."

"This is why I'm not an actor," Robert said.

Beckett slumped back in his seat. "Don't get me wrong. I'm

excited for people to see the season, but the process *sucks.*"

"So has it ever happened?" Callie asked, taking a sip of her water and shooting a smirk at Beckett.

"Has what happened?"

"You getting tired enough to say something interesting."

"Not that I recall," Beckett said blandly, which Callie would have taken for a yes even if Robert hadn't started laughing.

"It's on YouTube," Julie told Callie across the table in a stage whisper.

"What did you do?" she demanded, turning to Beckett. A small part of her was worried that it was going to be something mean or otherwise terrible that would make her reconsider her good opinion of him. But if Julie and Robert were also amused by it, hopefully it would just be one more thing she could have fun giving him a hard time about.

Beckett gave a resigned sigh and sat back up. "Okay, so interviews are like, you sit in this hotel room and every fifteen minutes they bring in another journalist and there's like water and snacks."

"And," Robert cut him off. "Some sort of media assistant who helps people get their snacks."

"Which is silly," Beckett retorted. "Anyway, I tried to be hospitable and pour this journalist water and accidentally dumped a whole pitcher of it on her. And then I babbled."

Callie clapped her hand over her mouth to hold in the giggle. Definitely not a terrible story, then. She could just see it — Beckett, in all his unselfconscious attractiveness, so determined to be kind and considerate, making a mess and then making everything worse by trying to fix it.

"That's why they have people who know how to pour water, Beckett," Robert said.

"Everyone knows how to pour water!" Beckett protested.

"Obviously not." Callie said, no longer bothering to hide her giggles.

"Yeahhhhhh." Beckett gave a resigned sigh. "It has like seventy thousand views online because of course the reporter was recording on her phone for 'cool behind the scenes media day exclusives.' The exclusive is, I'm a disaster."

❈

Later, after the kids had been put to bed, Robert and Beckett built a fire in the backyard firepit. They sat around it together with glasses of wine while Robert and Beckett told stories of youthful escapades they'd gotten up to together, with Julie helpfully interjecting at intervals. The story of the goat had nothing on their adventure with a pumpkin cannon. Or the taxidermied goose.

Callie tucked her legs up under her and leaned her head on Beckett's shoulder. He turned to smile at her, then wrapped his arm around her shoulders and pulled her close. He smelled like warm cotton and woodsmoke.

The cool night air and the quiet emptiness of it all reminded her of life on her boat, where sound was constant, but other people were almost non-existent. Being able to achieve that feeling here, in the presence of others, was a relief. She'd never managed to feel anything of the sort with her own family, who had always had big, loud opinions and no time for anything Callie had to say for herself.

Beckett's friends — and Beckett himself — were not, of course, without agenda, but everyone here trusted her to make her own decisions. They didn't question her ability to take care of herself. It never even occurred to them to make it a discussion.

She wanted to say something about all of that. But to do so, she would have to be more forthright about everything — the severity of the accident, her tumultuous relationship with her parents, the fact that she lived on a boat just because it was hard. Callie was going to have to untangle all of that, for him and in her own life, eventually. But she couldn't do it now, not all at once and not while they were guests at someone else's house.

The fire highlighted the planes of Beckett's face. He was so perfect he might have been a statue hewed from golden stone and so beautiful he made her ache. People didn't look like this in real life, and she was aware, not for the first time, that he spent a good amount of energy trying to hide it. She wasn't sure she liked that. Not for herself and not for him. It should be easier for a person to be who they were.

They'd been taking things slow, and hard questions between them were asked so much more often than they were answered. That had been as much her idea as his. More, probably. But Beckett was stunning; he was thoughtful; he was kind. Callie trusted him. And if she really was going to relax and enjoy being with him — Well. Callie was ready to be done with being cautious.

She lifted her head off his shoulder and turned to face him. "You —" She touched a finger to the center of his chest.

"Me?"

"Should come see my place. Next time your terrible show gives you more than twenty-four hours off."

Callie watched as Beckett's smile spread from one sly corner of his mouth to the other.

"I'd love to," he said, his eyes looking at her with wonder.

# CHAPTER 18

44°30'41.8"N 67°20'49.7"W
Temp: 64.9°F
Pressure: 29.86 inHg
Wind: 11.5 mph, NE
Visibility:  2.00 mi

OVERNIGHT THE WEATHER TURNED, and Beckett drove to work through a gray haze. By mid-morning rain started coming down, and by noon it was pouring buckets. The lunch tents were crowded with cast and crew escaping or at least taking a break from getting drenched, so Beckett grabbed his food and headed back toward the set town. There, he sat on the front porch of one of the houses that lined the little street leading to the quay, listening to the rain drum on the roof and patter into puddles in the mud. He wasn't technically supposed to do stuff like this, but he always made sure to tidy up after himself, and on a day like this everyone had other things to worry about.

A figure trudged up the street, hood cinched around their head and holding a travel mug — Robert, Beckett realized, when the figure was close enough for him to be able to distinguish his sodden rain jacket. He waved his friend over.

"What a day in paradise," Robert muttered, shoving his hood back. He dropped down to sit next to Beckett. "The rain is washing out all the track. We can't keep it steady in the mud."

"Joy." Washed out track meant a long day, or worse, a day where work that needed to get done couldn't, resulting in cost overruns and general misery.

"Yeah."

"Thanks for dinner last night," Beckett said.

"Of course. The kids loved Callie."

"What did you think of her?" Beckett asked, not without some trepidation. Callie had made a good impression, but that didn't mean Robert didn't still hold his doubts.

"I think she's perfect for you. I'm less sure you're perfect for her," Robert said.

"Okay," Beckett said slowly. "What does that mean?"

"It means," Robert said, "that if you're going to fall back into old habits, you're dragging an extremely nice person who's eighteen years younger than you along for the miserable ride."

"What makes you think I'm going to do any such thing?" Beckett's confusion was morphing into hurt. And maybe a little bit of irritation.

Robert scraped his fingers back through his rain-sodden hair, making it stand on end. "Because I know you," he finally said.

"What did you tell her?" Beckett was suddenly suspicious.

"Nothing you don't already know."

"Robert."

"Oh, turn that glare off. She asked why you're not already married with a bunch of kids. I told her because you fall too hard too fast."

"Why'd you do that?"

"Because it's true!"

"That was ten years ago!" Beckett's irritation increased. "I like, respect, and admire Callie. Do you have to try to sabotage this?"

"I'm not," Robert said steadily. Beckett recognized his patient father explaining things in small words to children tone, which didn't lessen his irritation. "She asked the question. And she deserved the answer."

"Thanks for that, then." Beckett knew he was sulking. And he knew it wasn't attractive. But he was long, long past trying to be anything but what he was in front of Robert.

"Buck up." Robert clapped him on the shoulder obnoxiously. "From what I was trying very hard not to overhear, none of that seemed to scare her off."

Beckett knew Robert was telling the truth. He and Callie already had their next date scheduled, this time at her place. He didn't want to read too much into that, but concerns about Beckett's ability to be a good boyfriend or partner were probably not part of the agenda.

A week later, Beckett pushed open the door to Sweet Claws to the now-familiar chime of bells over the door. Callie smiled brightly at him from her spot behind the counter but was clearly occupied with a highly indecisive carload of tourists. He wasn't about to interrupt her at work, so he found a seat at one of the tables by the window and pulled out his book, more than happy to bask in the scent of sugar and butter and the happy cadence of Callie's voice as she — very patiently — dealt with her customers.

"Sorry about that," she said as the door finally closed behind them. "I was just about to close up when they pulled in."

"No need to apologize." Beckett flipped his book closed and smiled up at her. "I like watching you work."

"Okay, flatterer." Callie frowned. "Why?"

"You're relentlessly competent. You light up whenever you're talking to someone. You love what you do and you glow whenever you're doing it. Also — is it weird to say? It might be weird to say. But your hands are captivating."

"I try," she said gamely.

But Beckett watched as she looked down at her hands, which were still slightly floury, and twisted her fingers together. A scar, presumably from her accident, ran from the back of her wrist up her arm. He'd clearly set off some train of thought in her head, but before he could ask questions or apologize, she tossed her hair back and seemed to recover herself.

"Want to help me close up? Emma's got a mural client over in Sealport this week."

"At your service, as always."

Once the work in the shop was done, Callie led the way to her truck. She took the road out of town and down the shore to where it turned to follow the edge of one of the inlets that eventually opened out into the sea.

"Hey, we've filmed down here before," Beckett noted as the road began to slope to the water.

Callie, slowing to take a particularly tricky turn, glanced over at him. "Yeah?"

"Yeah. I flipped my boat just over there," he pointed through the trees. "I remember that outcrop of spruce vividly."

"What kind of boat?!" Callie demanded. A smile was tugging at the corner of her mouth. Beckett knew he was about to be made fun of, and did not at all mind.

"Canoe. My brothers and sister and I used to go canoeing in the lake near our house when we were growing up, so I was all confident, but it turns out your weight distribution changes somewhere between the ages of fourteen and forty."

"I'm also assuming you didn't have all that muscle when you were fourteen."

"Oh God no. I was scrawny as hell. Anyway, it was right at the start of the first season. They had us come out early for boat and fish camp. First day in the water, I thought I was so cool — next thing I knew I was in the drink. Nobody let me live that down for weeks." Beckett chuckled. "But, looking back on it, it went a long way to getting rid of a lot of unnecessary hierarchy. I was just a guy with more lines than some of the other guys."

Callie cackled; there was no other word for the delighted sound she was making. "That is an image I am going to relish."

She turned down the rutted, bumpy lane and pulled off into a little gravel lot. Beckett was somewhat puzzled. They weren't in front of a house or an apartment building; he couldn't see any structures of any sort. There were just woods, water and sky. He had the thought, faintly, that this was how fairy tales, the old kind with monsters in the dark woods, began.

"Pretty out here," he said as he stepped out of the car. *Where the hell is your house?!* felt like an obvious thing to say, but also too bizarre to have to ask. The only sounds were the chirring of insects and, farther off, the gentle lap of waves on the shore. The water was visible through the trees, the lowering sun glistening across it in sparkles of gold and ruby. The breeze tasted of salt and pine.

"I know." Callie breathed out, a deep, contented sound.

"You're close to the water, aren't you?" Beckett asked as they made their way down the path. He didn't bother to hide his envy — assuming, of course, forest spirits or water goblins or who even knew what weren't lying in wait for them around the next turn.

"Pretty close."

"I'm jealous."

"You should be." Callie gave him an impish grin.

Her teasing was as enchanting as it ever was — but the hair on the back of Beckett's neck was still standing up. There were no houses down here. For all he knew she was about to drown him in the bay.

They rounded a corner of the path and were abruptly standing on a wooden deck, the trees falling away down the slope to the water and a set of stairs leading down to a dock, gimbaled to allow for the rise and fall of the tide.

Beckett looked around, expecting — hoping even — to see a little cabin perched on this breathtaking spot. But the only structure was a dock, with a houseboat — dark blue, white trim, gleaming cedar planking — moored at the end of it.

Callie was watching him expectantly. It was her face, half-laughing, half-anticipatory, that made it click in his head.

Beckett felt all the air rush out of his lungs in relief. "*This* is your house." There was no creepy magic lurking here in the woods or the water. His strange and wonderful girlfriend just happened to live on a boat.

"Yeah." She grinned broadly.

"You live on a boat?" He couldn't help but repeat the obvious. It was so wildly unlikely and also so perfectly obvious.

"Uhuh."

The last five years of Beckett's life had been consumed by a career in which he pretended to be a man who lived and died by watercraft and the sea. And now here he was, falling for a girl who wasn't even from here and yet, unaccountably, lived on a boat — no easy feat in these cold waters. He threw his head back and laughed. The universe was most certainly speaking to him, in all its peculiar and out-of-order glory.

"This is so fucking cool," Beckett exclaimed as he stepped onto the deck of the boat after her. On the side was a decal of a jauntily waving lobster perched in a taco shell wearing a sailor's hat. Beside that was the boat's name: *Lobster Taco*.

"Thanks." Callie unlocked the door and pushed it open for him to follow.

Inside was a trim little space decorated with more white paint and warm wood. There was a tiny kitchen, a cozy living space with a bench couch and table, and a neatly made queen-sized bed tucked under an expanse of windows at the bow.

"This is incredible." Beckett set down the grocery bags and looked around in awe. "You've been here the whole time you've lived here?"

"Pretty much. I wanted more control than I could get by renting, but I had a hard time finding a house up here that would work for just one person. Most of what I looked at was just too big

— I didn't need all that extra space. And then friends of friends were selling their boat. First of all, if you have the opportunity to buy a boat named *Lobster Taco*, how could you not? And then I figured that I'd already moved all the way up here and bought the shop. How hard could it be?" Callie gave a rueful laugh. "Turns out, pretty fucking hard sometimes. Especially in the winter. But I couldn't give her up now." She patted one of the beams, a fond smile on her face. "We've been through a lot together."

"Well, *Lobster Taco*." Beckett put his hand to the doorframe he'd just walked through. "It's nice to meet you."

He looked back to see Callie watching him, a soft smile on her face.

"You look good here," she said quietly.

"I'm glad," Beckett said, both earnest and solemn, not taking his eyes from Callie's face. She wasn't a water witch, or anything Beckett had been afraid of, but he could still feel the universe bending around her, around the both of them. This was one of those moments, a pivot point, from which every possible future extended. They just had to choose which one to grab onto. From the way Callie was looking at him, he was almost sure she felt it too.

"So." She rubbed her fingers along the countertop, sifting, he thought, through the strands of their future. "To be direct. I invited you here so you could spend the night. With the fucking that generally implies. Assuming you're on board. With the fucking."

"I am definitely on board."

She gave him that impish smile again and, God, he adored her. He was about to reach for her, but Callie wasn't done talking yet.

"I could cook first, and that whole thing, but I'm a great cook, which you know, and the food's gonna be rich, which you also know. So, um, do you wanna fuck now and then I'll make us middle of the night omelettes, which by the way will also be great?"

"You are perfect, you know that?" Beckett said.

Callie's eyes sparkled. With joy. But also relief. "I do, but you should keep telling me. So is that a yes?"

"Yeah," Beckett breathed.

With the space as small as it was, it only took him a step and a half to cross the kitchen, grab her head in his hands and kiss her. Callie's mouth opened instantly under his and she made a sound, half whimper, half triumph, that went straight to Beckett's dick and also steeled his focus. He wanted to keep making her make sounds like that,

"I want to take you to your bed," he growled in her ear. "And I want to fuck you. And I want to make it the most amazing fucking sex you have ever had."

"You sure set your bars low." Callie's voice was sarcastic but breathless, and Beckett kissed down the column of her throat while she tipped her head back and panted at the ceiling, her fingers tightening in his hair. Which was a great start, but Beckett wanted to do more for her.

He wanted to do everything for her.

```
44°28'46.3"N 67°30'54.7"W
            Temp: 70.0°F
   Pressure: 29.90 inHg
      Wind: 5.75 mph, n
 Visibility:  ≥ 10.00 mi
```

CALLIE HAD EXPECTED ENTHUSIASM — Beckett had never been anything but an eager partner — but the way he was guiding her backwards, towards the bow and her bed, one hand on the back of her head as he kept kissing her, the other expertly undoing the buttons down the front of her dress, was frankly next fucking level. Plus, no one was getting concussed on her low ceilings. *Victory all around!*

Her knees hit the back of her bed, and he stopped for a moment, their foreheads pressed together. Callie let out a faint whimper.

"Too much?" he asked They hadn't yet done more than kiss but he already looked so wrecked. His cheeks were flushed, his chest was heaving, and his hair was an absolute mess.

Calle got her fingers into the front of his jeans and went to work on the fastening. "Absolutely not," she said, holding his gaze. They were here, he was perfect, and she was going to enjoy this for as long as it lasted. "Not for me. You?"

He answered with another bruising kiss that toppled them onto the bed, a tangle of half-undressed limbs and bodies. Beckett finally got her dress unbuttoned and pushed it back off her shoulders, then stared at her, his face slack, as if he were gazing upon some ancient art object.

She preened a little at that, stretching her arms up over her head and arching her back.

"You are incredibly beautiful," he whispered, his voice reverent even as his eyes were still wild. With his fingertips he traced from her throat, over the curve of her breast and down her stomach.

She squirmed under his touch, heat pooling in her core and every nerve alight where he was touching her. Everything was already so much, but she still wanted more.

Beckett took his hands away. Callie was going to protest, but then she realized he was only finishing peeling his own clothes off. Which was something she was not going to complain about. The shirtless pictures she'd seen before didn't begin to do him justice. His shoulders were so broad, his chest defined, and his arms were so perfect she had to fight down that entirely unreasonable urge to bite them. And she'd never seen his ass before...or his dick. Both of which were well worth looking at. Which she did. At length.

He'd bared himself, she realized, leaving his own body naked and vulnerable before he divested her of the rest of her clothes. Which was not, in her experience, how these things usually went. Beckett was gorgeous — he had to know he was gorgeous; he was all muscle and texture and pure broad strength — but still, it was an offering to her. And a vulnerable one at that.

It was also incredibly hot.

He asked no questions and made no comments about the scars spiderwebbing their way across her body, just ran his hands over her skin like he couldn't touch her enough. They stared at each other for another long moment before, again, Beckett crashed their mouths together. This time, the scratch of hair and the tug of skin on skin made everything so much more. Callie wrapped a leg around his waist — she could feel the hard heat of his dick against her thigh — and moaned into his mouth.

Then, suddenly, Beckett grabbed her and flipped them so that he was on his back on her sheets and she was on top of him.

"Up." He tapped the back of her legs. Callie shifted herself onto her knees. The heat in her center became almost unbearable when Beckett closed his hands on her ass and pulled her farther up the bed.

She leaned her arms on the headboard, put her knees on either side of his face, and didn't even have to sink down. He grabbed her hips and pulled himself up to lick her open, before pulling her down to exactly where his mouth wanted her.

Callie let out a moan, louder than any before, and quickly slapped a hand over her mouth. She'd expected this to be good, but not so good, so fast.

He stopped just long enough to scold her. "Come on, I want to hear you." He tried to bat away the hand covering her mouth. She could feel his warm breath against her, which absolutely wasn't helping matters.

"Do you have any idea how sound carries out here?" she hissed at him.

"So apologize later."

"Beckett," she said, like a warning. But a warning against what, she didn't know. Just, if he wanted loud, he was going to get loud.

"What?" he said and twisted two of his thick fingers up inside her. He pressed them against her g-spot, which always felt different from other things. Like it would crack her open and make her cry. Not in a bad way, but it wasn't fair at all.

Too much, too much, this man was too much.

Then he had to go and speak again. "Apology doughnuts. It'll be fine."

She stared down at him, and the stupid, pleased grin on his wet face, and was just about to say something sharp and clever, because that's what they did. But then his mouth was on her again, and she really did scream, and oh well, apology doughnuts it was going to have to be.

After she came, Callie shuffled her way down on the bed so she could kiss Beckett, his beard damp and scratching against her skin in a way that set her already taxed nerves on fire. His broad chest was flushed, and the muscles in his arms shifted as he lifted his hands to tangle them in her hair.

"Been wanting to do this for a while," he breathed into her mouth.

"Eat me out?" Callie grinned at him.

"Oh yes. Very much so. But also your hair," Beckett said. "Like this." He twisted a curl around his fingers. His hand brushed her shoulder gently, making goosebumps break out all up and down her arm.

"You know what I have been wanting to do for a while?"

"No, but I would love to be enlightened."

Callie smirked at him, then lowered her head. She pressed a kiss to his bicep, then got her teeth into that skin, stretched over thick muscle, and bit.

Beckett gasped, then whimpered as she sucked a bruising kiss into his skin. His hips moved uselessly against the sheets. Callie managed to kick the bedding out of the way and sit astride him, his dick pressed against her stomach.

Beckett grabbed her waist, his fingers gripping tight enough to bruise. "How do you want this?" His voice was breathless again, and spots of color had appeared high on his cheeks.

Callie lifted one shoulder in half a shrug. "Whatever works for you." As long as she got his dick in her at some point tonight, she was going to be content.

"Oh no. No." Beckett's hips were still moving under her, desperate for the friction they couldn't get like this. "What works for *you*?"

"You do realize you just got me off with the best orgasm of my life?"

"And?"

"And I've never had a dude try to get me off more than once, so now it's your turn?"

"Oh, Callie." Beckett's eyes were glassy with desire, but they took on a determined edge. "It's time to change that."

"Oh yeah?" There was that challenge thing between them again. Beckett, confident, assertive, marginally in control, and determined to prove that his one purpose was to serve and worship her.

Callie wrapped her fingers around his dick, relishing the way his eyelids fluttered.

"Callie," he gasped, as she ran her fingers up and down the length of him, teasing velvety skin.

"That's me." She wanted to drink in this sight, Beckett's perfect body stretched out under her. She wanted to feel him in her hand like this, hard, heavy heat. She wanted, despite the fact that she'd just come, to feel him inside her.

"Callie...." Like her name was a prayer. Or a magic spell.

"Mmmm?"

"Please." The word was barely a whisper, and it was so hot Callie thought she saw stars.

"Well." She tried to hang onto the teasing tone, but this moment was quickly arcing past desperate for the both of them. "Since you asked so nicely."

Beckett held her gaze as she lifted her hips, one hand finding hers to help guide him inside her. His eyes stayed locked on her as she sank down on him in increments, hips shifting, adjusting to the feeling of fullness. His eyes were so very blue, like the ocean in the morning, and like the ocean, Callie felt like she could drown in them, be swept under and lost.

The prospect was not nearly as frightening as it should have been.

She started to move and could feel it when Beckett took a sharp breath, and then another. His arms were trembling, his fingers sharp points of pressure in her thighs.

Callie leaned forward, letting her hair fall across him in a curtain.

"Don't hold back on my account," she murmured.

Beckett surged up to meet her mouth. The kiss was bruising, biting, the way the kiss in his kitchen had been. Back when Callie hadn't quite been ready to fall completely into this.

But she was ready now. Oh, was she ready. She bit back, felt pleasure bolt through her at Beckett's hiss. He wrapped his arms around her, holding her there, while he lifted his hips to meet hers as she ground down onto him. The strength of him, the size of him...he was everywhere, around her and in her, and Callie kissed him and kissed him and let herself be surrounded.

She's been hopeful, but still, she couldn't help but be surprised when the need inside of her began to spark over to pleasure, Beckett's cock filling her, the nerves at her very core thrumming. Something of her surprise must have shown on her face, because Beckett laughed, the sound giddy and self-satisfied.

"Didn't think I could do it?"

"I'll never doubt you again," Callie said solemnly, or as solemnly as she could as their movements became more arhythmic.

"Doubt me as much as you want. As long as you let me prove you wrong."

He unwrapped one of his arms from around her, and Callie was going to complain about that until he brought his hand between them, his fingers exploring her folds, sliding through slick and sweat until they reached her clit.

"Oh holy fuck," Callie gasped as his fingers circled her there, drawing waves of pleasure that rose with every touch like the incoming tide. She dug her own hands into his chest. "There, there, Beckett, please...."

He kissed her again, mouth hot and desperate against hers, his fingers pressing just where she needed them as he thrust into her again and again, pleasure building until it crashed over her like a wave, shaking her from the inside, sparks of sensation rolling over her.

Beckett gasped, then gave a low, choked moan, and he was coming too, thrusting into her hard and irregular, drawing out Callie's own orgasm until they both slumped together onto her bed.

"Holy fuck," Callie said again, her face now smushed against Beckett's chest. Beckett laughed again, that giggle she loved so much, but now it was breathless and sated, almost disbelieving.

He lifted his head to press a kiss to her forehead.

"I agree."

Beckett's cheeks and chest were still flushed, and his hair was a wild mess. He was unspeakably gorgeous, and Callie sank back on the bed, the better to stare at him.

"It is extremely rude of you to just go walking around like this." Callie waved a hand to encompass the entirety of his being. "This much sexiness should not exist in one person."

"I can guarantee you I do not have a monopoly on sexiness."

"You know you're indecently good at that."

Beckett lowered his eyes, somehow demure despite the fact that they were a naked, sweaty, limb-tangled heap. "When I've got the right partner."

"Oh, stop." Callie laughed and rolled over, then scooted backwards so Beckett could curl around her. He draped an arm, heavy and peppered with bruises and bite marks, over her waist.

Callie traced the marks with her fingertips, mapping out patterns between them like constellations. "Er, sorry about that."

Beckett's laugh was a rumble that she could feel as much as hear. "Don't be." Callie felt him press a kiss to the back of her head. "Although the makeup people are definitely going to give me shit about that."

"Ooops?"

"They like giving me shit; it'll be fine."

Beckett ran his hand up and down her arm for a few moments, then spoke again. "You should come to LA with me. For the premiere. If you want."

"Wait, what now?" Calle craned her neck to try to look at him, but she couldn't see him from this angle.

"The season premiere I was complaining about at Robert's. It's in a couple of weeks. Do you want to come with me?" Beckett said, like she might have simply not heard him, rather than be surprised and a little overwhelmed. "You don't have to answer now," he added hastily. "But there will be a decent party and good weather. I'll be tied up with work for a chunk of it, but a bunch of the partners and what not usually do some stuff together or we can make an itinerary of doughnut places and LA food for you. There's the ocean —"

"I've never been on a plane before," Callie blurted.

"Whoa, really?"

"My family did camping trips growing up. And like road trips to national monuments. And then when I was finally planning a trip I got hit by a car." She and Sydney had been planning to go to Iceland. They should get back to that idea, someday.

"Ah," Beckett said.

"Yeah, wild right?" Callie wasn't bothered by any of those facts, but they were information Beckett should probably have.

"You're in for a treat, then, planes are great."

"Is a thing I have heard no one say, ever," Callie said skeptically.

Beckett considered that. "Okay, the idea of flying is great. And takeoff is fun."

Callie rolled over to face him. "You're a strange man," she said fondly.

"Does flying make you nervous?" he asked very seriously.

She shook her head. That was not the shape of the problem. "It's just...we've been dating for about five minutes and now you're inviting me to Los Angeles? For a big publicity event? It's a lot of new things at once."

Beckett propped himself up on an elbow and rested his chin in his hand. Callie didn't even bother to resist the temptation to run her fingertips along his chest, which got her a delighted smile.

"You bought a doughnut shop in a town you'd been to once," he said. "Decided to live on a boat, and said yes to a date with me of all people. You can definitely handle new. Also, to be honest...I don't love having to do industry stuff in LA, but it vaguely resembles time off, and I don't get a lot of that. I'm enjoying you — us — this thing — and I know this is a completely impulse ask, and I know you're running a business, but. I think it'll be fun."

"All right, then." Callie decided to let herself trust that

everything Beckett was telling her was true. "So long as you know you're being impulsive. But we're going to have a day where we sit down and prep and you walk me through everything."

"I always do a call with my people to go over the schedule of everything, so we'll just have you on that. They're more organized than me."

"Your people?" Callie said, her laughter mixing with horror. "Your people?!?"

Beckett winked at her.

"Are you messing with me?" she asked, laughing harder now.

"A little bit."

She slapped at him playfully. "You absolute fucker."

"There is a call! That part is true! But no, I don't call them 'my people.'"

"Oh my God, why is this happening to me?" Callie laughed. "Why are you happening to me?!" She did not fully understand the nature of the adventure she was on, but she was damn well going to enjoy it while it lasted.

Callie woke the next morning to the sound of birds, waves, and Beckett opening cupboards in her kitchen.

"What are you doing?" she asked sleepily, propping herself up on her elbows.

"Shit, sorry." Beckett looked over his shoulder at her. "I was just looking for mugs." He gestured at her kettle and the pour-over coffee maker he'd already found. He was wearing jeans, no shirt, and his hair was a sex-and-sleep destroyed mess. *Gorgeous.*

"Cupboard to your right. I didn't have you pegged for a morning person."

"Habit." Beckett shrugged. He pulled out two mugs and poured coffee into each.

"I can sympathize with that." Callie sat up and pushed back the covers. Beckett glanced up from what he was doing, and she didn't miss the way his eyes tracked over her naked body.

"Put a pin in that thought," she told him, pulling on a pair of pajama pants. "A girl has priorities."

"Like coffee?" Beckett pushed his hair out of his eyes and held out a mug to her.

"Like coffee."

When she took it, Beckett leaned over and kissed her, chaste and domestic, like this was a routine they'd had for years. Callie liked it.

They sat out on the little deck to drink their coffee, their feet propped on the bow railing. The sun was just coming up, burning away the night's fog and painting a glittering golden trail across the water. Callie was struck again by how comfortably they could sit here, with no need to fill the silence with conversation.

She was the one who finally broke it, pulling out her phone to take a picture of their two mugs sitting side-by-side on her little deck table, the bay awash in pink and orange behind them.

"So this is kind of a big ask," Callie said, studying the picture. If she was going to just enjoy this thing with him for as long as it lasted, she wanted to enjoy all the little bonuses that dating someone came with. Like being smug on social media. "But is it all right if I post this to the shop's socials?"

"Go right ahead," Beckett said easily, holding up a hand to shade his eyes from the rapidly brightening sky.

Callie posted the picture, captioning it simply *Enjoying the sunrise*. Then she tossed her phone onto the table between them. She had better things to pay attention to.

"It occurs to me," Beckett said. "That I invited you to LA before you've even been to set. We should definitely make sure that happens before we leave."

"Do I need to? I mean, I'd love to. Don't get me wrong. But isn't filming the show and — I dunno, doing publicity about the show — two different things?"

Beckett squinted against the sun now glaring off the water.

"You're not wrong. But TV's an industry like any other. I suspect you'll have a better time if you get a chance to meet more of the people involved and see how it all works before I drag you into the deep end with me. Also," he said. "This is gonna make me sound like an asshole, but — in LA, I'm going to be getting a disproportionate amount of attention. I don't want you to feel like an outsider. Or an afterthought. Because you certainly won't be to me."

Callie felt her own smile widen in understanding. "You want to show me off."

# CHAPTER 20

```
44°30'41.8"N  67°20'49.7"W
              Temp: 82.0°F
        Pressure: 29.99 inHg
           Wind: 9.21 mph, S
       Visibility: ≥ 10.00 mi
```

ARRANGING FOR CALLIE TO come to set was easy enough — everyone was excited to have the claw girl visit. And so, at lunchtime a week after their spectacular date on the *Lobster Taco*, Beckett found himself in the peculiar position of knocking on his own trailer door. Callie was hopefully in there, not too bored and willing to be subjected to an impromptu set tour, and it seemed only polite not to barge in.

But no answer came. He bit back a little stab of disappointment — something could have easily come up at the shop that she needed to deal with — and pushed the door open.

Callie was, in fact, there. On the bed at the far end, fast asleep, her shoes kicked off and her glorious hair spread everywhere. One of the dogeared paperbacks from his desk was open beside her, facedown on the covers. Her face was soft, her hand tucked under her cheek, and she was so stunning Beckett had to stop on the steps for a moment to catch his breath.

He managed to make it quietly across the trailer and sit down next to her without disturbing her, but when he brushed a curl of hair off her face she stirred and looked up at him.

"Hey," he said, softly.

"Hello there." Her voice was slightly froggy with sleep, and she cleared her throat. "Sorry, didn't mean to pass out, but I had to get up at three to open the shop and then I got here and was like, well would you look at this, a bed right here in your trailer!" She laughed, clearly not fully awake yet.

Beckett leaned down to kiss her. "I will never mind you doing whatever the hell you want in here."

"Good, because this bed is extremely comfy. Wait." Callie pushed herself upright, staring at him. "Is this what you look like out here? Damn."

Beckett squinted at her for a moment before he remembered that she didn't watch the show. Didn't, in fact, even own a TV. Her context for him at work, both in terms of the process of television and what he looked like on this set, was exactly zero.

"The costume department does a great job," he said modestly. He just showed up and did as he was told. There was no need for him to take credit for any of it.

She ran her fingers over the fabric of his sleeve where it was rolled up to his elbow. "I didn't think I had a thing for late-nineteenth-century menswear," she said, "but the scruffy fisherman look really works for you. Am I allowed to touch?" she asked, even though she already had, however delicately.

"Oh yeah, go ahead." Somehow, he was always at least slightly awed in her presence.

Callie touched his hair, which had started today artfully tousled by makeup and now was just a wind-swept, tangled mess Beckett couldn't even get his fingers through. Her fingertips brushed his cheek, and he had to focus so as not to let his eyelids flutter at that tiny touch.

"I see why the hair, now," she said. "I thought you were just being a hipster, but now you look like you don't belong in this century. It's funny." She traced her fingers down his cheek to his jaw. Goosebumps flared all over his skin but he sat motionless, pinned to the spot by her touch and her attention. "You always look so tame out in the real world."

"And I don't now?" Beckett's voice came out in a strangled whisper. He wanted to reach for her in turn. Wrap his arms around her, kiss her and perhaps show her exactly how not tame he could be. But Callie's gaze and her touch had him completely pinned in place.

"Not really." Callie's eyes were bright and curious, evidently unaware of the effect she was having on him.

"Do you like it?" Beckett asked, not particularly nervous, but wanting to be sure.

"Oh, yes."

He let out a relieved breath at the same instant Callie used her hand on his jaw to pull him towards her. The moment felt fragile, but the kiss was sharp and Beckett answered in kind. When Callie got up on her knees on the bed, he pulled her into his lap. She answered by pushing her hands into his hair, her fingernails scratching at his scalp. Heat rolled through him at the little zings of pain and he wanted nothing more than to get rid of their clothes, no matter what century, and be as wild as Callie wanted.

But they were in his trailer on set, and that kind of thing merited at least a conversation first. He pulled back, delighting in Callie's whimper of protest.

"Okay," he said, nosing along the soft skin of her cheek. "As down for it as I would be, I am going to guess you don't want to fuck in here on your first set visit."

Callie's eyes widened, and she leaned back so she could look him in the eye. "People do that?" She sounded equal parts scandalized and delighted.

"Long hours. Relative privacy. Hot people. And there are beds. Such as the one on which we currently find ourselves."

"Indeed." Her eyes narrowed, and she gave him that mischievous smile. "I guess people get good at being quiet, huh?"

Beckett gave her a playful shrug. "Guess so."

He was more than tempted to embark on this game together, to narrate to her the scenes that were now playing in his head, his fingers against her mouth as he fucked her from behind and whispered in her ear daring her to be silent.

But that wasn't what Beckett needed to be able to stay focused on his work, nor would it result in a very necessary set tour. And, perhaps most importantly, it was not quite where they were with each other yet, no matter how incendiary the chemistry and no matter how comfortable they were with each other. Beckett was trying to stay mindful of the experience gap between them; just because he felt like he was falling off a cliff for her was no reason to unbalance her world.

"But for today...." He tucked a strand of hair behind Callie's ear. If he wanted to be decent and considerate, then he actually had to be decent and considerate. "I've got a set to show you. Shall we go take a look around?"

Callie climbed off his lap with a theatrical sigh. "Fine. Let's go demystify Hollywood."

Beckett regretted losing the warmth and weight of her immediately, but made himself stand up. *Work face on,* he told himself sternly, and went to open the door for her, trying to adjust himself as discreetly as possible once he was turned around.

Beckett led them away from the trailers toward the set for a town that had never existed. He always liked giving set tours. He loved sharing all the minute moving pieces that came together to create the finished product and showing off all the thought and details that went into the work.

"This is Hidden Cove." He gestured as they walked down the main street, lined on each side with shops and houses. "Some of the buildings are just shells, but a lot of them are full sets inside too, which means we can do most of our shooting here instead of in the studio."

"Weather's not a problem?" Callie asked skeptically, peering into the windows as they walked.

Beckett shook his head. "Sometimes it feels like this whole job revolves around weather being a problem. But we have the studio up near Bangor we use in the winter when the dark and cold get real dangerous, or when we need to do a lot of shooting on the ship and thus can't actually use the real ship, because that shit is impossible. But as much as we can, the wind and the water and the mud is all part of the authenticity."

Despite his enthusiasm, he had to stop and judge himself for a moment. He wasn't as young as he'd once been, and he put his body through a lot of abuse for this job he loved so much. He was, maybe, a little weird to love it as much as he did, and there was the distinct possibility that he was out in the water and playing with boats because it was cheaper than therapy. Or dominatrixes.

"That seems unnecessarily hard," Callie said.

"Says the girl who lives on a boat." For better or worse, she wasn't any different than him. Not on this.

Callie shot him a sly sideways smile. "I didn't say that was a bad thing."

They were shooting in Hidden Cove today, and the set buzzed with crew and with extras in costume. Beckett stopped to introduce Callie to people as they went, and she was cheerful, warm, and invariably intensely curious about whatever the person's job was.

They ran into Robert, who was working on a rig with his lighting crew, and stopped for a brief chat.

"I see you've been dragged along for the tour," Robert said, amiably, but with a look at Beckett to show him exactly how much he was judging him for his choices.

Beckett gave him a wordless shrug. He was allowed to bring friends to set. Just last year he'd given his parents a tour. Showing Callie around was not at all an indication of wherever it was Robert thought he was doing wrong in his relationships.

"Beckett gets to see where I work all the time. It's only fair," Callie said. If she noticed the vibes passing between him and Robert, she gave no indication.

The set's big showpiece came at the end of their route, where the main street of the town led down to the quay and a rocky shore. There, riding at anchor, was the *Gambit*, sails furled and rigging crisscrossing the sky.

"Holy crap." Callie stopped to look up at the ship as they reached the docks. "That's pretty."

"Isn't she?" Beckett couldn't help the note of fondness in his voice. He and the *Gambit* had spent a lot of time together these last few years, and there was a part of him that felt like the ship justified so much of his life. Maybe acting wasn't real or important, but people had built that in order to tell a story with it.

Callie opened her mouth to say something, but was interrupted by the buzz of her phone. She dug it out of her pocket and glanced at it, then made an aggravated noise and shoved it away.

"Everything okay?"

"It's fine!" Callie said brightly. Too brightly, really. She looked a little wild around the eyes. "Just my mom."

"You can take it," Beckett hastened to assure her.

"Oh, no, it's fine. I can call her back later."

"If anything's wrong —" he started. Because something was definitely wrong.

"Nothing's wrong!" Callie's voice was getting higher pitched with every sentence. "Tell me about your ship."

The deflection made it obvious that there was a story with Callie and her mom, possibly beyond the usual way of parents and children. Whatever it was, she didn't want to deal with it — at least not in front of Beckett.

"All right," he said easily, like he hadn't noticed anything amiss. Inwardly he was concerned. He wasn't entitled to know everything, or even anything, about Callie's family life. But she was so open about so many other things that the difference here struck him.

But now was not the time to press. So he filed it away and instead said, "I can do better than tell you about the ship. Want a tour?"

They had finished poking around the *Gambit* and were heading back up the street when someone shouted Beckett's name. He looked up, squinting against the afternoon sun, to see Darcy standing on the front porch of one of the houses, in full mid-nineteenth-century getup, and waving.

People weren't supposed to hang out where they could accidentally leave modern stuff in a shot, but sometimes you just needed to be out of your trailer. He'd eaten lunch in all sorts of places he wasn't supposed to because it was more scenic. There was no reason to think other people — even flighty, hilarious, resolutely Los Angeles Darcy — weren't doing the same.

"What are you doing over there?" Beckett hollered across to her.

"Enjoying the sun," Darcy called back. Her hair was done in a low knot, blonde wisps escaping across her face in the offshore breeze. "Is that Callie?"

"Yeah!" Beckett shouted before turning to Callie. "Super quick warning," he said in an undertone. "God love her, but Darcy is a lot."

"She's very pretty. I see why Emma has a crush."

"Just wait," Beckett said, because yes, Darcy was pretty, but that was absolutely not what was remarkable or memorable about her. There was no way that Callie could anticipate what she was in for.

He watched as Darcy hoisted her full skirts in one hand and strode across the dusty street as rapidly as her high-buttoned boots allowed, hopping over a bit of track that had been laid down for the camera. A P.A., barely out of his teens, made a faint noise of protest, but she ignored him and marched up to Callie with an outstretched hand to introduce herself.

After the briefest exchange of pleasantries, Darcy threw herself at Callie and pulled her into a hug. The top of Darcy's head barely came up to Callie's chin and she was built like a sparrow, but Beckett could still hear Callie's *oof* of surprise.

*Told you so*, he thought to himself.

"I have been dying to meet you," Darcy announced, rocking Callie back and forth before finally stepping back to look up at her.

"I'm at Sweet Claws any time, but it's nice to meet you too," Callie said politely and with a definite hint of amusement.

Darcy leaned forward and affected a stage whisper. "Beckett will not shut up about you."

Callie raised an eyebrow at him. Beckett smiled shyly back. *Guilty as charged.* He hoped she didn't mind. He put a pin in that to address later, with an apology for not bringing it up before. There would certainly be no time now; Darcy, having begun talking, was rapidly accelerating through an obviously prepared welcome speech.

"I know sets are weird and you're not industry. But, like, they're also really cool? I hope Beckett is giving you a good tour, because I think you'd like some of the stuff we're doing today? So, just in case he's not, I wanted to invite you to come around with me."

"That's so sweet! But Beckett—"

Darcy ran right over her. "But first I wanted to say, because I know you might feel weird around me, or whatever. Beckett and I have *never*, you know?" She gave Callie a meaningful look that was meant to make it plain exactly what she was talking about, but Beckett wasn't sure the message was actually coming across.

"And like the kissing and the love scenes," Darcy went on, evidently not needing any sort of reply. "That's all just work and honestly kind of really awkward, it's always cold and he always gets to wear more clothes than me, and anyway I'm sorry I have to make out with your boyfriend on TV?"

Beckett watched, mortified and but also charmed, as Callie opened and closed her mouth several times. It had occurred to him at a couple of points to have that conversation with Callie, but she didn't watch the show, and it had never felt urgent. Now he wondered if he was going to wind up regretting that decision.

Callie didn't seem to be finding a response despite her obvious best efforts. Beckett couldn't blame her.

"Darcy." He rubbed his hand over his face.

"Yeah?" She turned to look at him.

"You are not making anything better." Beckett had been prepared for Darcy to be over the top and ridiculous. He had not been prepared for her to leap gleefully into a potential minefield. And despite his own, as he liked to think, formidable social skills, he had no idea how to proceed.

"Why not?" Darcy turned to him, her face eager. "It's all true."

Callie, to his extreme relief, finally found her voice. "I haven't seen the show," she said slowly. She even looked as if she might be trying not to laugh. "But regardless, just so we're clear, I'm not jealous." Beckett would have marveled at her poise, if he wasn't so damn grateful for it.

"You're not?" Darcy sounded pleasantly surprised. "Oh, good!"

"Because I am an adult who understands that making a TV show is not cheating," Callie said with a firm nod. She looked like she was trying to reassure Darcy far more than herself.

Darcy nodded back, and then, because she was Darcy, kept talking.

"Excellent. Because he's so kind and intelligent and thoughtful and just generally really awesome, you know? As a person and all. Beyond the obvious hotness."

"Okay, that's enough," Beckett said, his cheeks and the back of his neck aflame. There was only so much he could suffer in one five-minute conversation, and the limit was now officially surpassed.

Callie looked at him, gave a positively evil little smirk at whatever she saw on his face, and turned back to Darcy. "You're embarrassing my boyfriend," she said. "Which means we should totally have a chat sometime when he's not around."

Darcy whipped her phone out from somewhere in her voluminous skirts. "I'll give you my number!"

# CHAPTER 21

44°32'30.1"N 67°29'45.7"W
Temp: 73.9°F
Pressure: 30.06 inHg
Wind: 13.9 mph, E
Visibility: 9.94 mi

DESPITE THE NEVER-ENDING STREAM of surprises in her life, as the summer went by Callie strove to keep up a routine in her daily existence. When that worked, it was deeply soothing, kept her from being completely subsumed into the weirdness of dating a celebrity, and kept her business running. She devoted the hours between the pre-shooting day and after-school rushes to baking instruction for Emma, planning the claw production schedule for the next twenty-four hours, and doing what she could to promote the shop on its various social media channels.

The social media stuff wasn't going anywhere, but Callie knew she had to be persistent. *Hidden Cove* didn't shoot year-round, and no TV show ran forever. Getting a mail order business going would, she suspected, be essential to making sure Sweet Claws could continue to thrive.

Beckett dropped by several times a week, whether for an impromptu hello or a planned date. Increasingly, the line was blurring between the two as Callie and he fell into their own routines of comfort and desire. Both of their lives were horribly busy, but she was always struck by how much they both valued community and companionship.

"I have a question and a gift," he announced one sticky day in August, shaking his hair, wet from a sudden cloud burst, off his face. He usually entered the shop with a certain level of hi-honey-I'm-home energy that warmed Callie's heart — and sometimes, like now, made her burst out laughing.

"What are you talking about and *what* are you holding?" Callie asked. Because it looked like a lobster. And she didn't think her boyfriend should be carrying random crustaceans into her doughnut shop with his bare hands.

He waggled the object before setting it on the counter.

"Lobster. Don't worry, he's fake."

Callie touched it gingerly to confirm. It was, to her relief, plastic. "Okaaaaay."

"It's a show lobster," Emma explained from the back counter, where she was painstakingly shaping a tray of claws. "It means you're a friend of the show."

Beckett tapped his nose and pointed at Emma. "Right in one."

"Should I ask why there are show lobsters?" Callie asked. She had not anticipated this particular part of the celebrity-adjacent learning curve.

"'Cause we don't want to mess with real lobsters." Beckett looked incredibly earnest.

"You mess with real boats but you won't mess with real lobsters?" Callie laughed.

"We want to be nice to the lobsters. And the boats don't bite."

"Okay, that's fair." Callie looked at the peculiar blessing and smiled, first at it and then Beckett. "Thank you then. Now. You have a question?"

"I do." Beckett clasped his hands together. "And I don't know that the lobster is going to make up for it. But the premiere. I got an email today from the PR people and it's something I want to chat through with you before I reply."

"What is it?" Callie asked cautiously.

"Nothing bad! I just need your input on a thing. Since it's about you. And not me. Or should be."

Callie could tell he was starting to edge into that nervous babble that had so endeared him to her on their first meeting. And while it was just as charming now as it was then, she felt nervous. Her ongoing introduction to his world so far had been smooth, but she knew enough to know that fame wasn't always kind, either to the people who had it or to the people they cared about.

"I told folks I was bringing someone," Beckett went on. "And now like reasonable PR people doing their jobs, they asked me if you want your name and what you do attached to the pictures. Um, because there are going to be pictures. That you are in. With me. I probably should have mentioned that sooner. And the choice is entirely up to you, I told them I was going to ask you what you wanted, but...." He fastened her with that intense blue gaze of his. "In the interest of due diligence I have to tell you what's going to happen the minute people on the internet know your name and that I'm dating you."

Callie held up a hand. "Let me stop you right there. The thought has already crossed my mind, more than once and just now while you were babbling at me. I have in fact been a teenager on the internet."

Beckett gave a soft huff of laughter. "Yeah, okay."

"Mhmm. I have both been terrible and seen the terrible behavior online, and I do in fact understand intimately the thing you're trying to warn me about."

"Okay. Thank God." Beckett worried his bottom lip with his teeth. "So is that a vote in favor of, or against, me putting your name out there?"

"Not actually sure yet." Callie said slowly. She wanted to be brave, but if this thing with Beckett didn't last forever — and there was plenty of reason to think that might be the case — she didn't want to blow up her life for nothing. Or to be known as the girl who wasn't enough to keep her hot TV star boyfriend. "I need to think about this for a minute."

Beckett shook his head at her gently. "Of course. The situation is a lot."

"May I interject a thought here?" Emma looked up from her careful claw-shaping.

"By all means," Callie said.

"I get that you need to make this decision based on personal feelings, because that shit is important. Truly. But there's also a business angle here. That I would be remiss not to point out."

"Go on." Callie was trepidatious.

"You want to sell claws," Emma said. "And you've hired me to help you use social media to sell those claws. As your social media baked goods advisor, I have to tell you, nothing is gonna make your mail order business take off like having your name and the shop name associated with —" she pointed at Beckett. "*That.*"

Maybe Callie should have been more nervous about LA, but Beckett was plenty on edge for the both of them. Callie was clear that her main function on this trip was to enjoy herself and give Beckett someone to dote on. So while she played along as Beckett did his best to walk her through the stop-and-pose dance of the red carpet and taught her how to smile for a camera, Callie's main concern was leaving the shop for a few days. And even that wasn't too bad — with so many people in LA for the premiere, *Hidden Cove* was taking a few days off, which would cut down considerably on demand. Emma was more than capable of taking care of Sweet Claws in her absence.

She was excited, she was packed, she felt eager, and she was prepared — right until they got to airport security. *Crap*, Callie thought as she dug frantically through her purse. *Crap, crap, crap.*

The Bangor airport was slow and relatively sleepy to hear Beckett tell it, but she was not feeling that assessment at that moment. The backscatter machines were out of commission, and she'd just set off the metal detector twice. Now the handheld wands of the security screeners were whining over practically every part of her body.

The agents had pulled her aside, politely, and she babbled at them while looking for the damn form letter from her doctor about all the metal in her body. She had downloaded it as a precaution after the internet had been vague and confusing about whether it would set off security scanners, but she had assumed, or hoped, she wouldn't need to use it.

Reflexively she looked for Beckett, not that he could do anything about this. He was a good twenty feet away, already past the screeners, and watching her desperately. He wanted to help, that much was clear. But when their eyes locked she could just tell things would only get worse if he came back over to her, and they both knew it. He'd be too protective, she'd be too frantic, and it just wouldn't be good.

*Find the letter. Speak calmly. Get the hell out of here*, she told herself firmly.

She finally found the letter and took one very deep breath.

"Here," she said, thrusting it at the agent. "Hi. Sorry. I have metal. From surgery."

While she wasn't being particularly coherent the letter, at least, clarified things. Three minutes later and without needing to show anyone her scars, Callie finally rejoined Beckett.

"You okay?" he asked gently as he took her bag and jacket and the now-crumpled doctor's note from her so she could sit and put her shoes back on.

"Yeah." Callie still felt spiky with nerves and adrenaline. She hoped he wouldn't ask more questions than that. She already felt like all the screws in her body were about to vibrate right out of it.

But Beckett just sat, his body easy and relaxed next to hers on the bench.

"You know it's fine," he said, nodding toward the note now in his hand. "And it's okay to feel awkward about it."

Callie nodded, not ready to trust her voice yet. *It's fine right until you know how not fine it is*, she thought with a fury neither he, nor the world, had earned.

Rattled though she was, flying itself was not so bad. It also wasn't that interesting. Which was, in some way, exactly what she needed. Security might have been difficult, but she'd gotten on the plane and she had not, ultimately, had to give up her secrets.

Callie rested her head on Beckett's shoulder as they cruised above the clouds, and, worn out by weeks in the shop and the extra-early morning to catch the plane, slept until they landed.

She was still groggy as they deplaned. But once their luggage was in hand and they stepped outside the airport, Los Angeles slammed into her — the colors, scents, and temperature — jolting her fully awake. Even the very cast of the light was so different than everything she'd ever known.

Beckett was different here too: His posture was less relaxed, and his eyes squinted against the sun off the concrete. He offered her a smattering of tour guide narration as they drove, all of it odd. From an aviation-themed restaurant to the La Brea tarpits, Callie had to keep suppressing the urge to ask if Beckett was joking each time he pointed out another sight. Eventually, she figured out he wasn't. No jokes were necessary, or perhaps even possible, in a place as ridiculous as this.

"Hey," he said, startling her out of her reverie as they sat at a red light in a part of the city that seemed more densely populated with both people and buildings. "Don't look up."

"What?" Callie asked.

"Don't look up," Beckett repeated.

Callie looked at him. There were sparks of both mischief and panic in his eyes. Whatever was going on, she definitely needed to look up right now. She leaned her against the window and craned her neck until she saw what he must have been referring to.

There, on the side of a building, was Beckett's face, at least ten feet high, on a billboard for *Hidden Cove*.

"Holy shit," Callie said softly.

"Told ya not to look up." Beckett's voice was cheerful, but Callie doubted he really was.

"That must be strange. And it must be strange for you to have me here."

Beckett hummed. "Yup. Welcome to LA, where nothing is good, real, or normal."

The hotel was like nowhere Callie had ever stayed before. Aside from the top-tier service when they arrived (which had, as far as she could tell, nothing to do with who Beckett was and everything to do with the hotel's vibe), their room was stunning and modern and had a great view.

"Is it always like this?" she asked as she popped a chocolate-covered strawberry in her mouth and considered opening the white wine the hotel had chilling in an ice bucket for them.

Beckett paused to think about it as he unpacked. "Nah, this is a little nicer than normal, and it took a long time for my career to get here," he finally said.

Callie busied herself poking around the room, from the closet space to the extremely luxurious bathroom with the ginormous tub. All of it was bigger than the *Lobster Taco*. She sat down on the bed and bounced, which finally earned a smile from Beckett.

"I know I'm being ridiculous, but this is so cool."

"This is everything I am hiding from in Maine," Beckett said. "Well, not the hotel, but the rest of it. Rooms like this are lonely as hell when you're on your own. But your excitement is good for me. I'm glad you're here."

Callie was genuinely touched by that. "I know this place is hard for you," she said, hoping they could have a conversation about it.

"Sure is," Beckett replied. "But there's no reason that should change your feelings about this adventure. Nudge me if I get too glum. I want you to have a good time. Hell, if it's possible, I want you to show me how to have a good time."

Callie was exhausted from the day of travel and the intensity of so many new experiences, but she had also — perhaps inadvertently — been issued a challenge and a potentially sexy one at that.

"You should come here." Callie patted the bed beside her. She watched as Beckett stopped what he was doing, dropped the shirt he was about to hang in the closet on top of the dresser, and walked over to stand in front of Callie.

"There's a part of me that feels duty-bound to —"

"Oh no, Beckett. No no no no," Callie said. There was consideration and there was the fine fine line where that drifted over into old-fashioned misogyny. "Your sexual manners are impeccable, but you will not now, nor at any time in the future, imply that my desire is some sort of noble sacrifice about which you have concerns. Am I clear?" Callie asked.

Beckett nodded before he found his voice to answer. "Sorry. I just try to be careful."

"And it is appreciated. But I am a big girl who, if you are game for it, would like to take advantage of you, right now."

"Yeah?" Beckett asked. A sly smile was tugging at the corner of his mouth. "What's that going to look like?"

Callie pondered for a minute. She didn't actually have a plan because she hadn't thought she had needed one. But then Beckett had to go and be chivalrous in the middle of her seducing him.

*First plane trip. First red carpet. First celebrity boyfriend. Time to be brave, Callie.*

"You are going to lie on this bed, and I am going to ride you while you see how many times you can make me come before you lose control," Callie said.

She watched Beckett take that information in, wobble on his feet just a bit as it landed, and try to find his voice.

It took three tries. On the second, she reached forward to palm him through his jeans where he was already obviously getting hard.

"You...you really have my number, don't you?" He finally managed.

Callie reluctantly let go of him and scooted back on the bed. "You're a very good communicator, Beckett. Now get undressed."

"Can I ask an intrusive question?" Callie propped herself up on her elbows. Beckett was on his back, his arm thrown over his head on the pillows, far more relaxed than he had been all day. But he was still thinking. Loudly. And she had no way to access what it was about, except to pry.

"Please do."

"What do you want from your life?" Callie traced circles with her fingertips on his bare upper arm. "Like I get that technically you have everything most people would want right now, but what's your plan? Because coming back here...obviously isn't it."

Beckett looked at her for a long moment, his expression thoughtful but also, somehow, cautious. Callie wondered if she should brace herself. He flicked his gaze from her back to the ceiling.

"So, I can answer that question in an appropriate way," he finally said, his eyes still on the ceiling. "But you have to know before I do that I am concerned — no matter how appropriate and abstract I am about it — that that's going to put undue pressure on you."

Callie swallowed. "All the more reason to tell me."

Beckett finally looked at her. "Okay. Again, with the caveat that this is abstract."

Callie nodded.

"I want to get married. Build a house. Have kids. Somewhere as far from LA as I can get."

"In that order?" Callie asked. "With me?"

"I wouldn't have said I didn't want to put pressure on you if I meant with someone else. But yeah, maybe. If this keeps going the way it's going."

That was a deeply reasonable answer, even in the midst of a deeply unreasonable situation.

"What about acting?" she asked. It was easier to deal with that than any of the rest of it, including very much the realization that maybe Beckett wasn't just dating her because she happened to check his boxes, but because she was...her.

"Great," Beckett said. "I love my job. I just don't want to do it in LA."

"Okay. And you are worried about telling me this...why?"

"We haven't been dating that long."

"And yet here I am, in Los Angeles, facing your demons, professional photographers and possibly the wrath of the internet."

"Point."

"But?"

"I know we don't like to talk about the age difference, but I'm twenty years older than you."

"Eighteen."

"And I am extremely aware that you, or anyone, may be in an entirely different place regarding...all of that, than I am."

"You have a timeline," she said quietly. "And you're hoping that I'm the one that sticks. All while trying not to rush me and being totally in a rush yourself."

"Something like that," he admitted.

Beckett Brown, she realized, was a walking disaster. Callie didn't object to his fantasy life. Or being in it. Honestly, it sounded amazing. Terrifying, because she was just getting her life back under her own control, but amazing. Unfortunately, it also raised a lot of questions.

"I'm going to assume kids isn't the secret reason you asked out the much younger woman," she said tartly. She was pretty sure it wasn't, but she needed to be certain.

He looked horrified enough at the very idea that Callie was reassured. "Oh. Oh no no no no no. No. I tried to talk myself out of asking you out a whole bunch of times. I'm not into you for your presumed fertility. I also wouldn't presume. There are all sorts of ways to wind up with a family."

"How are you both *so* retrograde and *so* decent?"

He shrugged. "Therapy. Trial and error. So tell me, now that I've been a little too forthright a little too soon... what do you want?"

Callie tried not to splutter. A little too forthright? A little too soon? More like twenty-five percent of the way to a marriage proposal while on a trip that was stressing him out and had her so wildly out of her depth she might be swimming in the Mariana Trench.

"Are a nice little life and a doughnut empire mutually exclusive?" she squeaked out.

# CHAPTER 22

33°56'23.4"N 118°25'15.1"W
Temp: 70.0°F
Pressure: 29.71 inHg
Wind: 13.9 mph, W
Visibility: ≥ 10.00 mi

Beckett looked across the length of the bar to where Callie was deep in conversation with Darcy and one of the writers. She looked beautiful and like the demands of the endless day — stylists, the red carpet, the actual premiere party, and now this official after party at the sort of bar Beckett would never step into without obligation — hadn't exhausted her or been an extremely alien landscape.

"She's holding up okay," James, who had a recurring supporting role on *Hidden Cove* and who Beckett hadn't gotten nearly enough scenes with this year, said.

Beckett tipped his head in acknowledgement. "Glad someone is." While the day had gone smoothly so far and having Callie on his arm had been great, his general distrust of his time inside the actual fame machine that was Los Angeles had not lessened. In some ways, in fact, his anxiety about it felt worse than ever. Not only did he want to avoid the bullshit that made him unhappy, he now had someone he desperately wanted to protect from it, despite being the entire reason why she might be exposed to it in the first place.

"You're never gonna get comfortable with this stuff, are you?" James asked.

"Nope and never," Beckett said. "If I do, there's something wrong. Send help immediately."

"Speaking of...."

Beckett flicked his eyes to his friend and colleague, and found exactly what he expected there.

"Yeah, what the fuck is this meeting tomorrow?" he asked. It had been added to the schedule last-minute, and with little explanation.

"So I'm not the only one who has a bad feeling about this."

"Nope," Beckett said, wishing they had discussed this much, much sooner. Like when his agent had started being weird, but he had assumed that was just Steve being his usual self. "No you aren't. Darcy is Darcy, but I think she's rattled too."

"I'd trust her intuition like a spooked horse in a storm," James said.

Beckett chuckled. "I don't know what that means, but it sounds bad."

"Completely and at my own peril. Yeah."

The meeting — which Beckett had to miserably leave his and Callie's hotel bed for — turned out to be the most depressing sort of shitshow. Darcy, who Beckett would have expected to cry at news of what was basically a cancellation, instead cursed out the network executive and launched into a speech that strongly suggested she had an entire writer's room resident in her head. She only stopped — and thus managed not to get the three of them thrown out of their own cancellation meeting — when he and James each put a hand on her arm at the same time.

God, Beckett loved *Hidden Cove* and hated fucking Hollywood. Of all the things he had been dreading about this trip a cancellation notice hadn't even been on his radar. It didn't matter that that notice was being described as a pickup for a six-episode final season to bring the show to its 'natural and thrilling' conclusion. It meant the end.

And now, he had to dump this news on his girlfriend in the middle of their supposed vacation. Because what the hell was their future going to look like without Maine?

He brooded on all of it as he drove out to Santa Monica to meet Callie. But despite all of that, finding a parking spot and walking down to the beach helped. Los Angeles was what it was, but it existed in that form because the world here was beautiful. The ocean breeze, the late summer warmth, and the sound of the water were all legitimately soothing.

But best of all was texting Callie to say he had arrived and watching her from afar as she turned to look for him. Her face broke into a smile that outshone the sun once her eyes finally landed on him. She was wearing a turquoise bikini, and her hair was loose and blowing everywhere. She took his breath away. If he felt like the luckiest man in the world during any part of this trip, it was all down to her.

"Hey," he said as he finally got to her spot in the sand. He kissed her hello and dropped down onto her beach blanket next to her. "How's it going here?"

Callie set her book aside and sighed happily. "Magical."

"Oh, I definitely need to hear all about that." Beckett was eager for tales from a day less disappointing than the one he'd just had. Maybe it would help him put things in perspective.

Callie looked up at the sky. "Didn't it feel like a big deal, the first time you put your feet in the Atlantic Ocean?"

"Yeah, yeah it did." He'd taken a trip to the shore one weekend when he'd been in New York working in his very first play.

Callie pulled her knees up to her chest and rested her folded arms on them. "I got to do that with the Pacific today, and it felt pretty great. Everything in my life right now is an adventure I couldn't have imagined even two years ago. And I'm so grateful for all of it."

If Callie's joy was generally contagious, her sense of tranquility was even better. Normally Beckett thought of Santa Monica as little more than a tourist trap, but here she was radiating gratitude and possibility. He felt his heart rate slow down just from the smell of the ocean and the peace of sitting beside her. And it didn't make him want to keep secrets at all.

"You wanna hear about my day?" he asked.

"Was it good?" she teased like she couldn't imagine anything else.

"Not really," he said, staring out at the water.

"Tell me."

"So you know we're shooting season four right now, yeah?" He said.

"Yeah."

"And you know how I went down to New York for a few days back in June?"

"Yeah?"

"Here's the thing. I didn't want to go, but my agent was on me to think about the future, even though none of that seemed like something I needed to worry about."

"I think I can see where this is going," Callie said carefully.

"Yeah," Beckett said, glad she was quick on the uptake. "We're filming season five now, then there's gonna be six more episodes for season six. Which is enough time to wrap all the plots up, but that is not a full season and that is still a cancellation notice."

"Oh shit."

"Yeah."

"How much time have you got left, then?" Callie's tone was careful.

"Normally, we take a break from filming from January to like March. The weather is too dangerous to shoot outside most days, and we don't need that much material done in the studio. So everybody goes and takes a break or picks up extra work somewhere else. But this year, we're gonna come back in mid-January and keep working. We'll go through June, maybe July. And then we'll be done. Maine and having a job and all of that..." he held up a closed hand and then flicked it open. "Poof."

"That sucks."

"Yes it does."

"I know I should ask what that means for you."

Beckett shook his head. "I don't honestly know yet."

"Okay." Callie took a breath. "Because what I really want to ask is what it means for me?"

Beckett's heart clenched. He didn't want to stress Callie out with his job issues or make her feel like there was any sort of time limit on what they were doing. He knew it was early days still, but she was so steady and bright and certain of herself that it didn't actually feel that way. The conversation about their wants and dreams for their lives had been evidence of that. Whatever was next for him, he hoped that included whatever was next for her.

"You keep managing to ask me things where I have to keep finding ways not to put undue pressure on you," he said.

"Maybe I like pressure," she said. "I wanted to be a chef. Now I run a business. I spent yesterday on the phone with my employee because a metal antique ceiling tile almost fell on her head. And now somehow you've got me out here playing movie star. I can handle a lot of different types of things. Tell me what you want. The worst I can do is say no."

Becket stared at his hands and willed himself to be judicious. "I don't see you as temporary, and I hate LA, and those are the only two things I know. Is that enough for right now?" he asked, looking up at her.

"It is. But can I ask you something else?"

"Go for it."

"Why do you hate it here?" Callie had a look of wonder on her face and though he loved to see her happy, somewhere, somehow, it was making Beckett's heart sink.

"Don't tell me you're falling in love with it." Beckett tried to joke, but he knew his words were falling flat even as they left his mouth.

"Let a woman have her own taste. But seriously, what's your deal?"

Beckett went back to fidgeting with his fingers. Questions like this were easier to answer in the dark, after a few drinks or some great sex. It was absurd for her to ask him to be vulnerable in the midst of so much daylight and surrounded by all these people.

"I take it you don't want the easy answer about the traffic and the lack of seasons," he finally said.

"No," she said. "That's bullshit."

"That it is," he replied. Honestly, the city deserved better from him than he generally gave it. "Do you remember you asked me once if I know what I look like, and I said something funny and blew you off?"

"Yeah?"

"So when I'm here, everything comes down to what I look like. And I don't just mean how it's my job to look a certain way or that it's other people's jobs to make sure I look that way," he said. "I'm the last person on earth who's going to complain about that when women are dealing with that shit every day and aren't even compensated for it. But like... appearance is character, right? Not like, character as in someone's moral value," he clarified. "Character as in how we intuit things about people in fiction. You get that, yeah?"

Callie squinted at him and made a frustrated gesture. "Keep going where you're going. I'm not going to assume the point you're trying to make."

Beckett bit his lip, choosing the right words. Because this was about to be a lot. "Okay, so people see me, and they're like... Oh he's tall, he must be a leader. Or oh, strong jaw, he must be this type of man or that type of man. And in this city every second of every day is like that, because this is a company town and that company is the business of TV and film. Everyone gets reduced to a shorthand about what heroes and villains and men and women are 'supposed' to look like." He made irritated air quotes. "Never mind that the world is full of people who aren't any of those things. Does that make sense?"

Callie looked him in the eye. "You need to get to the part that is your reaction to all that," she said firmly.

"Okay. All of that adds up to a situation that's very high pressure and one in which I feel constantly misunderstood. I don't feel like I fit those molds comfortably. I never have. My body looks a certain way; that doesn't mean I'm an 'alpha male' — what is that? That's not even a thing! But it is what people assume about me, and I make my living off that. So how hypocritical of me is that? And it's  incredibly dehumanizing. Not just for me, to be clear. I mean for everyone that lives here and interacts with the industry machinery, and also for everyone watching at home." He stared down at his hands and started picking at his cuticles with a ragged thumbnail.

"You cannot be single-handedly responsible for our entire pop culture landscape," Callie said quietly.

Beckett nodded, but needed to keep going with what he was saying. "It's like this is a whole city of people who only get to succeed if they let themselves be flattened into the worst and most boring and toxic stereotypes," he said, and was surprised by the anger in his own voice. "And then people are supposed to have friends here? And families? And joy? I don't get how that works, and I am bad at playing along with it. Maine has meant getting to do what I love and getting to be a person who gets judged on my own merits, not just my face and my body. And now I have to get ready to give that up. I don't know what the consequences of that are going to be. I just know it can't be me living here."

Callie reached for his hands. "Thank you," she said.

It was only as she pried his fingers from each other — they had still been worrying at his cuticles — that he realized he hadn't looked at her once or even managed to see anything while he said all those words. Now that they were out there, he felt desperately vulnerable and unsettled. A raft of questions about identity and vanity and work and love were now all just sitting there ready to be picked up and used to dissect him.

But Callie, her curious and compassionate face aside, did no such thing. "I hope the person you are with me is the real you, because I like them a lot," she said. She smoothed her thumbs over the calluses on his palms.

Beckett huffed out a small laugh, still not quite able to look at her directly. He stared out at the ocean instead. Not the right ocean, but the roll of the waves was still soothing.

"I don't even explain my shit that well to my therapist, so definitely the real me, right there."

"I'm glad. About the real you," Callie said. "I'm letting you navigate that therapy thing all on your ownsome."

He snorted and took his hands back from her, wiping at his eyes. "Thank you." He wasn't crying, but a part of him sure felt like he should be. No more Maine? That was trash.

"We'll figure it out," Callie said. "Even if I do really like this beach."

"It's an all right beach. If you're on it." He offered her a half-smile, and she beamed at him so brightly in response he felt his entire mood lift. He was on a beach, with his beautiful girlfriend. Life could definitely be worse, and maybe he could let tomorrow worry about itself. At least for now. And if Callie was enjoying it here, he was not about to ruin their last day here with his moodiness.

"Do you want to go do the super cliché thing?" Beckett asked, pointing to the Ferris wheel up on the pier.

Callies face lit up. "I have no idea why," she said. "But I absolutely do."

They took the Ferris wheel as the afternoon shadows lengthened toward sunset, the water painted in brilliant stripes of crimson and gold and colors Beckett didn't have a name for. Callie took a picture of them at the very top, sunglasses on against the glare off the water, their hair loose and tangled in the sharp sea breeze, their smiles — even his own — electric.

She posted it to Instagram as they ate dinner at a conveyor belt sushi place not far from the beach. Beckett watched her as she concentrated, tongue between her teeth, on constructing the perfect meal as their options drifted by. Occasionally, he'd sneak a piece of fish off her plate, just because he could.

"Mine," she scolded, smacking playfully at the offending hand.

"Yeah, I am," he said.

Callie's eyes went a little wide and a lot soft at that, and he relished it.

Back in their room, Callie kicked off her sandals and flopped back on the bed. Beckett toed off his shoes, which surely still had sand in them, then looked around the room and sighed. He should start packing his things up to make tomorrow morning easier, but he didn't want to lose the magic of this bubble they'd somehow found themselves in.

*Somehow*. Callie was the magic, there was no doubt about that. As miserably as this day had begun, and as real as the challenges were that he would have to face back in Maine, while he was here with her he felt safe. Strong. Capable.

Packing could wait. He ignored their collective clutter — chargers, paperbacks, snacks, discarded pieces of clothing — and crawled up on to the bed with Callie.

"Why hello there," she murmured at him.

She made a soft, gorgeous sound when Beckett kissed her, so he threw a knee over her waist, cupped her face in both hands, and kissed her again. He wanted to stop being the mess of confusion and anger this city always made him into and be instead the person Callie deserved to have. To lose himself in her. To worship her.

He kissed his way across her chest, then cupped a hand under her back, intent on getting her shirt off. But Callie stopped him with a hand to the center of his chest.

"Save that thought for later," she said, looking up at him from under her eyelashes in a way that was not at all demure. Callie had liked to play with the constantly shifting power dynamic between them right from the start. So Beckett knew that look. It was a promise to take him apart. He wasn't at all sure if he was ready for that. Not today after the emotional wringer he'd already been through. But the thing he wanted most, always, was to be good for Callie. So he nodded.

She pushed herself upright and crawled into his lap, digging her hands into his hair and pulling him in for a fierce, bruising kiss. Beckett returned it, wrapping his hands around her thighs to pull her closer, their panting breath audible in the quiet room.

Already he was hard, nearly painfully so, and he whimpered as

Callie ground herself against him. She pulled his shirt over his head, then made short work of unbuttoning his jeans.

"Ass up," she muttered into his mouth, tugging fruitlessly at his waistband.

"You're sitting on me."

"Yes, I am sitting here staring at your body, Beckett. My God, you're strong enough for this."

The praise made him nearly dizzy with desire, and he did manage to lift himself up far enough that together they were able to get his pants off. Once he was naked, Callie nudged him backwards onto the pillows.

Beckett went, and caught the back of Callie's head to drag her down for one more kiss. She let him, for just a moment, before she bit the corner of his mouth and pulled back to give him that sly smile.

He closed his eyes and tried to control his ragged breathing as she kissed her way down his chest. But when she grazed her teeth against the sensitive skin by one of his nipples, he couldn't stop his gasp.

"This okay?" Callie asked, her words warm against his skin.

Beckett made a sound he meant to be affirmative but just came out as a moan. Callie, though, seemed to get the picture, and skimmed her teeth against his skin again, harder this time, then laved her tongue across the spot to soothe it.

"God, Callie," he begged. His cock was trapped between them, and he thrust up against her, desperate for friction.

She kept working at his nipples, one and then the other, until he was nearly out of his mind with pleasure. Then she slid further down his body, trailing kisses and bites as she went, Beckett only dimly aware of how loud his whimpers were in the quiet room. He couldn't be self-conscious about it, it just felt so goddamn good.

He very nearly came the moment Callie wrapped her lips around the head of his cock. But he didn't want this to end, not yet, not ever, and he mustered up every ounce of self-control left in his body.

The battle was still a losing one. Callie's mouth was too hot, too wet, and when he lifted his head to be able to see her she was staring at him, her mouth full of him. Seeing him for exactly who he was.

His orgasm wrenched out of him and he gave a strangled cry,

pleasure flattening him like a wave. Callie replaced her mouth with her hand, stroking him through it, then kissed him, deep and sloppy and tasting of himself.

As soon as Beckett could make himself move again he rolled them, covering her body with his, kissing her ferociously as he worked two fingers into her. She was slick and soaked and moaned into his mouth as he thrust into her and worked his thumb against her clit, and then she came too, her muscles clenching tight around his fingers.

*No one*, he thought, watching as pleasure washed across her face, *has ever made me feel like this.*

# CHAPTER 23

44°32'30.1"N 67°29'45.7"W
Temp: 84.0°F
Pressure: 29.81inHg
Wind: 13.9 mph, W
Visibility: 10.00 mi

R ETURNING TO MAINE FELT a little like going back to school after summer vacation — in both the bad ways and the good. In just a few short days Callie had gotten used to sleeping in, eating out, and spending almost every moment with Beckett. Returning to an alarm at three a.m. with no Beckett in bed next to her and then having to make breakfast for herself was all distinctly suboptimal.

Still, walking into her shop and hearing the bells over the door jingle was satisfying. Callie flipped on the lights, then laughed aloud. On the counter was Lobbie the plastic lobster, a piece of paper with *We survived! Even though the ceiling fell on our head!* written in big block letters propped in its claws. The lobster itself was perched on top of the stack of ceiling tiles in question.

Callie snapped a picture and uploaded it to the shop's social media. *It's good to be home,* she captioned it. *Thanks to Emma and Lobbie for holding the fort down.* Then, since she was on her phone anyway, she navigated to the app she used to manage the mail orders, just to see what she needed to deal with today.

She blinked at her phone in surprise. Sure, Emma had encouraged her to put the shop's name out there in connection with the premiere, and Beckett had predicted that appearing on the internet together would have an effect. It wasn't that Callie hadn't believed them. It was that she wasn't expecting to log in her first day back at work and find three times the usual number of new orders waiting for her.

*Today is going to be interesting,* Callie thought. She shoved her phone in her pocket, pushed up her sleeves, and got down to work.

❁

Emma joined her at the shop that afternoon and pitched in with cleaning up from the post-school rush while Callie dragged out her ladder to address the ceiling issue. Deluge of doughnut orders aside — they somehow kept rolling in as the day went on — she needed her shop to be in one piece.

She was on the ladder and using her phone as a flashlight to examine where the screws holding the tiles in place had failed when it rang in her hand. Callie glanced at the screen, hoping it might be Beckett with time to kill on set, but what it said instead was *Mom.*

"Shiiiiiiiiit." Callie hastened to swipe down on the phone, and stared at the blinking *call declined* notification, her heart suddenly pounding. She and her parents had been resolutely low contact since they had finally decided to believe she had really moved to Fly-Debate. The call from her mom while Callie had been on the set tour with Beckett — and which she should have followed up on — might have been just casual checking in, but there was no way this was. Nor could the timing, so soon after the trip to LA, be a coincidence.

Emma looked up from the sink where she was cleaning out the mixers. "What's wrong?"

Before she could reply, Callie's phone buzzed again — just once. Not a call. She looked at the screen again, dreading to see a voicemail notification, but what was there was, somehow, worse.

"My mom," she said dully. Her mother, who never ever communicated via text message, had texted her.

"Not good?" Emma asked.

"Not. Good."

Callie thought about ignoring the text as she had the call. But if she did, if she let that text sit on her phone, the awareness of it was going to haunt her for the rest of forever. She started to climb back down the ladder. Whatever this was about to be, she didn't have the focus to manage it from eight feet up in the air.

"You need backup?" Emma asked. Callie had discussed her parental issues with Emma even less than she had with Beckett, so she basically had no idea of the shape of the problem, but Callie appreciated the offer.

"Could use some moral support."

Emma gave her two soapy thumbs-up. "You've got this."

"Right. I got this."

Callie swiped open the text.

**Mom:** Callie! My baby, how are you doing? I saw your picture with that person in *People* magazine —

"FUCK." Callie deleted the text without reading the rest of it, then slammed her phone on the counter, face-down.

Emma jumped. "You still got this?" she asked, slightly wide-eyed.

Callie stared at her phone. It wasn't going to leap up of its own accord and bite her, obviously, but she definitely needed to remind herself of that fact.

"Fuck, fuck, fuck."

"Do I need to fight somebody? I wear the combat boots so I can fight somebody."

Emma's comment shocked a laugh out of Callie. "No. Thanks. But, question for you."

"Yeah?"

"Were you paying attention to any of the media and whatever about the premiere?"

"Dude. Darcy was there. Obviously I did."

"You know Darcy lives here," Callie pointed out, because talking about Emma's crush on Darcy was much better than dealing with the current situation.

"Yeah, but it's not like I see her out on the street!"

"Okay," Callie said. "Since you were following everything — were there by chance any pictures of Beckett and I in *People* magazine?"

"I dunno, I don't get *People*. But I can check." Emma wiped the suds off her hands and whipped out her phone.

"Thanks," Callie said faintly. She was fairly sure she already knew the answer, but she did not have the mental fortitude to go look for it herself.

After a few moments of rapid thumb-tapping, Emma held her phone out to Callie. "Yeah, here you go."

Callie took the phone tentatively, worried from her mother's tone that they were going to be some sleazy paparazzi photos of her and Beckett making out somewhere, even though she was nearly sure they had done no such thing. But there were just a few innocuous shots of them on the red carpet. Beckett's arm was around her waist, and they were both smiling, exactly as practiced and intended.

She handed the phone back to Emma with a sigh. "Thanks."

"No problem. So — can I ask? What's going on?"

"It's possible I never told my parents I was dating Beckett because there's a whole unrelated family drama going on where me and them don't talk much. And then they just found out because of the pictures in *People* and really, really want to talk now."

Emma laughed, a dismayed-sounding chortle. "Oh that's not good," she said, echoing Callie's earlier words.

Something about that snapped Callie out of her fear. "Wait," she said. "Why not? I'm an adult. I don't live at home. My parents don't need every tiny detail about my life. They've gotten by just fine for months knowing as little as possible."

"Okay, technically true," Emma said. "But I feel like dating an actor and going to a red-carpet event with him is maybe the kind of thing where you give them a heads up? Like, did you think they weren't going to find out?"

"Yes? No? I don't know. Rrrrrgh." Callie was frustrated. And suddenly acutely sympathetic to the thing where Beckett had never managed to tell her he was an actor. But her mother, calling Beckett *that person*... The caption and the pose made both identity and context perfectly clear. *That person.* Innocuous. And filled with judgment.

The more she thought about it, the angrier she was getting. Callie needed to deal with this or she was going to split apart at the seams.

"Hey, Em, can you keep an eye on stuff fort for a couple of minutes?".

"You got it, boss."

Callie took her phone out behind the shop where her car was parked next to the garbage cans, and leaned against the hood while she hit *call* on her parents' number. Her heart was pounding. Thank God they still had a landline and she wouldn't have to do two separate calls to deal with this drama.

Her mother picked up on the very first ring. She must have been sitting there, waiting for it. Which just annoyed Callie more.

"Calliope!" she exclaimed. "Is that you?"

"Yeah, it's me."

"Just a minute, let me get your dad."

"Mom, you don't have to —" Callie began, but then there was the click of another receiver being picked up and the tinny rumble of her father's voice.

"Callie!"

"Um, hi," she said.

"I'm so glad you called, baby," her mother broke in again. "We've been wanting to talk to you, to know what you've been up to, what you've been doing up there, up there, in…"

"Fly-Debate," Callie supplied flatly.

"What kind of a town name is that?" her father put in. "I know I've asked you that before, but it's messed up. Are they arguing about flies or what? Is that a fishing thing?"

Callie dropped her forehead into the hand that wasn't holding the phone. She'd been in Maine for well over a year and her parents were still obsessing on the town name like it was her fault.

"No, Dad, it's — Puritan. I think."

Her mother seized control of the conversation again. "That is not important right now. Do you remember Gina?"

"Yes, Mom, I remember her." Gina had been their next-door neighbor Callie's entire life. What Gina had to do with this, Callie was afraid to find out.

"Anyway she called yesterday," her mother continued, "and asked if I had seen *People* magazine, and I said no because what do I care about that, but she said you were in it with some kind of movie star and I said —"

"His name is Beckett, Mom."

"Is he a movie star?" Her mom sounded equal parts fascinated and horror struck.

"I mean, he's an actor? They're filming a TV show up here. We met —"

"He looks so much older than you!"

Callie made a frustrated noise. At least she knew the shape of the problem as her parents saw it. *It's not nothing*, a traitorous voice inside her own head reminded her. She'd been worried about the age difference at the beginning too. But her parents, she knew, were going to be completely over the top about it.

Her dad spoke again. "Yeah, and I looked him up on the internet, did you know he's forty-four?"

"Yes, Dad, I do know how old my boyfriend is."

"So he is your boyfriend!" her mom exclaimed.

"We went to LA together, what else would we be?" Callie hated that she was getting sucked into this conversations-by-yelling vibe that her family had, but she knew of no other way of communicating with them that worked even a little.

"Did you know he's divorced?" was her dad's complete non-answer to that.

"Yeah, I—"

"Tony down at the shop, he got divorced when he was forty-five and do you know how many twenty-somethings he's dated since?" he continued. "They all lasted maybe six months. Like, he's got a good job and a nice car, I get why girls go for him, but you don't want that kind of bullshit in your life. He has a good car though, doesn't he?"

"Are either of you going to let me talk at any point?" Callie burst out, tears of frustration stinging her eyes. "Because you're not telling me anything I don't already know, I get to decide what kind of bullshit I want in my life, and he actually has a really crappy car!"

"Well if he wants a recommendation, you know Marco's always got a good selection —"

"Dad! His car! Is not! The point!" If this were happening to anyone else, Callie might have found it hysterical. But unfortunately, it wasn't happening to anyone else, and it wasn't a brief scene in a book or a movie. It was her whole entire life and it was so godawfully loud.

"Thanksgiving's coming up, when are you coming home for that?" her mother asked, in what was probably not a good-faith attempt to change the subject.

Callie hadn't thought that far ahead; Thanksgiving was still months away. But now, trapped in the middle of this conversation, she realized she did not want to go home.

Or rather, she didn't want to go to her parents' house. Because Maine — Sweet Claws, the *Lobster Taco*, the morning fogs and the scent of the ocean, Beckett — all of that was home, now.

"I'm not going to make it back for Thanksgiving this year," she said crisply.

"What?!" her parents exclaimed simultaneously.

"Yeah. No. I..." Callie tried to put the words together. She loved her parents, and didn't want to hurt them, but also couldn't bear the idea of being stuck in a house with them and their overbearing concern. Or their incessant fretting about her dating life.

"Look," she said. "I didn't call to fight with you. I also didn't call because you wanted me to. I'm calling because it's the right thing to do, and none of us have been good at communication, but now that I'm telling you things I need you to actually listen to me, okay? Maybe I messed up by not telling you about Beckett, because I wanted space and wasn't informing you that I needed it, but you being all judgey and overbearing isn't making me want to be forthcoming, now or ever!"

"I guess it might be a good thing you're not alone up there in the woods," her mother said. "He does look like a capable man--"

"I do not need someone to take care of me!" Callie started pacing around her car. She was so angry she could barely see straight. She didn't need her parents' judgment on her ability to take care of herself. She also didn't need their assumptions about who Beckett was based on what he looked like. He'd spent so much time telling her how difficult he found all that, and now she had to listen to it from her own family?

"I am twenty-six years old," she said. "I run a successful business. I am dating someone who is so supportive and so thoughtful about letting me figure out things for myself when I need to. I have friends. And I keep rising to absolutely wild occasions, from, yes, dating a public figure to keeping a houseboat running in a Maine winter. And all I ever hear from you sounds like disappointment that I got better, that I'm not still hurt, that my injuries healed. So no, I will not be coming home for Thanksgiving. And if you want to know things about my life, you're going to have to ask, listen like you're actually interested in the answer, and maybe remember for half a minute that I am a grownup!"

Her mother started to say something, but whatever it was, Callie was in no position to hear it, or be productive in the face of it. She hung up the call.

And then she shouted, because as much as she hated that particular family tradition, it was part of her nature too.

"AUUUUUUUGH!!"

On the other side of the parking lot a squirrel startled and fell off a fence.

# CHAPTER 24

44°30'41.8"N 67°20'49.7"W
Temp: 80.1°F
Pressure: 29.85 inHg
Wind: 13.8 mph, W
Visibility: ≥ 10.00 mi

BECKETT WAS IN HIS TRAILER going over last-minute script changes. While such changes were common, he expected that more and more of them would be coming his way as the show navigated to its necessary conclusion. The word on that was now out amongst the cast and crew, and Beckett expected a public announcement within the next twenty-four hours.

His phone buzzed with an incoming call. Beckett glanced at it, then heaved a sigh. It was his agent.

"God, fuck this," he muttered to himself before he picked up the call. He didn't want to deal with Steve right now, but he wasn't going to want to deal with him later, either. "Hey there." He tried to put some kind of positive energy into his voice, and either he succeeded or his agent didn't care either way.

"Beckett! Lots of exciting things coming up!"

"Are there?" Beckett said sourly. "Or did I dream the thing where we got a cancellation notice and now you sound happy about it?"

"You got the rest of this season and half of another! That's hardly a cancellation."

Beckett was not in the mood to argue that particular point, so he said nothing. Steve took that as an invitation to continue.

"So look, I know you're going to tell me you're above it, but I've been chatting with one of the casting directors who's been working on that whole superhero juggernaut and things are ramping up for the next wave, and look, she thinks you're interesting. Acknowledged the undeniable charisma and the ridiculous jawline, and is willing to have you send in a tape. Obviously this is hush-hush; there's going to be an NDA just to breathe in the vicinity of this thing, and I'm sure the sides they send you are going to be totally unrelated. But will you be a good boy and actually cooperate? This could be very big."

An alert from his family group text flashed on top of the screen, and Beckett opened it, only half listening to Steve. Superheroes would be fun — but that was the kind of gig A-listers got, and it was hardly going to be worth the time to try.

**Christine:** Hey Becks, something you wanted to tell us?

"Yeah, totally," Beckett said to the text message that couldn't hear him and the agent that thought he cared. Evidently the cancellation was public knowledge now, if his family and his agent were both hellbent on pestering him about it at the same time. *At least that's more efficient*, he thought crankily.

A link from his sister came through. The last thing he wanted to do was read about his show being over. He already knew the details. But then the preview of the link popped up and Beckett realized that he was very, very wrong. Pictures of him and Callie on the red carpet at the premiere were out in the wild. Beckett's pulse sped up.

**Taylor:** Oooh, she's cute.
**Taylor:** AND she owns a doughnut shop?? Beckett you've been holding out on us.

Meanwhile Steve was still talking.
"And in any case, being back in LA full time is going to mean — "

Beckett snapped back into awareness of the phone call. "I don't want to move back to LA."

"Beckett. You're an actor," Steve said.

"I'm aware," Beckett said dryly as texts from his family continued to come in. He was going to die from a thousand digital paper cuts.

**Thomas:** wjiiene22wwwwwwww
**Thomas:** Sorry, Teagan got my phone. How did you not tell us!
**Christine:** I'm calling Robert, he MUST have details.
**Mom:** What a lovely young woman. You both look so happy! <3
**Knox:** GUYS SHE DOES MAIL ORDER DOUGHNUTS.

Beckett groaned to himself. He *should* have told his family earlier. Callie was important to him, and he owed it to everyone to share this particular piece of news himself instead of letting his family learn about it from a random article on the internet. But in the whirlwind of preparation for LA it had completely slipped his mind.

He typed back rapidly as his agent nattered on about a future that seemed designed for someone else.

**Beckett:** 1) Technically, they are claws 2) Please don't call Robert, he's currently dealing with a crew that just found out we got a cancellation notice and 3) I hate all of you.

When he tried to navigate back to the call with his agent, Beckett realized he'd accidentally hung up on him. *Oh, well.* Steve probably wouldn't even notice.

He tossed his phone onto the desk and blinked back frustrated tears. He looked around his trailer, so cozy and familiar. At his pile of highlighted and dog-eared script pages on the desk. The stack of board games in the corner. Several plastic lobsters on top of a cabinet. This was home, so much more than any place in LA ever had been.

Beckett stood up. Time to see about getting lunch. He still had to deal with the script changes, but he needed a break first.

He wound up at a table in the corner with James, speaking in hushed tones. The mood on set was, predictably, not great. They both should have been part of the solution — Beckett, particularly, as the first person on the call sheet each day — but he had no idea how he was supposed to fix this.

"In what world," Beckett asked, "is it normal to accidentally hang up on your agent and then he just doesn't call back? That's weird right?"

"You don't sound like you wanted him to call back," James pointed out.

"I mean, yeah, but —"

As if summoned, Beckett's phone rang. He fully expected it to be Steve connecting him to someone in LA real estate, but when he fished out his phone it was Callie. He frowned, surprised. She usually texted when she knew he was at work.

"Hey, sweetheart, what's up?"

"Are you busy right now?" Her voice wobbled.

Something wasn't right. He got up from the table with a nod to James to try to find a little more privacy for whatever was going on.

"No. It's lunch. Are you okay?" he asked, his heart in his throat.

"I just had an awful fight with my parents, and I know everything's a mess on your end too, but —"

"It's fine," he soothed. He'd known something was up with her and her family for a while, and clearly, he should have asked for details before it had done… whatever it had clearly just done. "What about? How can I help?"

There was a long pause that felt nearly unendurable while Callie gathered her thoughts.

"It was about you," she said. "Or *People* magazine, at least. You probably haven't even seen it. And you probably don't even care, it's not like being in a magazine is weird for you —"

Beckett felt both relieved and miserable all at once. Whatever this was, it likely wasn't a tragedy or something that couldn't be fixed. But it was also his fault, which was never his idea of a good time, especially when it made someone he loved hurt.

"My family saw it too," he said. "And gave me more than a bit of shit for not telling them about you first. Do you want to come over? To set?"

"I don't want to interrupt."

"Callie," he said firmly. "What are they going to do? Fire me from my canceled show?"

Callie, when she arrived at Beckett's trailer, was not crying, but she obviously had been in the not-too-distant past. She stepped into his arms with a silent relief.

When she told him about the conversation with her parents in more detail he was relieved the situation was nothing worse, but he knew enough not to say so. It had been so long since he'd been a young adult with overly protective parents, and the last thing he wanted to do was offer useless advice with a side of condescension. Instead, he did the only thing he could do: Apologize.

"What on earth for?" Callie asked in reply.

"I spent so much time trying to make sure you were comfortable at the premiere and with photographers and with the internet's potential reaction, it never occurred to me to ask where your family might be with any of it."

"You're not responsible for me, you get that right?"

"I do," Beckett said, aware Callie was probably afraid he would be one more person who didn't treat her like the adult she obviously was. "But I am responsible *to* you."

"You're gonna make me cry again," Callie protested. "That's a compliment, by the way."

"Clarity, appreciated." Beckett smiled at her.

"How are you doing?" Callie asked. "I know nobody's having a good day here."

"Yeah, not particularly. But we'll get through it." Beckett tried to be optimistic on that point, but he wasn't feeling it yet. The rest of the day was going to be emotionally draining, that was for sure, and Callie wasn't the only person he was responsible to. The rest of the cast would be looking to him for leadership, and it was on him to provide it. He glanced at the clock. "They're going to need me soon. But you're welcome to stay here and hang out. Or I can come meet you at the shop or your boat tonight. Or you can come to my place. Whatever you want."

"I should get back to the shop." Callie blew her nose again. "We got a bunch of mail orders this morning, and they keep coming in. Which at least is a good thing. Here, look."

She pulled out her phone and flicked through it — and then clapped her hand over her mouth.

*Oh no.* "What's wrong?" Beckett asked, his heart sinking. Fake orders with mean messages from internet haters suddenly struck him as a likely possibility.

"Well," Callie said, drawing out the word. "We just had a bunch of orders come in and either it's a giant coincidence and a bunch of people with your last name just ordered a whole lot of doughnuts...or, it's all your siblings. And possibly your mom. Here, look."

She passed him the phone. Sure enough, there were his family's names and addresses, alongside pretty sizeable orders.

"Yeah, that's them." Beckett was horrified — until he realized Callie was on the verge of laughter, not more tears.

"I am so, so sorry about them," he said, nonetheless. He should have told them all to knock it off in the family group thread.
Callie shook her head. "Don't be! It's great business. Plus I can troll them on the packing slips." She gave him a smile that was clearly brighter than she was actually feeling. "It's gonna be great."

<pre>
44°28'46.3"N 67°30'54.7"W
            Temp: 39.0°F
   Pressure: 30.59 inHg
      Wind: 3.45 mph, W
   Visibility: ≥ 10.00 mi
</pre>

NORMALLY, CALLIE AND BECKETT didn't spend nights together in the middle of Beckett's filming week; it was too disruptive for both of them. But with everything that had gone wrong or strange that day, they had dinner together and then Beckett slept over on the *Lobster Taco.*

Sometime in the early morning, Callie was jolted out of sleep by a sharp pain in her thigh. "Oh, fuck!"

"What's wrong? You okay?" Beckett said muzzily, rolling over to face her.

"Just a charley horse. I'm fine."

"Mmmkay." Beckett let out a contented sigh, draped a heavy arm over her side, and fell asleep again. Callie stared into the darkness, listening to the slosh of the waves against the hull and Beckett's peaceful breathing, willing her heart to slow down.

*Weather's changing,* she thought. This had happened last year, too, when the temperatures began to drop: The occasional aches in her leg and wrist where all the pins were would give way to sudden stabs of pain unless she was extremely judicious about staying warm and doing her physical therapy, and sometimes even then. But she hadn't wanted to have any of that conversation with Beckett before LA, and she didn't want to start having it now. Not when there was so much that would need to be told, if she ever started.

She hadn't even begun to drift back into sleep again when Beckett's alarm startled her all over again.

"It's so early," she muttered, while Beckett fumbled for his phone to silence it. Early mornings were the norm for both of them, but it did not feel reasonable to get up yet.

"Studio day." Beckett sat up and shoved a hand through his hair.

Even tired and in pain as she was, he was distractingly beautiful, with his chest bare and his hair falling in tangles to his shoulders, his gaze on her soft.

"Extra fun commute day," she mumbled.

Beckett reached for his shirt and pulled it over his head. "Yep. I won't be back 'til late, and once I do get back I'll have to go over my pages for tomorrow, but do you want to come over anyway? I'll grab food."

"That sounds nice. I have stuff to do for the shop all day, but let me know when you're headed home?" Apparently, they were going to keep up the weeknight thing. Callie didn't at all mind, even if it was one more schedule element for them both to manage.

"Of course." Beckett stood up, and Callie immediately missed the warmth of him next to her. He leaned down and pressed a gentle kiss to her forehead.

She waited until he had left and the sound of his footsteps had faded away down the dock to throw back the covers and ease herself, slowly and painfully, out of bed. The first order of business was to turn up the heat. The second was going to be doing her physical therapy exercises.

Callie expected that her parents would call back, after she had screamed at them and then hung up — after all, conflict aversion was not a thing for any of them. But they didn't. And Callie's relief at that quickly faded into a kind of terrible weight in her stomach. Should she call them herself and face them? Probably. But she suspected she'd be the one who wound up doing all the apologizing and they wouldn't change anything. She was better off letting that lie.

She and Beckett started spending almost every night together. That was different from what they'd been doing before LA, and made their early mornings even earlier, but it was also lovely. Beckett would sit at one of the tables in the shop while she sanded and painted ceiling tiles, or next to her in bed while she did bookkeeping and social media for the shop, his reading glasses on and his forehead furrowed in concentration, both of them quietly enjoying each other's presence. Callie didn't know what that change meant in light of the now-impending end of *Hidden*

*Cove*...but that ending was also months away. She could safely put off worrying about that.

The mail orders for doughnuts continued to come in. Callie was glad for the work, and only occasionally annoyed by the messages on the mail order requests. Beckett's mom put in an order almost every week, which she thought was adorable.

And so the fall rolled on — crisp days that were rapidly shortening, foggy nights that grew longer and longer, work and her town and the sea — and Beckett.

The day before Thanksgiving, Callie unlocked the door to the shop, pushed it open — and stopped in her tracks. An entire strip of ceiling tiles were lying on the floor.

"Oh, for fuck's sake," Callie said aloud. When they'd fallen while she was in LA only a few had come down. Now there were a dozen.

She dumped her bag on the counter and went to find paper and a marker for a sign to put on the door.  She was already tired, her hands were cramping, and her leg hurt. Travel along Route 1 was picking up thanks to holiday travel, which meant more customers, and the mail orders were still coming in at a steady clip. She was in the middle of perfecting a Thanksgiving-themed turkey claw (pumpkin spice filling, with a cranberry glaze). She was not in the mood, nor did she have the time, to deal with one more thing on her plate.

The bell over the door jingled behind her.

"Oh damn." Emma stopped and stared at the mess.

"Yep," Callie said, scribbling out her makeshift sign. *The gremlins have struck again, Forgive the dust while we tidy up after them.*

"Any idea why they fell down?" Emma asked.

"Not a fucking clue." Callie went back to the door to tape her sign to it, then turned back around to survey the damage. They'd have to pick up the fallen tiles, put them somewhere safe for now, barricade off the area under the rest of the restored tiles lest they decide to fall down too, sweep the floors and disinfect the counters again, just to be safe. After all that she'd have to start the usual morning shop tasks.

"Normally," she said, "I'd call my dad and ask for help, but—"

"I have been working with you for months. Never have I once seen you call either of your parents for help."

"Yeah, okay. But this is desperate. However, my parents are pissed at me, and if I show weakness now they're just going to think all over again that I'm not an adult who can do things on my own."

"That sounds like a you problem to sort out." Emma started picking up tiles, evidently unconcerned by Callie's angst.

"Do you think it's an omen?" Callie wondered aloud to Emma. This was all so terrible it was just possibly ticking over into the absurd.

"An omen for what?"

"I dunno. Maybe that I am not cut out for a doughnut empress after all and when Beckett leaves Maine I should go with him."

"Uhhhhhh..."

"Or maybe Beckett and I are just doomed and I should cut my losses now?" Callie shot Emma a teasing look to show that she was joking. Mostly.

"Maybe it really is gremlins," Emma mused. "D'you think the health code has anything in it about gremlins?"

"If they do, we are well and truly fucked."

<pre>
44°36'29.6"N 67°8'22.9"W
        Temp: 41.0°F
   Pressure: 29.73 inHg
     Wind: 5.75 mph, NW
    Visibility: 5.00 mi
</pre>

AS CALLIE NARRATED THE LATEST edition in the saga of her shop's ceiling, Beckett navigated the familiar route out to Robert's house. In the backseat of the car, several boxes of Callie's special pumpkin-spice-and-cranberry Thanksgiving claws were stacked. A few bottles of wine — Beckett's own contribution to the gathering — clinked together gently whenever he turned a corner.

"So after that," Callie was saying, "I wanted to go to Sealport to talk to the people at the hardware store and get some ideas about what to do next, but with Thanksgiving being today everything was closed by the time Emma and I got out there and I have no idea what to do now. And tomorrow's Black Friday and the traffic up the coast is going to be intense and half my shop is a disaster zone." Callie sighed dramatically and slumped against the passenger side door.

Beckett couldn't blame her — the situation was miserable. She wore a festive leaf-patterned dress over tights and boots, and her hair was twisted up in pretty coils, but her pale skin was dark under her eyes. He thought he might be able to help — but first, to be sure such help was wanted.

"Do you want me to make a suggestion? Or do you just want to rant? Either is totally fine. To be clear," he said.

"Please, I'll take whatever suggestions you have."

"You know who's been dealing with construction issues in this climate for going on five years now?"

"Who?" Callie asked.

"Robert."

"I mean sure, but Robert's got eight hundred things going on right now. One of which is hosting Thanksgiving at his house." Even Callie's laugh sounded tired.

"Still, you should ask him. Or I can, if you want. But I know he'd be happy to help. And between you, me, and the fencepost...I think he'd be glad for a concrete problem he can actually solve."

Robert's house buzzed with holiday chaos. The boys had the parade on the TV but were mostly paying attention to the giant matchbox car track they were constructing around the living room. Dahlia was in her highchair, thoroughly engrossed in coating herself with what looked like the contents of an entire can of pumpkin puree.

"She's happy, don't judge," Julie said with a laugh, hugging Beckett and then Callie hello. Robert helped put the turkey claws on top of the fridge, out of reach of children and their racetrack.

"You know I would never." Beckett bent over to kiss the top of Dahlia's head, only to get splattered with pumpkin as she giggled and slapped her hands into the mess.

"Probably should have seen that coming." Beckett grabbed a paper towel to wipe his sweater off. "What can I do to help?"

"You and Rob can bring the rest of the folding chairs up from the basement. And then you, Beckett, keep Robert from setting fire to himself."

"Hey! That was one time!" Robert protested, already heading for the basement door.

"One very memorable time." Julie laughed.

When Beckett emerged from the basement he found Callie deeply engrossed in arranging stacks of paper plates and plastic silverware on a card table covered with a festive tablecloth and fake fall leaves.

"I should have brought Lobbie," Callie said when she saw him. "This would make a great pic."

"If you need a lobster for a shot," Julie said from where she was crouched down plugging in a series of warmer plates. "You can use ours."

"You've got one too?" Callie looked amused.

"We've got a bunch. Beckett likes to bring them to people."

Callie gave him a laughing glance over her shoulder.

He shrugged. "The kids all needed their own."

"He's like a cat." Julie stood up, brushing her knees off. "Leaving chipmunks on your doormat. Except instead of beheaded rodents it's plastic crustaceans."

Once things inside were under control, and Robert had shown Callie the current state of the peapod, Beckett, Callie, and Robert tromped out to the backyard to embark on the adventure that was cooking turkeys in trash cans. Callie perched herself on the woodpile to watch, clearly amused while Robert consulted his phone for instructions and Beckett made himself useful by clearing several circles of stones and twigs.

"Okay, I'm going to stop you there," Callie said as Robert started unrolling aluminum foil and then struggled to cover the first of several stakes with it.

"Why? What did I do wrong?" he asked.

"Nothing yet, but it's gonna be a lot easier if — here." Callie took another stake and another roll of aluminum foil, and deftly wrapped it. She handed it to Beckett, and gestured to the rubber-headed mallet lying on the ground. "You, bang this in, and then we'll do another layer of foil around the stake and then on the ground."

"You've done this before?" Robert asked.

"No, but I know basic cooking engineering and food safety."

"Fair enough."

Callie supervised the rest of the process — putting the turkeys on the foil-wrapped stakes, inverting the clean metal trashcans over each one to make an oven, lighting the charcoal on the trash can lids.

"Hey, Robert, I've got a question for you," Callie said as they worked.

"Sure, what's up?"

"Prefacing this by saying Beckett volunteered your expertise, but all the ceiling tiles in my shop are falling down, I can't figure out what to do about it, and I have possibly reached the end of my rope as to what YouTube, Emma and I can figure out on our own. And for reasons.... I can't call my dad."

"Oh!" Robert paused in the middle of tearing off more foil. "Tin ceiling, right? Original to the building?"

"Yeah."

"We had almost the exact same problem a couple of years ago

in some of the houses on set. Not tin ceilings, wrong era, but the same idea and you would not believe the cost in time and dollars when shit like that ruins a shot. One of the local PAs finally figured it out. The salt air rots the nails right out of the wood. You need composite plywood and — there's a particular kind of screw that works great, but you're gonna want to cap them, if you want to keep the period look. Where do you get your supplies?"

"Sealport."

"Perfect, that's where we get a lot of our stuff too. You want a hand getting everything to the shop?"

Callie stared at him, evidently surprised by the offer. Beckett grinned to himself and kept wrapping the stake he was working on.

"Normally I would say no," she said slowly. "But it's possible my pride has been eroded by the ceiling gremlins."

"It took me about two years, too," Robert smiled at her. "But trust me, life gets easier after that. What are you doing for the rest of the break?"

"I was gonna be winterizing my boat, but now I'm dealing with this, too."

"Oof. That's a long weekend."

"Yes, it is!" Callie sounded, for the first time since Beckett had known her, slightly manic at the prospect of the work to do in front of her.

"I'll get you a list of the stuff you want to pick up," Robert said. "And you let me know when's a good time for me to swing by and lend a hand."

"It's Thanksgiving!" Callie protested, but Beckett could see the relief in her eyes. "I can't ask you to do that."

"You're not, I'm offering. Besides." Robert gave her a friendly nudge with his elbow. "Can't let the claw lady down."

Beckett was already watching Callie's face, so he got to watch Robert's statement, so casual and sincere, hit her. He was less surprised than she was — he knew Robert would jump at the chance to lend a hand — but it settled something in his heart to see her know she was a part not just of the Fly-Debate community, but of the *Hidden Cove* one, too.

❧

Other people, many with their partners and families, began to arrive as they finished with the turkeys. Soon the house and even the yard, chilly as it was, were abuzz with people.

The main topic of conversation was, unsurprisingly, what the hell everyone was going to do next. The upset of the initial cancellation announcement had settled, for the most part, but the stress of figuring out what happened after *Hidden Cove* was very much still there. Some people couldn't wait to get out of Maine; others, like him and Robert, now had lives so entangled with the state that leaving was as much of a problem as staying. But for most people the situation was less one of choices or celebrations and instead a matter of extremely stressful logistics of money and housing.

Beckett realized he shouldn't have been resentful of Steve's insistence that he think ahead. The sooner he had a post-*Hidden Cove* plan, the sooner he could drag as many of the people here as possible along with him. He couldn't solve everyone's problems, but his own next moves could go a long way to helping chunks of this cast and crew not have to freak out about their future paychecks. *For that*, Beckett thought, *I will even send in the tape for that superhero thing*. Of course, nothing was ever going to come of that in a million years, but he should still try.

"My turn to ask a favor," Beckett said to Robert, as they worked side-by-side at the outdoor faucet to clean off the tools they'd used to prepare the turkeys.

"Yeah?"

"I've got a self-tape to do and I want it not to look like shit. You willing to help?"

Robert gave him a skeptical look as he scrubbed a pair of tongs. "You know it's called self-tape for a reason. And even if it wasn't, you're perfectly capable of doing that yourself."

"I know. But it's for one of those things that's too high profile for me to actually name and there's definitely an NDA involved. So the bar's gonna be high, and you're the best."

Robert gave a disbelieving laugh. "First you don't want to leave Maine and now you wanna audition for something like *that*? What the fuck?"

"It's never going to happen. But maybe something else will come of it." Beckett shrugged. "In any case, I gotta go through the motions."

# CHAPTER 27

44°36'29.6"N 67°8'22.9"W
Temp: 43.0°F
Pressure: 29.77 inHg
Wind: 13.8 mph, NW
Visibility: 10.00 mi


AFTER DINNER, WHICH WAS a riotous, joyful affair, and cleanup, which was hardly less convivial, Callie went to see about finding Beckett, who she'd lost track of somewhere in the chaos. She had half a mind to ask him what he and Robert had been whispering about together before dinner —

Callie stopped, the breath literally catching in her lungs. Beckett was in front of the sliding doors that led out to the deck. He was crouched beside Dahlia, who had her face pressed against the glass, one gentle hand on the baby's waist to help steady her as she stood. The mellow early-evening light fell across his face, making the gray in his hair and beard glow and highlighting every perfect angle of his face. His eyes, turned up to the sky, were at once thoughtful and intent.

"There, right up there," he said, pointing with his free hand. "You see that bird on the branch? That's a downy woodpecker."

Dahlia slapped her tiny hands on the glass. "Twee! Twee twee twee twee!"

"Shhh, shh shh," Beckett hushed her softly. "We don't want to scare it away."

"Twee," the baby whispered solemnly, and Beckett's face lit up in a silent laugh. That smile wasn't for anyone but him and Dahlia, and it was the most gorgeous thing Callie had ever seen.

*What if that was our baby?* For a moment Callie let herself indulge and imagine it. A toddler with her red curls and Beckett's blue eyes, Beckett a tender and attentive father, in a house of their own where they could raise a family, not just one baby but a whole houseful, a life full of joyful chaos and affection.

She withdrew back to the kitchen, not willing to disturb the tableau but also needing a moment for herself. She'd liked Beckett from the moment she'd met him; had been lusting after him for nearly as long. But now Callie realized she had at some point — possibly this very moment — gone from having an unreasonable amount of fun with the hottest man she'd ever seen, to having a deep affection for him, to being completely in love with Beckett. And that was kind of a lot to take in, at his best friend's house on Thanksgiving Day.

Robert was true to his word, and on Saturday morning he, Callie, and Beckett all made the trip to Sealport for construction supplies and then back to Sweet Claws. There was enough holiday traffic that Callie couldn't keep the shop shut down for too long, and Robert had his family to get back to, so they didn't have time to fix the entire ceiling. But they made enough progress, and Callie learned enough from Robert, that she was confident that the ceiling nightmare would eventually end.

Unfortunately work didn't end when she left the shop. There was still the *Lobster Taco* to get ready for winter. Fortunately, Beckett seemed to be game for any and all physical labor, even during his days off. Callie was glad both for the extra set of hands and his cheerful, capable presence at her side as they flushed the external water lines, scrubbed the scuppers, and reinforced the insulation.

The work was physically taxing, and the cold and the wet made everything more difficult and more painful for Callie. But Beckett was always there, to tie knots when her fingers were too stiff and make her take breaks and entertain away the tedium of the work with stories and chitchat.

She suspected, however, that he was using the labor to work off his feelings about *Hidden Cove.*

On Sunday afternoon, they were out on the deck putting the finishing touches on the electrical heating tape that would keep her pipes from freezing. The mist was cold, and clinging, and Callie was thinking longingly of being done with this last task and spending the remaining few hours of the day burrowed beneath the blankets in her bed. Surely Beckett would be willing to bring her tea and wrap her up until she stopped feeling so damned cold.

"Have you got plans for Christmas yet?" Beckett asked as he reached for a fresh roll of tape.

"I haven't even thought past tomorrow." Callie said with a rueful laugh. Which was true enough. "What are you doing?"

"Seattle. See my folks and everyone." Beckett paused while he tore off a strip of tape with his teeth. "Do you want to come with me?"

Callie stared at him. His hair was escaping from under his knit cap, the wind tugging at the damp strands. His face was earnest and open.

"To Seattle?" she asked.

"Yeah."

Callie knew she should be happy about this invitation, especially in light of her own family situation, but something in her felt on the verge of panic. "For Christmas?"

"Yeah," Beckett said, a faint note of caution in his voice now.

"For how long?" she asked, stalling for time.

"I leave on the twentieth. And get back after New Year's. You could come for just part...if you wanted..." His voice trailed off in a way that strongly suggested he saw some sort of horrified look on her face.

Callie shook her head slowly. "I wish I could. I really do."

And she did. She wanted a world where she could accept that invitation with no more consequences than when he had asked her to go to Los Angeles with him, but things were moving too fast, not so much in terms of their feelings for each other, but in terms of the impact it was having on their lives at a moment when way too much was up in the air.

"It's all right," Beckett said, seeming to track her trepidation. But Callie couldn't stop talking.

"It's just — all this work with Sweet Claws and the boat, the crisis with the ceiling... my body is exhausted. I can't put all the holiday work at the shop on Emma. And oh my god, Beckett," she said, twisting a piece of insulation around in her hands. Her whole body was turning to panic. "Neither of us even managed to tell our families we were dating until they saw the pictures from the premiere. My family situation is a mess and I adore you but Christmas is not the time to dump me on your parents."

The next morning at Sweet Claws Callie kept turning Beckett's invitation over and over in her head. She'd already said no, but she wished it hadn't been necessary. There was no logic she could come up with that would let her change her mind, however. And the more she thought about it, the more she hyperfixated on all the other issues that had to be addressed long before she could entertain such an invitation.

"Fuck, I have to do something about my parents."

Emma looked up from where she was kneading dough at the counter. "What?"

Callie knew she'd spoken out loud; she had done that a lot during her first months putting the shop and her life in Fly-Debate together. She had, however, forgotten that she had an audience now. She punched her own lump of dough.

"Beckett invited me to Christmas with his family, and I freaked because family Christmas is like... a really big deal? And I said no? Because I can't leave the shop for the holiday, obviously —" Even as she tried to explain herself, Callie knew she just sounded scared.

"Hello, I'm not chopped liver," Emma said. "I can handle the shop."

"You can, yes! But the holidays are hard on both people and entrepreneurs. And all of that aside... how can I go meet Beckett's family when I'm not even speaking to mine?"

Emma shrugged. "I dunno. You make the choice? Or you don't. So, what's the deal?"

Callie took a deep breath. "My grown-up boyfriend —"

"You mean old," Emma interjected.

"Ignoring you!" Callie laughed. "But he wants to introduce me to his family at Christmas, and when we were in LA together stuff got intense because of the show cancellation and also he said some stuff that felt like, twenty-five percent of the way to a proposal. Which was a lot but fun at the time and the right amount of serious, and now this feels like, ten percent closer to a proposal and not the right amount of serious?"

"Wait, wait WHUT?" Emma asked. "Because if you marry Beckett, that basically makes Darcy my friend-in-law, so like you definitely need to do that."

"I'm not saying he proposed!" Callie flapped her hands in a panic. Her life could only get worse if a rumor like that got around.

"Well, what did he say?"

"Just... we were talking about what we wanted out of our lives and how he wanted a spouse, and kids, and soon, and he didn't want to put pressure on me by telling me all of that, which is the sort of thing you only say to someone you'd want to be doing spouse and kids stuff with."

"Okay, yeah. That's big. By the way, as a rule, you should breathe every few words," Emma said. "But why was that okay but him wanting you to meet his parents is too much?"

"I don't know!" Callie threw up her hands, distraught. Everything was a mess and she was making everything more of a mess. "I am super into this, to be clear. Like I would love for him to bring me home for Christmas, and I do not want him to slow down. But everything also feels real and serious beyond my ability to keep up. And it would be fucked up to pretend that I'm an adult he's bringing home to meet his parents when I'm not even enough of an adult to call my parents back after yelling at them in a parking lot and scaring the squirrels."

"I got the impression that was justified," Emma said.

"Maybe? I don't know. I haven't called them back. That's kinda fucked."

"I will note they have not called you back either. So everyone seems like they're learning from the best, here." Emma punched at her dough. "Ever consider your parents aren't adult enough to fix shit with you?"

"Every damn day. Pretty sure we all suck, though. And I do not know what to do."

"I've been doing a mural at a beauty salon, and they keep a lot of daytime TV talk shows running in there," Emma said. "So I've been learning a lot about family drama and pop psychology, and they would say that you need to keep the lines of communication open without making concessions you don't want to make."

Callie narrowed her eyes thoughtfully. "Why does that sound reasonable?"

Emma shrugged. "Stopped clock, right twice a day."

"Okay. Fair. Now how the hell am I going to do that?"

"I dunno. Send them doughnuts?"

# CHAPTER 28

47°37'14.8"N 122°12'51.7"W
Temp: 43.0°F
Pressure: 29.65 inHg
Wind: 11.5 mph, E
Visibility: 7.00 mi

Beckett usually felt a certain sort of relief landing at Sea-Tac. This time, while the relief was still there, there was also a feeling of being off-balance. Home was Washington, yes. But home wasn't *only* Washington. Not anymore. That had probably been true since he'd first moved to Maine for *Hidden Cove*, but arriving here without Callie underlined the point, possibly more sharply than he cared for. He understood why she wasn't here with him, but he had a sense of foreboding in terms of what it meant for their relationship.

He shook his circling thoughts off as much as he could. There was no use in dwelling and doing so would only make him a terrible guest. Besides, Knox was picking him up, and of everyone in his family he was probably the person who most needed and deserved his full attention. Acting was a hard career, and the differences between their respective success were not great for their relationship. It behooved Beckett to take extra care.

"Can I ask you a thing?" Knox said as they pulled onto the highway.

Beckett stopped himself from groaning, but just barely. Knox only asked for permission to have a conversation when the topic was serious. Beckett wasn't sure if he had the bandwidth for it under recent circumstances and without even a day to acclimate first.

"I just got off a plane and am entirely useless right now," he said. "But sure, go."

"I'm thinking of quitting," Knox said without preamble.

It wasn't a question, and it made Beckett sit up from where he'd been slouching in the front seat. But whether Knox wanted his advice or just wanted a target for his frustrations remained to be seen, especially within the confines of the drive home.

"What's that about?" Beckett suspected he knew. The job was a brutal one and Knox, talking about this here and now, likely wanted an answer and the ability to make a grand announcement over the holiday. Beckett sighed. *What a shitshow.*

"Like you never thought about quitting," his brother said instead of properly answering.

"I *never* thought about quitting," Beckett shot back. "I wished I could have, sometimes, but I'm not good at anything else. I didn't want anything else." He paused and bit his lip. "This conversation should not be about me. Do you still like the work?"

"I don't know," Knox said. "I don't know if I've ever liked it."

"Really?" Beckett prompted. Sure it was possible, but he suspected Knox just needed to talk himself through a thing.

"Maybe? Maybe I just want to be other people... not like, act."

That was interesting. It was also more of an existential crisis than Beckett felt prepared for, especially when his own life was ... the way it was right now. Between the Callie situation and the top-secret superhero situation which wasn't going to amount to anything but was still happening, Beckett doubted he was in any shape to give anyone advice about their own life. But still, he loved Knox, and he was always happy to mentor or advise where he could.

"Okay. Look," he said. "This job is not worth suffering for if you don't enjoy it. And it's not worth throwing away just because it's hard if you do. If you don't like the very act of pretending, of play, then yeah maybe it's a bad fit. But honestly, I'm happy to be a sounding board, but I'm not here to nudge your bad mood into one decision or another, okay?"

"I'm not —"

"You are," Beckett cut him off. "Because I did shit like this to other people when I was in the despair place. And, frankly, I know my character flaws and can't say I won't do it again."

"Seriously?" Knox shot him a disbelieving look. "You're the lead on a show and —"

"That's ending," Beckett said tersely.

"Surely, you're going to get all sorts of crazy offers."

Beckett wanted to talk about this. But he wasn't sure if he was ready to. Also the NDA he had ultimately had to sign just to have his agent send in the self-tape was, unlike most such documents, genuinely scary. But scary documents were what happened when you tangled with some of the most lucrative and litigious IP in the world. He'd have to find a way to talk around this as best he could.

"I had a self-tape I had to do right before I came out here."

"I fucking hate those," Knox said.

"You shouldn't. More control than an in-person audition. Although, make friends with a DP."

"Yeah, I'll just magically make that happen," Knox said. "So what's it for and why are they making you do one? Aren't you important enough now to just skip the audition thing?"

Beckett snorted and shook his head. Didn't he wish. Things were easier now, yes, but the business was full of genuine stars. He was still just a guy who worked hard and had gotten lucky. Whether he would keep getting lucky remained to be seen.

"Three words," he said.

"And they are?" Knox asked, all impatience.

Beckett knew he shouldn't tell. Not even a little. But he couldn't stop himself. Plus, half of Hollywood had put themselves on tape for this sort of thing at one time or another. It didn't mean anything.

"Super. Hero. Shit," he said.

Knox let out a low whistle. "Between that and your girlfriend who isn't here, your life is doing some things, isn't it?"

While Beckett was happy to accept a bit of ribbing from Knox — it was the best possible sign that he wasn't as down in the dumps about the acting thing as he thought he was — Callie felt like a sore point and his sense of worry spiraled again.

"Don't rub it in, okay? I'm not thrilled about that," he said.

"Trouble in paradise?" Knox asked.

Beckett shook his head. "Nah, we're fine. She just runs that shop and has some family stuff that's stressing her out. Coming out here felt a little too weird and a little too soon for her. Which, you know, is a bummer, but it's also fine." Maybe if he kept saying it, he'd eventually believe it.

Knox rolled his eyes. "You're so reasonable."

*Don't I wish.* "Yeah, well, someone has to be," Beckett said genially. "It sure as hell isn't you."

❀

Beckett did not feel reasonable as the week before the holiday got underway. Seeing everyone — his parents, his siblings, the extended chaos of niblings and cousins — was great.  But he missed Callie desperately. He wasn't proud of it, but he was jealous of Thomas and Christine having their partners there with them. And he struggled to stay focused on the people right in front of him.

His job made so many interactions awkward.  Acting didn't merit more attention than any other career, but it always engendered curiosity. But it was the sort of thing it was impossible to make small talk about with anyone other than Knox. And Knox definitely didn't want to hear about it in the midst of his own struggles.

Beckett found himself staying quiet in ways that felt awkward. He didn't want to talk about the emotional weight of the impending end of *Hidden Cove* and he'd already said too much to Knox about the next steps he was taking professionally. Curiosity about Callie was great and welcome, but Beckett didn't feel comfortable speaking for her — about her life or her future or why she wasn't here.

His parents, of course, clocked his restless discomfort right away, asked him about it, and gave quiet heavy sighs when Beckett explained that he was just out of sorts. He felt ashamed about it, as if there surely had to be some way he could just be normal and engaged and not famous for the week. But whatever the secret to that was, he was failing to discover it.

Also not helping the situation? How much his phone kept going off. He and Callie were exchanging brief texts around the bakery's schedule and the time difference, but those were lovely and great. It was the professional texts that were sending him around the bend.

Not just because they were vague and incoherent, although they were. But because every time he got into an exchange where he ultimately had to ask for more information the other person was seemingly pulled away from their phone by the holidays. The self-tape was still a long shot that wasn't going to go anywhere, but the cryptic exchanges meant that Beckett couldn't help but fixate on the faint hope of a possibility.

Steve asked repeatedly if Beckett had heard anything about the self-tape, which was absurd and infuriating. If there was anything to know, Steve would know it first. Thus, he was either asking a question that didn't make sense (perfectly plausible) or knew something and was refusing to tell Beckett, which also sounded like his speed.

The only reason Beckett didn't think it was the second option was because it was now late December, and no one was casting anyone in anything until January. Which he continued to think right up until the director of the project texted him and asked if they could get on a video call for an informal chat with "a couple of the guys from the studio."

Beckett had to resist the urge to text back and ask if this was a prank. Doing so would have been bad form. And if it was a prank, and he just wound up looking foolish by the end of this all, so be it. He had meant what he said to Robert — an opportunity like this could mean a lot of work for the folks from *Hidden Cove* if he got cast. If there was an actual chance here, he had to not fuck it up by being flippant and insecure.

Beckett wound up taking the call in his dad's little woodworking workshop, which was just a mud room in their half basement, but the internet came in there and thus it had the strongest signal in the house. The facts that ambient noise was limited and no one was likely to interrupt him also made it an obvious choice for conveying some vague degree of professionalism.

He'd just have to live with all his dad's half-finished projects cluttered up behind him.

Those half-finished projects turned out to be the least of his concerns as the call got underway. The first thing he was asked was if he was in a private location where no one else would overhear the discussion. The second thing he was asked was whether he minded if a few more people joined the call.

The import of the situation was becoming very clear, very quickly. Beckett may have been an actor, but he was not capable of acting like any of this was normal, because it wasn't. The only way he was going to be able to get through it without fainting was to acknowledge what the hell was going on.

"Um, I realize there's a lot of stuff we can't say out loud at this stage," Beckett began. "And I am sure I'm not the only person you're talking to today, but I also want to acknowledge what's happening here, which is that it's two days before Christmas and there are *eighteen* people on this call?"

Beckett had never been on a studio call with more than five participants before. And he'd certainly never seen one come together this quickly with this many different schedules involved. *The beauty of the holidays.*

When it was done Beckett put his head down on his dad's workbench and tried to gather himself. While he remained sure there were several other people still in contention alongside him, that call had been very, very serious, and not just because of how many people were on it at a time when no one wanted to be working.

No, they had wooed him, zoning in on his points of hesitation about submitting in the first place and knocking down those concerns one by one until Beckett was kind of convinced that the project was going to be thoughtful, aligned with his politics and ideals, and possibly committed to not destroying his body. That was the one he trusted the least, frankly.

Beckett moaned to himself. What the hell was he supposed to do with this massive unofficial, uncertain-but-definitely-possible secret? There were eighteen people on that call! How was that even a thing?

He didn't know. He didn't know any of the people who did the superhero stuff, so he had no gossip, no knowledge, and no way to ask. Did this mean something or was the whole process just like this?

Did he even want to be a superhero? He wasn't sure. But more now than when he'd put himself on tape, that was for sure. Work was work, and work like this would give him the freedom to do anything he wanted for the rest of his damn life.

But right now, there was only one thing Beckett wanted. Too bad she was tremendously far away due to doughnuts and good boundaries. Still, that wasn't going to keep him from whining.

"I just want my girlfriend," he whispered miserably to the gods of awkward crafts and basement sawdust.

But they didn't answer. Which was probably for the best. Because now he couldn't say anything to anyone about this. Even accidentally. While he was trapped with his entire family in his childhood home.

<pre>
44°32'30.1"N  67°29'45.7"W
          Temp: 33.1°F
    Pressure: 29.38 inHg
      Wind: 20.7 mph, N
    Visibility: 0.75 mi
</pre>

WITH BECKETT AWAY, AND Callie all in on making the season entirely about her business, making the shop festive had been as much a priority as baking endless claws for the holiday demand. She and Emma had decorated the shop with pine garlands and twinkling lights. Robert, Julie, and their kids had stopped by to bring them cookies and a jug of mulled cider. Callie had dinner with them one day and with Sydney and her grandmother another, before returning to Sweet Claws to pack up the latest mail orders and get a jump on the next day's prep work. Somewhere along the way, Lobbie the Lobster acquired a Santa hat.

As busy as the pre-holiday rush was and as dissimilar as the week was to Christmases past, there was a peace to it all that Callie had never known growing up. Her days were under her own control, and evenings either on her boat or visiting with friends were quiet and peaceful. No one was yelling in anger or in joy, and while some part of her missed the convivial chaos of her upbringing she was grateful for a choice, to see what suited her best.

The one thing looming on the horizon was a storm. Callie knew to keep a close eye on the weather. Life in Maine, and on a boat, necessitated it. In the last year and change she liked to think she had become an expert at assessing the actual threat posed by weather as opposed to the predictions of the forecasters, which tended to be distinctly alarmist. This storm had her worried. She'd have to make sure both the boat and her shop were fully prepped.

Her phone rang as she was in the shop's utility room, checking the insulation around the pipes. If the power went out, the risk of the pipes freezing would increase significantly. And that was a potential disaster neither she nor her business could afford.

She fished her phone out of her pocket and smiled. Beckett.

"Hey, how's it going?" she asked as she answered the call.

There was a quiet, unhappy sigh on the other end of the line, and she frowned.

"I'm all right," he finally said.

"You don't sound it," she said bluntly as she poked at a spot where the insulation had come loose. *I'll need more duct tape.*

"There's some stuff going on here."

"What kind of stuff?" Callie was concerned. She was pretty sure only one of them should be having family drama at a time, and she had that booked in solid for the moment.

"Nothing bad," Beckett said hastily. "Things are just kind of a lot."

Callie made a sympathetic noise. "So tell me about them."

"I dunno." The line crackled as Beckett blew out a breath. "To be honest, I'm feeling down and kind of lonely. And thinking that I should have stayed in Maine for Christmas. Or tried harder to woo you out here, even for just a few days."

"Beckett," Callie said seriously. "You didn't have to stay. And it wasn't right for me to go, so don't lose sleep over any of that. The shop and the weather have me plenty busy. Now either tell me what's wrong or tell me something else."

"What do you think of me coming back to Maine?"

"What?" That was neither of the options Callie had offered and she was sure she must have heard wrong.

"I miss you. I miss Maine. There's more we should have talked about before I left. Hell, there's more I want to talk about with you now. And I still don't want to put pressure on you — that's the last thing I want. So if you'd rather not, I won't. But also, I'm looking at plane tickets. For tonight."

That was a lot to process all at once. And while it hit all the too-much-too-fast buttons that had resulted in them spending Christmas apart in their first place, Callie realized she did, however selfishly, want him with her. The stuff that was stressing her out was real, but it wasn't Beckett. He wasn't the source of the expectations she felt; everyone else was.

But all of that aside, what Beckett wanted to do — was offering to do! — was impossible.

"Christmas Eve is tomorrow!" Callie gave a disbelieving laugh even as her whole being yearned to have him back for the holiday.

"Have you seen what the weather's doing? And what are your parents going to say? I don't want them to hate me before they've even met me!"

"My parents will be fine and you are not responsible for my choices. But what's that about the weather?"

"There's a nor'easter forming," Callie told him. "It's off New Jersey right now but it's going to get bigger and faster. Even if it doesn't get any worse, which is a huge if, we're looking at some serious wind and snow, not to mention waves. Unpleasant and worrisome for me, but also the sort of thing that cancels a lot of flights."

"Is the *Lobster Taco* going to be okay?"

Callie was touched by the thought. "The inlet's relatively sheltered. We'll find out if 'relatively' is good enough. But whatever the storm is going to do, it's going to do. I've got the shop to hunker down in if that seems safer."

"Would me coming back be too much? I don't want to make things harder for you. Or for you to think I don't think you can handle a storm."

"I appreciate it. Truly. But, if you want to come back —" Callie gave a disbelieving chuckle. She did want Beckett with her for the holiday, of course she did, even if she thought he was signing up for more of an ordeal than was wise. "Come on home. After all, you're the one who's going to be sleeping in an airport when your flight gets delayed."

After their call, Callie went back to storm prep. The insulation on her pipes was somewhere between fine and nothing she could solve now, so after applying some duct tape to it she went back to pre-treating the sidewalk outside the shop and making sure she had working flashlights on hand should the power go out. It was easy enough work, but difficult while also managing the holiday rush of customers. Having at least closed the mail order business until after New Year's was the only thing affording her even some small amount of breathing space.

But as much work as there was to do, and as many things in her life that were unsettled, Callie couldn't have imagined being happier than she was right now, the scent of ginger and cinnamon in the air and the snow beginning, gently for now, to fall.

She assumed — hoped, even — that Beckett would think better of his sudden urge to return to Maine for Christmas. If he could have magically transported himself, or her, she would have been delighted to spend the holiday with him. But this was a long, unplanned flight towards a major weather event on an already unmanageably busy travel day. She could love him from afar for a few more days if she had to.

Instead, when she woke up the next morning, there was a text from him, sent the previous evening, to tell her that he'd gotten a flight out of Sea-Tac later that very night.

**Beckett:** With any luck, will see you for Christmas Eve lunch.

Callie smiled to herself as she replied, even though judging by the timestamp of the text, he was likely still on a plane and out of communication.

**Callie:** You are making dubious choices. But I'm here whenever you get here.

Her phone pinged with an incoming message almost immediately.

**Beckett:** I am. I am also in Chicago.
**Callie:** Was that part of the plan?
**Beckett:** No. Weather already. And planes in the wrong places because. I'm trying to solve it, but...
**Callie:** You'll do what you can. I am okay. You make sure you are okay. If we have to have Christmas on the phone, that was the original plan anyway. Yes?
**Beckett:** Yes, ma'am.

Callie had been baffled the first few times he had called her ma'am, back when they'd barely known each other. Now it made her fond. It also made her want to take him to bed.

❀

Beckett kept Callie updated on the status of his attempts to get another flight. His tone, even through text, became increasingly frantic. Callie felt for him and also tried not to burn too many cycles on why he'd decided to take on this mission to get back. He had told her it was nothing bad and, as unsettled as he sounded, she had no choice but to try to believe him.

As his texts continued to come in, it became very clear to what degree he was racing the weather that was already more than dusting the sidewalks of Fly-Debate with snow.

He did, finally, manage to get a flight that would get him to Newark. It was progress but Callie was fairly sure he'd get stuck there for the duration. At least he had friends in New York. It would be unfortunate that he was neither with her nor family, but it wouldn't be dire.

**Beckett:** *Arrived in Newark...running to catch connection to Bangor.*
**Beckett:** *Shouldn't have bothered running...plane is being de-iced.*

For a while, Callie had no idea what had happened after that. Beckett was silent as lunch came and went.

**Beckett:** Plane is STILL being de-iced.
**Beckett:** I am stuck in an eternal hell of de-icing and they're canceling flights by the minute. Auuuuuughhh.
**Callie:** Maine will be here. Whenever you get here. I promise. Breathe!
**Beckett:** ACTUALLY BOARDING NOW.

Callie may have told Beckett to breathe, but now she needed to do the same. Because there was a very good chance that the plane would not get off the ground or would land at a different airport.

This whole story would, she knew, be funny someday. And it was strange to think about the future in which that was true. Her and Beckett living happily ever after... or not. But it would still be a story she told, about that one year she dated a celebrity who needed her in ways she hadn't understood at the time.

She sure didn't understand them now.

Callie shoved her phone in her pocket and turned her attention back to her shop, and her customers, and the increasingly necessary breaks to go outside to shovel off the next layer of snow and put down fresh salt.

By four o'clock the sky was dark and the snow and wind were picking up. Callie saw off the last of her customers, flipped the sign on the door to closed, and started cleaning up. With luck, she'd be able to get the shop in order and be on the road to her boat before the weather got any hairier. With good luck, Beckett would make it to Bangor in one piece and be able to hole up in a hotel tonight. And with extraordinary luck, the roads would be cleared and he'd be able drive down to Fly-Debate tomorrow morning.

There was a banging at the front door. Callie, in the back of the shop washing down the mixers, ignored it. The shop was closed, it was Christmas Eve, and frustrated doughnut-seeking travelers could take themselves away. She needed to get out of here before that became impossible.

The banging continued. Callie sighed and threw down her dishtowel.

"We're closed!" she yelled, coming to the doorway, ready if need be to march out from behind the counter.

Instead, she froze. Beckett was outside, hand raised to knock again.

"What the fuck!" Callie ran to the door, laughing, unlocked it and pulled it open. Beckett tumbled through, collar pulled up to his ears, snow in every crease of his coat. "How did you get here?"

Beckett shook his head, shaking snowflakes out of his hair. "Easy. I flew and then I drove."

Callie laughed in disbelief. She was giddy with his presence and baffled that he was actually here. "You didn't tell me you landed!"

"There was no time. I wanted to get on the road. It's worse in Bangor and it was looking like every minute mattered. And I think it did."

"You're out of your mind."

"Yeah." Beckett's gaze was intense, his blue eyes fixed on her. "Yeah," he repeated. "I needed to see you."

Callie still couldn't figure out what was going on with him, and was just about to ask when he swept down on her and covered her mouth with his. She dug her hands into his hair instinctively, the snowflakes in it melting rapidly to little specks of cold against her fingertips.

*Maybe I needed him back here more than I realized.*

Beckett whimpered as she tugged at the strands. It was the faintest sound, but it immediately sent a bolt of heat through her to her toes. She had so much power over him. He'd spent a day traveling in this storm to get to her, because she, somehow, had become home too.

Callie combed her fingers through his hair, before digging in. This time, intentionally, she pulled.

Beckett made a sharp desperate noise. Not quite wounded, but definitely lost.

"Oh God," he managed as he pulled back from her mouth.

She looked over his face, so close to hers, but just far enough away to study without the world going blurry. He looked dazed.

*I did that*, Callie thought. *He lets me do that. Needs me to do that.*

Dazed was a very good look on him. She stood on her tiptoes to kiss him again.

It was not enough for either of them.

Beckett picked Callie up and set her on the counter that ran along the back wall. With one hand he caught the back of her head and kissed her, his beard dragging over her skin. There was a sharpness to it that she had come to love. She hoped the beard would stay after *Hidden Cove* was over, but she knew it probably wouldn't.

There was no time to consider that particular issue though, as he slid his other hand up under her dress until he reached the waistband of her leggings.

"Wait, wait, wait... we cannot do this here," Callie protested, not that she wanted to.

Beckett paused, looking at her incredulously.

"I'm sorry but like, we're about to violate half a dozen food safety regulations and the shop window shades are not entirely opaque."

Beckett stared at her, devastated or too turned on to parse what she was saying, she wasn't sure. "The storm. We're not —" he began.

"Shhhhhhhhh," Callie soothed. She hopped down from the counter where he had placed her. "Come on. Shop office. It's not all that comfy, but it's less... all this." She gestured vaguely, running out of words herself. Talking was not what she wanted to be doing right now.

*Beckett. Beckett is what I want to be doing right now.*

She led him by the hand through the door to the back of the shop and to the left, sliding back the barn door to her "office" into which she had squeezed a desk, a small Ikea bed, and about a million shipping boxes for the burgeoning mail order business.

"You have a bed," Beckett exclaimed with such wonder that Callie burst into laughter.

"I do, and we should make use of it."

With that instruction Beckett wasted no time, getting his hands back up under her dress to tug down her tights. He backed her into the desk as he did so.

*So much for the bed.*

Callie didn't even understand why he'd done that until he slid to his knees as he peeled the tights off her. His cheeks were flushed, and his chest rose and fell in time with ragged breaths she could feel on the now-bare skin of her thighs.

Beckett kept reminding her just how much he liked being on his knees for her.

She ran her hands, gently now, back through his hair, wanting to soothe and cherish and praise. His eyes fluttered closed. They hadn't even done anything yet but he already looked wrecked. Callie didn't know how this had gotten so out of hand so quickly, but then, that's how they always were, wasn't it?

"Callie—" Beckett's voice was rough.

"I know," she said. "But that's not what I want right now."

It was true. She didn't. What she wanted was him inside her and for them to fuck the weird chaos of this entire holiday season away.

Beckett, however, was a little slower on the uptake.

"What do you—" He swallowed, looking up at her still with glassy eyes, his throat bobbing. "Anything."

She used the hand in his hair to pull him upward. "I want us on the bed and you in me. Now."

He made a noise as he climbed to his feet — not quite a growl, but something all want and need and deeply animalistic. As soon as he was standing, he crashed their mouths together. Callie frantically fumbled with her clothes and his by turns, determined only that they get just naked enough to actually do this.

Beckett was a little more together on that front; he loved her body and despite the baggage of his work, loved living in his. He helped her pull her dress over her head and then yanked off his own clothes as quickly as he could while watching her every move.

Callie couldn't blame him. Her tits really did look spectacular upon escaping a bra.

"Bed," Beckett said.

Callie didn't think he was capable of more words than that and scrambled to comply. This was one of the things she loved about sex with him. As eager as he was to give her pleasure and make her the star of the show and serve her, he was always willing to be assertive about it. For Callie, these particular power dynamics were the best of both worlds. Others might have had different tastes, but hers were well satisfied, and they fit together. They just fit.

He prowled onto the bed after her. Callie was in awe, not for the first time, at the play of muscles in his arms and chest. She reached out to touch him, but lost her focus when he swiped his fingers through her folds. Testing, she was sure, to see if she was wet. How could she not be, when he looked like this and had flown across the country in a storm because for some reason he needed her more than he needed anything else?

"Ready?" he asked from where he was sprawled across the little bed, his cock hard and eager, and his face made of wonder.

Normally, Callie made a point of answering such questions verbally. They served an important purpose of consent, yes, but also of dirty talk. This time, however, she pawed at Beckett's hips, and when he got close enough grabbed his cock and lined him up.

"Ready," she finally said.

Beckett wasted no time, and Callie gasped into his shoulder as he thrust into her. He paused for just a moment to gather himself, but Callie had no patience for it, and nudged him to start moving with the heel of her foot. That was all it took, and Callie laughed smugly as Beckett's hips quickly became too frantic to find a rhythm,

"You feel so fucking good." Beckett breathed the words into her ear and then slid his hand from her thigh to the center of her, pressing his thumb against her clit.

Callie moaned. Why was he so good at this?

"Yeah, just like that." Beckett panted, his thrusts growing even more unsteady.

Pleasure sparked throughout her body, and Callie could feel the warm build of her own orgasm begin.

"Beckett…" She didn't know what she wanted to tell him. She just wanted to say his name, to be there with him, to make sure he knew how utterly overwhelmed she was in the best possible way.

"Yeah?" He was goading her to put words to this moment.

"You are perfect," she said.

"No, no," he protested as his hips snapped into her. "We are perfect."

Callie grinned at that, so silly and precise and sweet in this moment where she barely had a brain. But then he kept talking.

"I cannot wait to put a baby in you," he gasped in her ear.

The words, dirty and shocking and hot, closed some sort of circuit in her brain. Combined with Beckett's hand on her clit and his cock deep inside of her, her entire body arched up into the idea of him filling her up like that. She sobbed with the filthy pleasure of the thought, and when Beckett next circled his thumb on her clit, an orgasm rushed through her with a ferocity she was not prepared for.

He followed moments later, pulsing inside her, both of them gasping for air.

She whimpered as he slid out of her, not ready yet to lose that fullness even as her muscles ached and definitely not ready to think about what had just happened. Beckett reached for tissues to clean them up, but she caught him and dragged him back, to kiss him again, to feel the warmth and texture of him while her skin sparked with aftershocks.

After Callie could finally bear to let him go long enough to put themselves to vague rights, Beckett flopped down on the bed. There was enough space for the both of them if she wedged between him and the wall, which she did. She was asleep before she could have a cogent thought.

She woke to Beckett's arms wrapped around her and the sound of his words echoing in her head. *I can't wait to put a baby in you.*

Callie was instantly awake. That had been hot, undeniably, in the moment, which was a kink Callie hadn't even known she'd had.

But then, maybe it was just Beckett. He definitely brought out the try-anything-twice vibes in her.

But out here, in the real world, she and her very reliable IUD were having some feelings. *Who even says something like that when it's not the clear agreed-upon agenda?* Was it weird? It felt a little weird. Was it a thing she should be upset about? Her body, which was suddenly wildly tense, sure seemed to be telling her yes.

She sat up carefully, so as not to wake Beckett. The clock on the wall said it was three in the morning — time to start work, on a normal day. Which this was not. Callie scooted to the edge of the bed to retrieve her clothes and slowly wiggled into them. *Boots too*, she told herself. After all, they were still in her bakery.

"Okay, Callie, puzzle this out," she whispered to herself as she finally slipped out of the office, checking on the progress of the storm, before she headed to the stool behind the register where she always sat.

There, as always, waited Lobbie the Lobster in the little hat Emma had made for him. His dopey plastic face stared at her impassively. What strange and at times imaginary friends she had in her chaotic life.

Callie knew Beckett wanted kids; he'd been upfront about that in as gracious a way as possible — taking pains not to pressure her, not being a possessive asshole about genetics or adoption. And she'd seen enough of him with his friends' kids that she suspected he was actually up for the hard work of it all. Crying babies, diapers, the sudden panic of a seven-year-old. Like the acting thing, Beckett was not just into the idea of being a parent for the glory.

So far so good; Callie liked kids, too, and raising a family with a partner eager to share in the bad days as well as the good frankly seemed like the fucking dream. But when she followed that thought, she was left with the logical conclusion. Her, pregnant. With luck, happily and healthily so. But even the easiest pregnancy in the world meant doctors and hospitals and her body — once again — fragile and not under her own control.

Her breath caught once more, but this time, not in a good way. Her vision seemed to narrow, and sound receded to the roaring of her own heart.

*You're having a panic attack*, she told herself sternly. She took a deep breath and closed her eyes while she tried to remember her lessons from therapy. *Breathe. Keep breathing. You're scared. But you're not in danger.*

Eventually, the tightness in her chest lessened, but the heaviness of a realization remained.

"God," she whispered as she looked around at her shop, at the snow, and at this man in her bed. "I do not know if I am ready for the future I think you want."

# CHAPTER 30

44°32'30.1"N 67°29'45.7"W
Temp: 33.1°F
Pressure: 29.81 inHg
Wind: 11.5 mph, NW
Visibility: ≥ 10.00 mi

BECKETT WOKE SLOWLY TO the smell of coffee and his own deeply disoriented body. Even before he opened his eyes, he didn't recognize the feel of the bed he slept in, and for a moment wasn't even sure what state he was in.

*Maine... Callie... the shop... great sex...and my own incredibly stupid mouth...*

Beckett snapped his eyes open to see the tin ceiling of Callie's shop. He was in the small bed in her office. The door to the public area of the shop outside of it was half-open. The shop was closed today both for the holiday and presumably for the snow; the bluish glow of a post-snowstorm morning was filtering in from the front. How bad had the weather gotten?

His musings on the weather ended when he saw Callie, sitting at the counter, with a mug of coffee. She was fully dressed and her body language was crisp and sharp. He'd never been so sure someone was about to have the bad kind of talk with him in his life.

"'Morning," he said, and then he shut up. A feat he was only able to manage because his job was listening to people, not anticipating them. Sometimes he was even able to apply the skill to his real life. Usually when he was already in a mess of trouble.

*Probably like right goddamn now.* Beckett tugged at the blankets on the bed. He was way too naked for whatever this situation was about to be.

"I had a bike when I lived in New York," Callie said quietly. "It made it easier to get around. Made me feel like I had more control. You really only survive getting chewed out by a chef instructor once for being late because someone 'got sick' on the train. That means the train hit someone, by the way."

Beckett nodded dumbly. Knox had told him that once. At the

time, he hadn't believed him. He believed Callie now.

"New York is outrageously dangerous for cyclists," Callie continued. "But you probably know that. Like, it's obvious. But you never think it'll be you. Until it is."

Beckett knew where this was going now. Knew it from the scars on her body and the note at the airport and the frantic, panicked way she never wanted to talk about the amorphous Before of her life.

He wished he could stop her. That if he could prevent her from telling the obviously terrible story she was about to tell, he could somehow undo whatever had happened to her.

"Do you know what dooring is?" Callie asked.

Beckett shook his head, although he had a guess.

"It's when someone opens their car door into another road user," Callie explained. "Depending on the timing you can get knocked off your bike, or flipped over the handlebars, or just slammed into really hard and bruised. Usually, it happens on the sidewalk side, because that's the sane way to get out of a car."

"Oh no," Beckett whispered.

Callie went on like he hadn't spoken. "That was not the way it happened to me. I got doored into moving traffic. Or so I hear. I don't really remember it. Actually, I have no idea what happened after I had breakfast that morning. Brains are weird, by the way."

"I am so sorry that —"

"Of course you're sorry that happened to me, Beckett," Callie snapped. "But let me finish the damn story. I had to live it. You can at least hear it and let me get to the point."

Beckett swallowed. "You're right. I'm sorry."

"Okay," she said. "Good. So, I bounced off a moving car and I broke a bunch of stuff. Some ribs. I've got metal in my left wrist and leg." She touched her arm and then her leg; Beckett didn't think she was even aware of the gesture. "I broke my cheekbone and had to have plastic surgery. I don't actually look like the pictures of me from when I was a kid. That's fucking weird." She shook her head, her gaze sliding away from him. "And I'm fine, you know I'm fine. No one would even know. Even the scars don't really convey what happened. I had a lot of physical therapy. Like, months to be good at walking again. The arm stuff was a fucking bear for culinary school. And you could not pay me to get back on a bike like ever again. Wear your helmet though, if you feel impelled. I am...extremely lucky to be alive."

"I'm glad you are."

"But here's the thing," Callie said. "And this is where we get to the point. Actually, a few points. I never watched your show because I can't stand TV. It's on constantly when you're in the hospital and the rehab center and I just...it's weird. It's a thing I'm working up to. But the other thing is, after that accident, for months, my body was extremely public property. Because of doctors and nurses and rehab and the investigation and the lawsuit, and then my parents wanted me to never leave the house again and my teachers were adamant I'd what...? Never be able to chop onions fast enough again? Handle the really big jugs of olive oil? So I fucked off up here. And decided to do every impossible thing I could."

"Of course you did," Beckett said. Everything made sense now. Her self-sufficiency. Her confidence. Her relationship with her body. Everything.

"Including you," she continued.

It sounded fond, and a laugh burst out of Beckett. He couldn't help himself. In the middle of this terrible, serious conversation, there was Callie. He loved her so much. She was so impossible and funny and sharp and capable. Not because of what had happened to her — he hadn't even known about that, not in any detail — but just because she was who she was.

She smiled at him sadly.

Beckett felt his entire body go cold. And not just because he was still naked in her secret bakery office bed in the middle of a blizzard.

"I know I am just as guilty as you are in terms of the pace of this thing," Callie said. "I may have acted otherwise at points, but I get that I am absolutely also on the hook here. It is so easy and extraordinary to be with you. You're the first person who has ever cared about me and my body who has also totally understood that it's mine and just mine and no one else's. And you've never doubted I was capable or smart or an adult. But last night —"

Beckett hung his head for a moment. "I said a thing."

Callie nodded, and there was a laugh he could see there, under her tears which were also threatening. He wanted to wipe them away, even though he knew he was a cause of them too.

"You said a thing," Callie repeated. "And look, no lie. That was hot in the moment."

"You're extraordinary," Beckett breathed.

"I'm trying to be."

"It both was and wasn't a fantasy," Beckett admitted. Maybe that was foolish, but lying to her, trying to protect her from his own issue, was unforgiveable.

"Yeah. And look. I love you. and I love kids. Every moment you're not exhausting me with the speed of this thing I'm like 'I think this is the guy... get me a dress, get me a ring and get me to my happily-ever-after.' But I am twenty-six-years old, and my life has been a mess and my parents hate me because I'm trying to be more than some girl who got hit by more than one car."

"You are. My God. I didn't even know," Beckett said. "And I am only sitting in this bed and not coming to you right now because I am still naked and I get the sense that that —"

"Would be awkward and also a health code violation, yes," Callie put in.

"Should I....?" Beckett trailed off and gestured awkwardly.

"Get dressed? Before I break up with you? Yeah, probably."

Beckett heard it like a record scratch. Despite all the ominous everything of this entire conversation he had hoped, believed even, that somehow this moment could be dodged. Hearing it felt impossible.

He scrambled over the side of the bed for his shirt, for his jeans, for anything he could find. Callie sat there quietly as he dressed, sometimes looking at him, sometimes fidgeting with her hands to give him privacy, he assumed. Not that it mattered now. Goddamnit. This girl was going to make him cry.

Callie must have seen it on his face, because she frowned, and was silent for a long time, even after he was dressed and perched on the edge of her office bed, still painfully far away from her.

"If I have babies with you in the next five minutes, Beckett, which it doesn't matter what you say, it feels like that's what you want — that's strangers touching my body and infinite medical stuff and all of this everything I am just so not into right now. And that shouldn't impact you. It shouldn't impact us. But you want what you want, and you want it now. And I am who I am and my ability to go there may never change. I have very real trauma to work through here and as much as part of me wants to get on board, my reflexive reaction is panic right now. And that's bad. All

I want to do is be sure I belong to myself first."

"You do," Beckett said. "Of course you do."

"Yeah but I don't know how to belong to myself and want the things you make me want. And I need a break. To sort out my shit. And you, by the way, need to sort out yours. About this place and work and your fucking shit about Los Angeles."

"There is stuff going on there," Beckett said reflexively. Because *oh God*, half the reason he had flown back was because there was a chance he was about to have the starring role in a major superhero franchise and it was fucking with this head. What was more sorting out his shit about work and LA than that?

Callie threw her hands up in the air. "That's great. But that's no longer an us issue."

"I flew back here because —"

"No," Callie said, holding up a hand. "No, you are fucking with my resolve, and grownups tell each other things on the phone. They don't fly into snowstorms for dramatic sexy reunions that involve fantasizing about getting people pregnant without taking about it first!'

"Can we at least acknowledge I wasn't the one flying the plane?"

"Beckett —"

"Okay, I will stop being clever, but would you give me a goddamn chance please?" Beckett snapped. He knew he had fucked up. In more ways than one, but this didn't have to be an insurmountable set of problems unless Callie wanted it to be.

Callie let out a frustrated sigh. "I gave you a chance, Beckett. I gave me a chance. Us. But we have fantasies about each other we can't live up to. You'll be leaving Maine forever in a few months, and I have a business and a life here."

"There are ways to figure that stuff out."

"No there aren't! I can't give up everything I've fought for because you want to have babies and need someone to hold your hand every time you're in LA!"

Beckett couldn't believe what he was hearing, except he could. Small mistakes added up, amplified each other, and cascaded exponentially. That was the human condition, that was why his life had involved so much love and all of it punctuated by near misses and the disaster of his profession. And now he was angry. At her, at himself, and at his whole wretched industry.

"You know what?" he said. "I appreciate that I screwed up here. But you expected me to know something you never told me, despite all the times it kinda sorta came up. And fine, I can be the asshole for what I said to you in bed, but making me the only guilty party in flying back here — you could have said no and you didn't."

"You are not real great at giving a girl space to say no," Callie shot back.

"You didn't even trust me with who you are!" Beckett snatched his coat off the floor and stood. "Anyway. Message received and worst Christmas ever. At least you won't have to worry about seeing me around town soon."

And with that, Beckett attempted to make the most dramatic exit of his career. Too bad that when he opened the door to the shop, a waist-high snow drift fell onto the tiled floor.

Beckett stared at it in horror. Neither he, nor Callie, were going anywhere for quite a while.

# CHAPTER 31

44°32'30.1"N 67°29'45.7"W
Temp: 33.1°F
Pressure: 29.84 inHg
Wind: 10.4 mph, NW
Visibility: ≥ 10.00 mi

THE WORST THING ABOUT breaking up with her boyfriend in her doughnut shop in the aftermath of a blizzard was that there was no way for either of them to escape. Both of their cars, not to mention the road outside, were buried under multiple feet of snow. Callie didn't know what she was supposed to do. Grab a shovel and start digging?

She didn't think her body could take it. And even if it could...there was no way the roads home would be clear for either of them.

"Well then," she said, trying to will herself to look up from the snow and at Beckett. They were, for better or for worse, going to have to solve this together.

"Do you have a shovel?" he asked.

"Of course I have a shovel," she snapped. Just because she didn't have the strength to shovel this much snow, didn't mean she wasn't prepared.

"Well, hand it over," he said.

"Even if you clear the door, the roads —"

"We gotta start sometime," he said. "No matter how much you hate me."

"I don't hate you, Beckett," she said as she fetched the shovel out of a storage closet and handed it over. "I'll put on some more coffee. Thank you for doing that."

"Cool," he grumbled. "Appreciated."

She looked at the forecast on her phone before tossing it on the table to start the coffee. The snow was only going to keep them busy for so long.

*What a nightmare.* Eventually, they were going to have to make small talk, assuming Beckett didn't give himself a heart attack shoveling.

Her phone buzzed with a text, bouncing along the counter. She grabbed at it, desperate for even a momentary distraction.

**Emma:** How are you doing with the storm? Did you get home okay?

Callie fought back something an awful lot like a sob.

**Callie:** Still at the shop. Beckett and I broke up. And now we are trapped here together by snow.
**Emma:** SHIT.
**Emma:** Don't worry. My dad's got a truck with a plow. We'll get you out of there.
**Emma:** Do you still have heat? Water and everything?
**Callie**: Yeah. We're fine except for how we're not.
**Emma**: Cool. Stay safe. See you in an hour.

Callie had no idea how that was going to be feasible, but she appreciated the thought.

She looked up from her phone to see Beckett by the door, surveying his handiwork.

"I think I made enough progress to actually shovel from out there. You'll be able to close the door at least."

"Please promise me you won't do more than is reasonable? You don't need to be out there freezing to death."

He shrugged. "Helps to have something to do," he said, before going back out into the cold.

Callie could stare at him and question her recent decisions, or she could make herself useful.

She ended up taking inventory of everything in the supply room — or at least going through the motions of taking inventory. She couldn't keep track of numbers and kept finding herself with a bag of flour or a box of yeast in her hand, staring into the distance while her thoughts rolled on a continual loop. From outside came the repetitive sounds of Beckett working away at the snow

Sometime later, she wasn't sure how long, came the much louder and deeper scrape of what sounded very much like a plow. She hurried out to find a pickup truck, plow attached to its front, rock up in front of the shop. Beckett, shovel in hand, stepped hastily back as it parked along the curb, throwing up a huge mound of snow as it did.

The passenger-side door opened, revealing Emma, well bundled in a parka and a bright pink hat. She said something to Beckett that Callie couldn't hear, and he turned back to the door and pulled it open.

"Emma says she and her dad want to give me a lift. They say the road down to the marina is already clear. Are you going to be okay?"

"I'm going to be fine."

It both was and wasn't true, but now was not the time for any of Beckett's chivalry. She needed him gone.

Beckett looked like he wanted to say something more to her. Instead he just nodded, once, and pulled the door shut tightly behind him. Callie watched long enough to see him climb up in the cab of the truck beside Emma, then that door closed too and the truck pulled away.

As soon as she was alone in the shop, Callie once more pulled out her phone. Since the *People* magazine and parking lot incident, she and her parents had had no contact beyond the claws she had sent them which had, thus far, been met with silence. But there was no one else right now whose voice she wanted to hear than theirs. Plus, she thought morosely, they'd probably be thrilled with the news.

Still, she thought she could hold herself together — until her mom answered the call with a warm "Callie! Merry Christmas!"

Callie broke down in sobs.

"Are you all right? Callie, baby? What's wrong?"

For once, Callie wasn't annoyed at the level of concern in her mother's voice. "I'm okay," she managed to choke out. "Um, I think Beckett and I just broke up."

"On Christmas!" Her mother sounded outraged. "What kind of asshole —"

"No, no," Callie broke in. "It wasn't him. Or well, not like that. Just, we had a fight, and —" Callie's breath hitched, and she paused to gulp in air. "He's wonderful, he could be it for me, but this is all moving too fast, it's too much. He has such a determined trajectory I got scared there was no room for mine!"

"Why, what happened? Did he propose?"

Despite her misery, Callie gave a choked laugh. "No. No, not exactly."

"Are you pregnant?"

Back to crying apparently. "Also no."

"Oh, my baby. This is exactly what I never wanted for you, and exactly why we were concerned."

Callie wanted to bristle at that. Callie did bristle at that. She didn't want her parents to be, as she had feared, happy at this turn of events. But she also didn't want to get off the phone.

"What? Why?" she asked.

"You know I had you when I was twenty."

"Yeah, I know. Which I kinda judge you for but not my life and also I am not twenty, and it's not happening anyway, so!" Callie knew, even as she said the words, that she judged her mom for it a lot. But that was decidedly a her problem.

"It wasn't a plan, Callie. Your dad and I were dating, I got pregnant, and we got married, because that seemed like the thing to do."

"God, why?" Callie asked. They had more than had options.

"You try having parents and grandparents and cousins and aunts who started asking you why you weren't married and having babies yet while you were just trying to graduate high school. There'd been some pressure. For some time."

"How have you never told me this before?" Callie demanded.

"It never came up and you didn't need to hear all that old country high drama. That was an entire past that had nothing to do with you."

Callie made a disgruntled sound. The past was always relevant to the present, as she and Beckett had just found out.

"Anyway, we got lucky," her mother went on. "We've been happy enough. I can't even tell you if I had another plan for my life, but I sure never got to explore it if I did. We didn't want you to wind up in the same situation, or feel that pressure. And yet now here you are, calling me in tears because someone's moving too fast and you feel trapped."

"Wait, hang on," Callie said. "I don't feel trapped, because I got out of the situation. And also, I have some opinions here about you not wanting me to get married and pregnant young and so instead decided to keep me stuck at home when I got hurt. You have completely discounted the career I've made for myself here, and haven't offered any advice or curiosity about Beckett when we were still together. There was so much help I could have used before all of this!"

"Callie —"

"No," she said firmly. "Listen to me. Everything I've ever wanted to do you've 'helped' only by telling me it's too hard or too dangerous or too far away."

"Callie, you live on a boat."

"I know! Okay, I know." She lowered her voice. "You've been trying to keep me safe, I get that, but I feel like you've just been trying to keep me attached to your hip instead of actually helping me figure out my life. And now I don't know how to talk about the things I want. Especially when they involve other people."

"Oh, Callie." There was another long pause, and then what sounded suspiciously like a sniffle. Was her mom crying? "I am so, so sorry."

"...Thank you.? Callie hadn't expected that and had to blink back more tears of her own.

"I never meant — you're just, you're so driven. You never seemed like you needed any help."

"Yeah, well. Two things," Callie said. "Maybe I had to step up because I felt like it was the only way to have anything that was truly mine. And maybe I've achieved all I have, not because I'm not frightened but because I know fear lies so I did everything — *do* everything — in spite of it."

"I'm so sorry," her mother said again. "If there's anything you need to talk about, or want to tell me — I'm here, I'm listening, and I will try not to do that again. Also we got your claws and let me tell you, they were *delicious*."

"Thanks. Right now — I just. I broke up with my boyfriend on Christmas, and that sucks, and in retrospect I should have given him more information so the things that got said didn't get said when they did, but God he's a *dumbass*."

She laughed wetly, and, to her strange delight, her mother laughed, too.

"Oh, my baby, I can only imagine."

*Oh no,* Callie thought, *you definitely can't.*

She was never ever going to tell her mother what Beckett had actually done or said. The entire situation sucked, and she was still desperately sad. But she had a boat she needed to get back to and check on. And she felt a little better to have, even if just for today, a parent who paused long enough to listen to her. Maybe that wasn't everything. But it sure was something.

# CHAPTER 32

44°36'29.6"N 67°8'22.9"W
Temp: 28.9°F
Pressure: 30.06 inHg
Wind: 12.7 mph, W
Visibility: ≥ 10.00 mi

WITH AN ASSIST FROM EMMA, Beckett got home to his little apartment, albeit without his car or his luggage. He was so deeply grateful that the owners of the house had shoveled out his front door so he could actually get in that he didn't care. And while he regretted that his marathon trip back from his childhood home had led to this disaster with Callie, he was grateful to be as exhausted as he was.

He could sleep off Christmas and start again tomorrow.

No matter the circumstances, the morning after bad news always felt the same. Waking up and not remembering, then waking up more and deciding the pain wasn't that bad, and then actually being fully awake and realizing that no, everything was terrible and was going to be for a while.

The only good news, as far as Beckett was concerned, was that the roads were clear enough for him to retrieve his car and that Robert, having heard the misery in his voice, was perfectly willing to have him come over — even without explanation.

Beckett felt somewhat bad about interrupting what was surely family time, but at least he'd waited until after Christmas Day. He was assuredly not, however, going to stop and get doughnuts as a gift for his hosts.

"Oh dear." Robert stood in his open doorway, regarding Beckett on his porch. "What happened to Beckett?"

"Do I look that pathetic?" Beckett asked as he took vague stock of himself.

"Your hair's a mess, your posture is shit, you have epic bags under your eyes, and that charming, dimpled grin thing you do is nowhere to be seen. Yeah, you look like shit."

"Well, that all is the first appropriate crap I've done this week, so thanks, I guess."

Robert heaved a sigh. "Come on in and tell me what you did then."

The Christmas tree was lit in the otherwise dark living room, sending a soft glow over the kids' scattered toys and the stray bit of wrapping paper. Zoe was stretched out in front of the fireplace, paws twitching slightly in her sleep.

"Where's everybody?" Beckett asked softly, reluctant to break the quiet of the house.

"The boys went sledding with friends. Dahlia's napping, and Julie's upstairs, getting caught up on reading, I think. You want coffee?"

"Sure."

While Robert got the pot brewing Beckett fidgeted with the pieces of a Lego set someone had left out on the counter, sorting the pieces first by color and then by size. He couldn't look at Robert while he was saying the things he knew he had to say.

"Callie and I broke up," Beckett told the Lego pieces as Robert pushed a steaming mug across the counter at him.

Robert froze, his own mug lifted halfway to his mouth. "Shit."

"Yeah."

Robert set his mug down. "I'm sorry to hear that."

"I said something exceptionally foolish." Beckett did not want to admit to what he had done, but at the same time he knew he had to confess it and confess it specifically if he had any hope at all of not obsessing on his clumsiness and associated self-hatred.

"Oh no."

"Yeah." Beckett took a deep breath, a long drink of coffee, and did not look Robert in the eye as he admitted, "I said I wanted to put a baby in her. While we were —"

Robert burst out laughing.

"Hey!" Beckett protested. Honestly, he wanted to burst into flames. Or sink through the floor. What he'd said was awful because of the human emotions involved, but he didn't need to get laughed at for the heat-of-the-moment horniness factor too.

"You said this while you were fucking?" Robert asked.

"My mind was not entirely functioning."

"Clearly! Oh my God. Wow." Robert was still laughing. "You are so incredibly foolish, my friend, but even I did not know you were this absolutely clueless."

"Yeah, well, in the moment, it was working for both of us. And then when I woke up, she was up and dressed and telling me details of the accident she'd been in. Which is about when I realized I'd accidentally walked right into her trauma about medical shit and like...being a human in the world and set it off."

"Shit," Robert said.

"Yeah and then she dumped me and then I was super not graceful about it."

Robert cleared his throat. "*Wow*. Okay. I don't even know what to say."

"You think? God... like, I'm not even here to ask for advice. I'm here to unburden myself so hopefully I can exist as something other than a ball of pure shame."

"That's good, because there is no advice," Robert said.

They contemplated that point together in silence for some moments.

"Question." Robert said, eventually.

"Yeah?"

"Why are you even here? Until you called to come over I thought you were in Seattle."

"Oh. Um."

Beckett was stuck. With Callie, he might have been able to talk around the bizarre superhero related call in a way that vented his feelings without letting on more than he was allowed to. But Robert had helped get Beckett on tape and knew the industry in the same way Beckett did. He would know exactly what Beckett was talking about and be able to read between all the lines.

That risk was too big. He also didn't really want to think about it. On this side of things, with everything going the way it had with Callie, Beckett assumed he had gotten as far in that casting process as he was going to. And, much like with Callie, he had let his emotions get way out ahead of reality.

"I missed Callie and was having feelings about my career," he said. Which, while not the entire story, was certainly true.

"You mean in terms of what you're going to do next?"

"And where I'm going to go. Yeah," Beckett said. Robert was, very kindly, handing Beckett an out, and Beckett wasn't going to not take it.

"You still want to stay here?" Robert asked.

That was a big question in light of the mess he's just made. But he didn't want to go back to LA except when summoned. He liked Maine, even if this one particular town was now a world of awkward for him.

"I don't know," he confessed. "I wanted to, when the only problem was that it's hard to have a career from here. But it's a lot more complicated now no matter how much I like it. And maybe I'm just enjoying this little village we've all made together and when everyone else goes home, I'll regret being left behind. It's hard to know right now. I'm not fucking going back to LA though. And Knox and I will both be better off if I leave New York to him."

"Not everyone's going home," Robert said.

"What do you mean?" Beckett asked.

"Julie and I are staying; the kids don't really know anything else. So we're looking for a house to buy, and if we can make it work, you can make it work."

Beckett blinked in disbelief. "You're staying? When did that happen?"

"We've been talking about it for a while. And you've been...busy," Robert said.

Beckett grimaced. Robert wasn't saying it in so many words, but Beckett suddenly recognized that he'd probably been falling down on his friendship duties for a while now. That was something else he'd have to solve, but he was going to take Robert's grace and put that off for another day when he could give it his undivided attention.

"I'll work on East Coast shit for a while, do commercials if that's what makes sense," Robert explained. "Julie can work from anywhere. We can keep renting this place 'til we find something, but there's another house a little farther up the coast we've got our eye on. A little less isolated, more kids around. Closer to an airport. But still enough land and trees that you can't see your neighbors."

"Like it's just that easy?" Beckett felt, not for the first time in recent days, as though he'd been hit by a truck.

"It is that easy. And if I, a DP with a wife and three kids, can make it work and honestly make it work comfortably, I somehow suspect your charming self can figure it out as well."

"It's not that simple," Beckett said.

"But it is," Robert said. "You've been the lead on a very successful show for years. You're ridiculously good looking, actually talented, and not a nightmare to work with. I know you feel like this was your first big gig, but it really wasn't. It's not like you're going to have to go audition. And who knows where what you do next will film? If you want this to be home base, make this home base. Sure, you might be gone months at a time, but Maine's not going anywhere."

Beckett's heart was screaming in his chest to be able to talk about the superhero situation, just to exorcize the demon of possibility there. Because everything Robert was saying couple apply to that — it was just all so messy and so much.

"My agent's pretty insistent on LA being the next step," he said, in lieu of anything useful.

Robert shrugged. "So fire him."

"Wait. What?" Of all possible responses, Beckett had not expected that.

"Fire. Him," Robert repeated slowly. "He works for you, remember?"

"He got me this gig." *Hidden Cove*, yes, but also, Steve had set Beckett up for whatever was going on with superheroes right now. "And all the ones before it, really."

Robert shook his head. "You know who got you this gig? You. He got you in the room, but you did the rest. And what was right five years ago — or even one year ago — isn't necessarily what's right for you now. Because I know you like doing as you're told. But *really*. You've complained about him forever. I get there's a lot of upheaval right now and I guess most of it feels negative, but why not take the opportunity to blow everything up? Make a life you want?"

"Without Callie," Beckett said, the limits of his choices slamming back into him in the form of petulance.

"Sure. But you can fix your shit for the next opportunity," Robert said. "And you can figure out how to make yourself happy. It's not a prerequisite for partnership, but it can sure make some of the work of it easier."

All Beckett could do was latch onto the part of this conversation that didn't make him want to cry. "Fire my agent when I'm already out of my head and we're all trying to find the next big thing?"

"I mean, find someone else first, but then fire him. Also, seriously? You're ready for the big boys."

Beckett knew what that meant — all the variously acronymed agencies that constantly fought over who was representing the biggest of the best movie stars. Those agents didn't even glance at people who weren't household names. Or about to be.

"Call them up," Robert continued. "Talk about your vision — and your needs. Show them you're willing to fly out there and be well-behaved and take a meeting or two. They will fall all over themselves to rep you. And not nag you to move back to LA."

Beckett took a deep breath. Everything Robert was saying seemed logical, even possible, and made him feel some glimmer of optimism for his currently very messed up life.

"There's just one problem," Beckett said.

"Only one?" Robert asked. "What's that?"

"I'm an actor. My entire existence is about getting out of the way and letting other people tell me what to do."

Robert laughed. "That's above my pay grade. And you need to check in with your therapist. But try to remember, out here in the real world, you can't blame the careless shit you say on the writers. No matter how done and over it is, Callie's going to deserve a real apology from you at some point."

# CHAPTER 33

44°32'30.1"N 67°29'45.7"W
Temp: 26.1°F
Pressure: 30.29 inHg
Wind: 4.60 mph, S
Visibility: ≥ 10.00 mi

CALLIE BROKE THE NEWS of her dumping Beckett to Sydney a couple of days after Christmas while Sydney was helping her out at Sweet Claws. She even managed to get all the words out without crying once while bracing herself for a slew of half-joking recriminations. But Sydney actually seemed somewhat relieved.

"Honestly, this makes me feel better. He really did seem too good to be true. My faith in the balance of the universe has been restored." Sydney didn't even give Callie a hard time about breaking up with him before having a chance to introduce him to her.

"So do you want to watch *Hidden Cove,* now that you hate him?" Sydney asked.

"Ah, no," Callie said. She wasn't sure if she hated Beckett, honestly, but the point was moot. If she hadn't watched the show when they were together, she definitely wasn't going to watch it now.

"He gets beat up a bunch," Sydney offered.

"No!" Callie exclaimed with a laugh. Which was probably what Sydney had been going for in the first place. "No, I just want to forget that this entire ridiculous interlude ever happened."

And that's all it was, she told herself. A few very intense months. Nothing to be devastated or derailed by. If she looked at it like that, she could view the whole thing as a win. She'd tried dating again and survived. Her business was going strong. And the *Lobster Taco* had escaped the storm entirely unscathed. Maine was still hers, and she was still happy. More or less.

But with the holiday rush over, Callie couldn't settle down into a routine again. The quiet week between Christmas and New Years was really quiet. There — for once — wasn't enough work to keep her hands or her mind busy.

Which led to a plan. Emma strongly disapproved, but Callie thought it was brilliant. The internet needed to know she and Beckett had broken up. The internet also needed claws.

So two days before New Year's Eve, she, Emma, and Sydney gathered at the shop to put it into action. Sydney would film, Callie would talk, and Emma would warn her this was all a terrible idea.

"As your social media advisor, I need to tell you that you do not understand what is going to happen if you make this video," Emma said, her arms folded across her chest as she leaned back against the mural she had painted for the store when it first opened.

"I am done trying to predict things," Callie said, brushing her hair back over her shoulder. "Because it never works out. And this can't be worse or weirder than when I wound up in *People*."

"That was mediated. You could blame others and ignore the direct feedback. This is not," Emma explained tersely.

"I think it's a great idea," said Sydney, who was standing ready with Callie's phone.

"Yes, well, some people just want the world to burn."

"It's going to be fine, Emma." Callie said.

Truthfully, she had no idea it would be any such thing. But whatever was going to happen with this wasn't going to be as emotionally wrenching as the last few days had been.

She picked up Lobbie, and nodded to Sydney to hit *record*.

"Surprise!" Callie sang into the camera. "We're back early for orders. And by we, I mean me, my lovely shop assistant Emma, my friend Sydney, and this here plastic lobster — whose name is still Lobbie and who I still like — given to me by my now ex-boyfriend. I have a lot of feelings to work off, so if you were thinking about ordering some claws, now is the time to order some claws. Mainly so I have something to do with mine in this time of woe. We will not be taking any questions at this time except about flavors and ingredients!"

Emma had been right; Callie was absolutely not prepared for the consequences. Although the consequences were mostly good, albeit with a hearty dash of peculiar.

First, the volume of online doughnut orders doubled from their usual level. Then, they tripled. But the number of orders — in retrospect, she absolutely should have had a cap on what she would take — was nothing compared to the contents of the "Extra Info" field people were putting in.

Many were sympathetic and offered encouragement or attempts at solid pieces of wisdom. Others were in the spirit encapsulated by one note in particular, that made Emma laugh so hard she'd asked to print it and bring it home with her.

*Oh good! You're not fucking my man anymore, now I can order doughnuts from you!*

Callie was glad she had Emma to remind her of the inherent ridiculousness of the situation and to laugh at it with her. If left to her own devices, she would have driven herself crazy dwelling on all the ways people were getting involved in her business — very much including the thing where she'd broken up with Beckett because she couldn't deal with the prospect of people being involved with her business.

As she tried to move away from the past, and not dwell on the absolute mess of the present, Callie found herself inevitably looking toward the future. Now that she was so thoroughly detangling herself from the mess and the pressure of the things Beckett wanted, she was left with the question *What do I want?*

"What's more fucked up?" Callie wondered aloud to her friends as they struggled to keep up with the deluge of claw orders. "Having a successful mail order business because you're dating a celebrity or having a successful mail order business because you broke up with one?"

Emma didn't look up from where she was deftly twisting claws into shape. "That, my friend, is a question only you can answer."

"I just want to have a business that has nothing to do with him. And that was true even when I was together with him!"

"That was never going to happen," Emma said. "Every celebrity spouse or ex who has a thing deals with this is my guess. You consider it compensation for the bullshit and make that money."

"How do you even have this perspective?" Callie asked.

"I watch a lot of reality TV," Emma said. "I'm thinking of putting it on my resume."

Callie sent Emma and Sydney home at five in the morning and then stayed herself, cleaning up and generally getting the shop in order. Finally, at seven, with mountains of overnight boxes stacked up for the mail carrier to pick up, Callie was at the door, dressed for the elements, her keys in her hands when who approached the shop but Beckett.

Callie stared at him. Even swathed in a parka and knit hat he looked just as beautiful and fuckable as ever, if maybe a little more tired and pale.

"Um, hi," he said.

Callie had to work not to stare at the way his mouth moved when he talked. He was just so goddamned magnetic, and that fact was incredibly not useful to her. Now, or probably ever again.

"I was just passing through town and thought I'd stop in. I just...wanted to see how you are." He paused. "So, um, how are you?"

Callie adjusted the strap of her bag over her shoulder; she didn't believe him.. "I've been here all night because I told the internet we broke up and then got more orders than I could handle."

"Yeah, I saw your video."

"Oh shit." Callie should have assumed that would happen, but until this moment it hadn't occurred to her. Should she have checked with him before she did it? Maybe. Did she care? Also maybe. But it was too late now, and she had no regrets. Not about that anyway.

Beckett gave the ghost of a smile. "It's cool. My agent's pissed, but that's not your problem. I thought it was great."

"I feel like you should know," Callie said. She wasn't going to let him off easy for whatever his plan was with regard to waltzing in here and trying to make all the hurt better. "Half of the orders are coming from people who are thanking me for breaking up with you because you are now available for their various fantasies."

"Oh. Yikes," he said.

"Yeah, yikes!" She knew it wasn't something he could control, but not being with him meant she could stop feeling so obligated to be understanding about some of the more challenging parts of his life.

"Are you doing okay?" Beckett asked, with the same level of attention and care he'd almost always used in speaking to her. To anyone. Which was deeply irritating. Why couldn't he just be awful and make it easier to let go of him? And give her someone to fight? A part of her definitely wanted to fight. But that would not benefit either of them.

"Yeah, I'm fine. Thanks," she said. "This is a small town and we're both in it. At least until your show is over."

Beckett winced slightly at that, even though her tone hadn't been sharp. Which made her keep talking.

"Are you okay? What's going on?" she asked.

"I'm mostly just here to apologize," he said.

His voice was low and earnest but his eyes slid away from her like he didn't know where to look. Which made two of them. But then he looked right at her, his gaze steady and direct.

"I fucked up, and then, when you were explaining that to me, and telling me more about yourself, I was not gracious, and that has been weighing on me. I'm trying to get my life organized and prioritized so I can be more clear and appropriate and have better timing with the people in my life. I didn't do any of that with you. And I'm sorry. I don't have any kind of ask, I don't need anything from you, I just wanted to say those things."

"Thank you," Callie managed. She was trying to stay breezy, but it was hard. In reality she was staggered at how quickly Beckett accepted the situation, saw his blame in it, wanted to make it right, and most importantly, realized he couldn't. "I appreciate it."

She expected him to launch into a speech or more groveling, but he was true to his word. He didn't ask anything more of her. He just nodded at her as if satisfied he had discharged his responsibility to apologize.

"Good luck with the claws," he said.

And then he was gone.

# CHAPTER 34

<pre>
33°56'23.4"N 118°25'15.1"W
             Temp: 30.9°F
       Pressure: 30.21 inHg
          Wind: 10.4 mph, S
     Visibility: ≥ 10.00 mi
</pre>

HIS APOLOGY MADE, BECKETT was left to the remainder odd, empty time between Christmas and New Year's. If he'd stayed in Seattle, as perhaps he should have, there would have been plenty of gatherings and activities. But here in Maine *Hidden Cove* was off until mid-January, Robert was occupied with his own family, and Callie had dumped him.

Aside from catching up on his sleep — and he seriously needed to catch up on his sleep, working TV hours was horrific — Beckett kept himself busy as best he could. He cleaned his apartment. He did all his laundry. He went snowshoeing. He checked an unreasonable number of e-books out of the library and even read some of them. And throughout it all, he tried to ignore how deafeningly quiet life on his own was. He'd been alone for years before Callie; hell, he'd even been through a divorce long before her. This wasn't the end of the world.

But sometimes, it felt like it.

New Year's came and went, quietly and soberly, although Robert and Julie had the kindness to invite him for a New Year's Day brunch. After that he threw himself into hiking, both for the distraction and to get his body at least active again before he had to dive back into filming.

He had just finished one such hike — out of the range of any reliable cell service and probably foolish to do on his own — and returned to the trailhead and his car to find a series of voicemails on his phone and then a series of emails in his inbox all following up on each other. The gist of it all was he was wanted in LA. In 48 hours. About the superhero thing.

Beckett wondered if this was the moment he was supposed to have an out-of-body experience about this particular process.

*Not yet*, he told himself sternly. *They're still talking to at least three other people. They have to be.*

But whether that was or was not the case, apparently there were people who should have been in the call right before Christmas who hadn't been. Those people wanted to talk with him now. And everyone who *had* been in that meeting wanted to see him in person, not just via his laptop from his dad's basement workshop. Meanwhile, the  footage he had sent them for his self-tape had been good — of course it was, Robert had shot it — but they wanted footage of him on their own cameras. Or that was the excuse to see if he was a jerk about feedback.

Beckett had four days left before *Hidden Cove* was supposed to restart in which to make this happen. So much for his life being too quiet.

"Fuck!" he shouted at no one but the cold emptiness of Maine. "Fuck fuck fuck."

After he replied to the various emails to confirm that yes, he could get out there, and yes, they should just book him tickets and tell him where to be when, he did the only thing he could other than getting into his car to get warm.

He called Robert. Because fuck the NDA. He was losing his mind here.

"Hey, sorry to keep interrupting your break," he said as soon as his friend picked up the call. "But you know that self-tape you shot for me?"

"Yeah? You got complaints?" Robert asked with a laugh.

"No. I've got a flight out to LA tomorrow."

"Shiiiiiiiiiit," Robert said. "They're going to make you an offer."

"No, they're not." Beckett may have called because he was experiencing an intense mixture of hope and fear, but it was Robert' job to talk him down, not encourage it.. "Stop prognosticating before I tell you the rest of the story."

"There's more to the story?" Robert asked.

"Yeah." Beckett paced back and forth next to his car. "Remember when you asked me why I was back in town and I just mumbled at you?"

"Yeah?"

"I had a call with the studio right before Christmas. Like, they asked if I was cool to jump on a call with a couple of people and then it wound up being almost twenty people."

"Beckett," Robert said. "That is not normal."

"I know that!" Beckett yelled, startling some small wildlife in a nearby tree. "Which is why I freaked out and wanted to get back here to see Callie."

"You should have told me," Robert said.

"You know I couldn't do that."

"Really? Because I'm the one who put you on tape. You'd already broken the rules. You know I'm good for secrecy. Why were you sitting with that on your own? Did you tell Callie?"

Beckett ran a hand over his face. "I don't know. Maybe I knew you had enough perspective on how unusual that call was that I was sure you wouldn't talk me down. Maybe I didn't want to jinx it. And yeah, I was probably going to tell Callie, but that wound up not happening for reasons you already know. Anyway. Help?"

"They're going to give you an offer," Robert said again, although more slowly this time, with each word enunciated as if in desperate hope that Beckett might choose to understand them.

"No way." Beckett kicked at the snow at his feet. "There's gotta be three or four guys still in the process. I'm the backup to the backup."

"Is that what your agent thinks?" Robert asked.

"My agent's an asshole."

"Okay, I don't know if you called for advice or not, but here's some, because I am sick of you griping about your agent. You get off the phone with me, and you call up every big agency in LA, explain that you'll be out there in the next couple of days for some very high-stakes, hush-hush, final rounds of negotiations or whatever and that you have some concerns about your agent's ability to deliver. Then you ask them if they would be willing to have a chat about representing you going forward and maybe also tag teaming this very big serious deal you can't name with your current agent."

Beckett opened and closed his mouth several times before he remembered that Robert couldn't see him. "That is some high-level bullshittery."

"You're an actor aren't you?"

"Yeah."

"And you hate your agent?"

"Yeah."

"So regardless of this offer you think you're not going to get —
but you are, Beckett, goddamn you — don't you think you should
exploit it to get yourself a team you like better as *Hidden Cove*
wraps up?"

"No one gives a shit about me," Beckett said, before realizing
how it sounded. Were his current issues overlapping? Probably
quite a bit. He needed to pull himself out of this pit. And to clarify.
"Especially when I can't even tell them what's up."

"Oh but you can," Robert said, and Beckett could hear him
smile down the line. "When they offer you a muffin or suggest a
lunch meeting or want to know if you take cream in your coffee,
you say 'Alas, my trainer has me on a really strict regimen right
now.' They'll put that together with the NDAs and all the rest of it,
and understand that you are in tights and a cape territory."

"Disordered eating is not a negotiation tactic," Beckett said
firmly.

That was not a road he could go down. Not for himself, not for
younger actors who might not have the ability to resist the
industry's pressures, not for his ex-girlfriend the doughnut lady,
and not for the audience. The last thing he wanted to do right now
was have a fight with Robert on top of everything else, but he was
prepared if necessary.

"Hey. I am not endorsing our trash industry and its worst
behaviors, I'm just telling you how to manipulate it. If you can find
a better way around the NDA, go for it."

Beckett still hated LA, but it was easier with a strict itinerary and
a studio being an extremely good host to him. It was, to some
degree, unnerving. Wasn't he supposed to be here to convince
them to hire him? Yet they were just shy of wining and dining him.
Business class flight out. Very nice hotel room in which a
ridiculous basket of fruit and snacks and overpriced mineral water
awaited him.

Beckett couldn't help but think about Callie and how much she had enjoyed those amenities when they had flown out for the premiere. This was even nicer... except for the part where she was back in Maine and they were never doing this together again.

Instead of squishing those feelings down and just focusing on the task at hand, Beckett let himself feel what he was feeling. He was either going to get this role for being exactly who he was or he wasn't. Maybe, he could save the playing pretend for the actual character and just, for a change in this city, try to be himself, Consequences be damned.

When they offered him the muffin at the first of his agent meetings, he took it and ratted Robert out.

"So, my buddy who shot the self-tape for me on the thing I can't talk about but is why I am out here and talking to you... he said the way I should covertly let you know what the project is, was to be weird about food. But here's the thing, that's dishonest and toxic. And if I really am in serious consideration for this project, one of the things I am going to need from anyone negotiating on my behalf is a commitment to my well-being."

"Meaning that even if you have to save the world by throwing cars and planets around, you still get to eat the muffin?"

Beckett nodded enthusiastically while he finished chewing. "They're pretty good muffins."

With that as an icebreaker, it suddenly felt easy to talk about his career and what he wanted from it, his history with his current agent, and how he wanted to create a working life for himself that meant LA existed for him only as a commuter destination.

The conversation, in which his potential future agent actually listened to him with the same deep attentiveness and curiosity as the best scene partner, gave him the type of hope he hadn't experienced from this part of the business maybe ever. He suddenly knew what his advice was going to be to any young actor — including his brother — next time he was asked. *Find the best scene partners and trust them.*

"So," Beckett finally asked. "Where do we go from here? I haven't done this particular dance since before I had a career."

"You go deal with the reason you're really out here. You go meet with my competitors. And then hopefully you call us back and put me in touch with your current agent so we can work out a deal around this current situation that is fair to everyone and as undramatic as possible."

With that heartening conversation behind him, Beckett went into his actual cape-and-tights meeting — he was going to keep calling it that even though he wasn't sure there was even a cape still involved for the character in question — with a sense of newfound ease. Whatever would be, would be. If he didn't get what he wanted this time, maybe he would some future time. Because while he'd always known he couldn't force things, lately he was learning he couldn't rush them either.

"Hi," he said as he walked in. "I'm so glad to be here."

He meant it too.

Four hours later, after a lot of introductions, talking, reading some sides, and some more talking, Beckett found himself face to face with the question he should have expected and yet hadn't even occurred to him.

It was about Callie. And her video. No wonder his soon-to-be former agent had been so testy about her Lobbie the Lobster breakup video.

"Honestly? It's a big deal because I feel quite sad about it, but It's undramatic," Beckett said, echoing the words of his prospective agent in regard to the much broader contractual situation. "We're just at different places in our lives with what we want and it wasn't going to work. We've had some friendly chats since, and it's fine. I certainly harbor no ill-will about the video. My presence in her life was complicating through no fault of hers or mine."

"Okay, this is just a high-profile situation with a reputation at stake..."

Beckett nodded to himself. "Have you seen what people on the internet call me?"

"Saint Beckett."

"Yeah, and to be frank, I'm not a fan of it. But I have no meaningful skeletons in my closet and Callie and I are fine. If you need to be in touch with her, I get that, but I'm going to be cranky about the intrusiveness."

"Of course, you understand —"

"Just let me warn her, if that needs to be a thing. It's not a problem for me."

When Beckett was finally released to the wild and without any further meetings until the next day, he was at loose ends, but the day had gone well. There had been a lot of promises to talk soon and one stray admonishment to keep his phone close, but Beckett mostly felt as if, for no particular reason and without grief, he had come to the end of this particular road. He'd go see a superhero movie in a couple of years and laugh quietly to himself about a thing that had almost happened and didn't.

For the first time, despite the traffic and the exhausting effort it took just to exist walking down the street, he couldn't help but see some of the magic of LA as Callie had seen it.

Here, people went into offices and came out with stories. The weather, even in January, was at least attempting to be perfect, and there was a vibrancy to people on the street and eating outside at restaurants. He forced himself to admit everyone around him wasn't networking or trying to be seen. Some of them, most of them probably, were just living their lives.

He would never want to live here again. He could never do that and be well and happy. But maybe he could warm up to the idea of visiting it and accepting that other people took pleasure in the place.

He found himself taking pictures, which he had rarely done in the years he had lived here, always afraid to seem like a tourist, or a newbie actor (honestly, there wasn't much difference between the two). Perhaps, most surprisingly, he found himself posting some of them to social media. Palm trees with the sunset behind them; a dog being walked in a stroller; a late-in-the-day decaf and — yes — a selfie with a doughnut from a trendy spot in Silver Lake.

*Different coast, different doughnuts,* he wrote, *but we're all just doing our best.*

# CHAPTER 35

44°32'30.1"N 67°29'45.7"W
Temp: 25.0°F
Pressure: 30.53 inHg
Wind: 5.82 mph, N
Visibility: ≥ 10.00 mi

THE BUSINESS OF SWEET CLAWS continued to consume almost all of Callie's waking moments, both because that was the sort of entrepreneur she was and because she needed the distraction in the wake of her breakup. But there were still slow moments.

Today there had been a rush just before dawn, as filming got started again on the conclusion of *Hidden Cove*. There was another as parents dropped their kids off at school and/or headed somewhere more populated for work. But now, in the space between the start of the workday and its end, there was little for Callie to do but catch up on mail orders, get organized, and perhaps even close down for a couple of hours so she could catch a nap.

She scrolled through her phone as she stood at the counter in her blessedly empty shop. Beckett had posted pictures to social media a couple of days ago. He didn't do that often, and it reminded her that she still followed him there. Perhaps she should unfollow. But she didn't feel ready yet. And it was a good heads-up mechanism, she supposed, for when he finally moved away for good or started dating someone else.

The pictures were from Los Angeles and sent a stab of loss through her. They were already broken up, there was no reason to miss him more if he was in LA than if he was here in Maine. But she thought back to that inexplicable moment a couple of weeks ago when Beckett had wandered into her shop, to apologize and tie up loose ends. This was what he'd been working toward, apparently. His own next big thing, whatever it might be — which was what he needed and deserved — while Callie carried on with her life in Maine, with her supposed doughnut empire and her boat.

She was glad he'd found something worth documenting in a

city in which he'd been so clear about having never felt at ease in.

Amongst the photos was a selfie he'd taken: a doughnut in his hand and a tired-looking smile on his face. The caption, even more than the picture itself, made her breath catch in her chest.

*Different coast, different doughnuts, but we're all just doing our best.*

Not an apology, which was fine. He'd already done that in person. This wasn't even explicitly directed at her. No request made or expectation formed. Just a gentle statement, tossed out into the world, that she had mattered in the story of his life, and that he was still there and maybe still trying. Not to win her back — just to live his life. Just like she was.

She considered replying, but boundaries were her friends. If there was going to be continued rapprochement between them, which there would need to be to survive them both living in Fly-Debate for the next few months, it didn't need to happen in public. Still, she settled instead for tapping the little heart. He'd been generous about the breakup video; she could be kind about this.

The door of her shop jangled open, and she looked up to see who her customer was. She knew most of the locals and show crew by now, if not by name then definitely by sight.

But it wasn't just any customer. It was Beckett. Callie nearly fumbled her phone out of her hand, across the counter and at his feet in her hurry not to get caught looking at his social media. Luckily, the phone landed face down at the edge of the counter, and she leaned forward to scoop it up and stow it behind the register.

"Sorry," he said. "I didn't mean to startle you. I am here at the command of people, I am not here...for whatever... Just... I didn't get hair and makeup doughnuts this morning on my way in, and they're mad at me. And now there's a big shooting delay because a piece of track for the camera broke and I've been sent here with an order?" He held up a scrap of paper awkwardly.

"You're not banned, I don't know what you're babbling about, but you're not banned."

That much was true, but Callie still wasn't sure how much pity she should take on him.

"Thanks. I appreciate that." Beckett glanced at the ban list on her chalkboard, evidently making sure.

"Do you want to recite that to me or do you just want to hand it over?" Callie held out her hand for the slip of paper.

Beckett stammered some more and eventually passed it to her. Their fingertips brushed lightly.

"I, um, I should tell you something too," he said. "I was in LA —"

"I just liked your social media crap like five seconds ago. So I know. Glad it didn't seem to suck." So much for playing it cool, but what else was she going to do?

"They asked me a bit about our breakup, 'cause of the video...."

"Still not taking it down," Callie said, as she started to get out boxes for the order.

"Still not asking you to," Beckett fired back. "There are just some concerns that maybe I was trouble."

Callie snorted, but Beckett soldiered on.

"There's a vague possibility someone might call you about it, just to make sure there's not a scandal brewing."

"If you want any response from me other than uncontrollable laughter, not sure that's gonna happen," Callie said. "But no, I'm not gonna fuck up your career, Beckett."

"I know that. I know you wouldn't," he said, obviously frustrated by both this turn of events and Callie's lack of emotional investment in them. "I just thought you deserved a warning about a weird phone call that I probably can't prevent from happening."

Callie tipped her head to the side. "Okay. I can appreciate that."

And then, as if on cue, Beckett's phone rang. Callie was grateful. It meant way less of all the intolerable small talk.

She did her best not to listen in. It seemed just like a telemarketer at first, with Beckett trying to figure out who was calling him based on the edge of impatience that crept into his voice.

But then something shifted and his tone became one of true urgency.

"Wait...what? Who...Say that again."

There was a long pause; the other side of the call was giving Beckett some sort of information.

Callie looked up from where she was boxing two dozen of the signature lobster claws. Beckett was frozen in place, breathing hard, and pale. On one level, she was concerned. On another... her famous ex-boyfriend had better not be about to have a heart attack in her shop.

*He's old enough for that, right?*

"Okay," he said with an obvious quaver. "Thank you. I know you're on it, but I'll make sure everyone is in touch."

Beckett dropped the call... and his phone. Callie stared at him as he bent over, hands on his thighs, obviously trying to get himself together and failing.

"Are you okay?"

Callie pushed the claw box order aside, and, never taking her eyes off him, frantically turned to her sink to get him some water. Maybe water was the wrong thing to do, but she had to do something.

"Just shock," Beckett said. "Give me a minute."

"You need to sit down," she said firmly.

She left the water on the counter and went to his side, her only goal to nudge him into at least sitting in a chair before he fainted.

He apologized breathlessly, then tried to assure her, again, that he was fine.

Once she got him seated she fetched his phone and shoved the cup of water at him.

"You are not fine. What the hell is going on?"

He looked up at her with huge eyes. "I can't tell you."

Callie was not falling for that. "The hell you can't tell me. You're having either a panic attack or a medical emergency in my store."

"I really, really can't." Beckett's eyes were pleading, and his voice sounded wounded.

"Nope," Callie said. "Not how we're going to do this."

She went to the door and flipped the sign to closed before locking it. Then she turned around and glared at Beckett.

He took a sip of water. "Shades too," he croaked out.

"You better not have been secretly a spy all along," Callie said sharply as she yanked the shades down.

Beckett shook his head. "I really shouldn't tell you this. And you can't tell anyone. Because it will make the thing that is happening not happen and it will affect so many more people than me."

"It's not like I actually give a shit about celebrity gossip or television."

Beckett took a deep, slow breath. Callie approved.

"Way back in the fall, I was asked to put myself on tape for something," Beckett said. "I didn't take it seriously, but had

Robert shoot it so it looked good. A couple of days before Christmas — which is a messed-up time for any of this to be happening — the director asked me if we could chat. I still didn't take it seriously, because, well, you'll see. But there were almost a dozen people on that call —"

"And you started to take it seriously," Callie supplied.

"Maybe. I figured, oh I'm a finalist for something I'm not going to get. No big deal. Happens all the time, although the project is a very big deal. Anyway, I was in Seattle, I missed you, Knox had been freaking out to me about his career, I was in my parents' basement taking this incomprehensible call — and I just wanted to be here."

The why of what had happened was starting to make sense.

"So you flew back," Callie said, "to get comfort from me, about a thing you couldn't or wouldn't tell me about, and planned out your whole life around it, culminating in —"

"Ungood things I have said during sex, yes."

"Okay, so assuming no one died, they obviously just called you to tell you you got the part. Now what the fuck is it?"

Beckett looked up at her, eyes beseeching, as if she could deliver him from his own success. "Only one of the most iconic superheroes of the last seventy-five years."

Callie stared at him. And then pulled out a chair so she could sit down too.

"Well, well, well. Saint Beckett. Truth, Integrity, and Light, huh?"

"You never told me you knew comic books," Beckett said.

Callie shrugged. She used to read them as a kid with her grandfather. It was one of the things he told her that always felt the most like America to him.

"You never asked," she said. "Also, I'm very happy for you."

Beckett gave her the lopsided smile she felt sure he had used to charm his way into every role he'd ever had.

"I miss you," he said.

"Yeah. Me too," Callie said, and placed her hand on the table between them palm up. "But here we are."

He took her hand. "We should talk about it. Sometime. If you want to. Us, I mean."

Callie wasn't sure what the offer meant, and beyond that, if there was any use to it. All she knew was that she needed to remain firm in her boundaries, not necessarily about Beckett, but absolutely about Beckett's issues.

"I can't be your security blanket for this project," she said. "And I won't be the girl you woo so you can check off your baby-centered to-do list."

"I know," Beckett said.

"Okay," Callie nodded and felt the edges of her resolve wavering very cautiously. "Then we can talk about it. Sometime. After you get your head screwed on about this movie, because that is not my job. Clear?"

Beckett chuckled to himself, looked down at their joined hands, and squeezed. "Yes, ma'am."

Callie squeezed back.

# CHAPTER 36

44°30'41.8"N 67°20'49.7"W
Temp: 26.1°F
Pressure: 30.46 inHg
Wind: 8.06 mph, N
Visibility: ≥ 10.00 mi

Somehow, Beckett made it back to set, although the fact that he was able — or even allowed — to drive under such circumstances was a bit alarming.

In light of extremely recent events, acting was at least as bizarre. But being his character was easier than being himself on this particular day. Every time his mind started drifting in the direction of *Beckett, welcome aboard...* the world started going swimmy again. It took all his years of training and experience to separate himself from the work and actually be present for the rest of the day.

Back home that evening, he sat in stunned silence staring at the walls. He had no idea how to absorb this piece of information or all the ways his life was about to change. Nothing had prepared him for this — and the singular nature of the moment, not to mention the NDA, meant he could confide in absolutely no one. He really, really should not have even told Callie. She had demanded it of him, and Beckett wasn't particularly worried she would carry the secret further, but it still hadn't been fair to saddle her with it.

He had no other option except to soldier on as usual while he waited for the massive machinery of Hollywood to chug along with its business of lawyers and contracts and press releases. So soldier on, he did.

Which involved, among other things, re-incorporating a stop at Sweet Claws back into his morning routine.

"Back again?" Callie asked the next morning when he arrived, sounding surprised, but not unpleasantly so.

"Hair and makeup," he explained. "I've learned my lesson."

"Have you now?" Callie's tone was dry.

They were definitely talking about more than one thing, but

now was not the time to claim true personal reform.

"So far as crew and pastries go....yes," he said.

"How are you doing?" Callie asked quietly, as she started boxing up his order.

"Ahhh...." Beckett tried to find words, failed to find words, and instead gestured with the hand holding the cup of coffee he'd just picked up, spilling a few scalding drops. He hissed and set the cup back down on the counter so he could shake off his hand. "About like that," he admitted.

Just then the bell over the door jangled, and Beckett jumped back from the counter, as if his secret could be guessed just by his proximity to Callie.

"Maybe less caffeine," Callie offered, a hint of amusement in her voice, but it wasn't cruel and was no more than he deserved. Beckett knew he was being ridiculous.

"See you!" he blurted out as he grabbed his claws and fled.

Back in his car and on his way to set, Beckett scolded himself in the safe silence of his own mind. *You are going to have to get your shit together if you're going to survive until the announcement.*

*Yeah,* some other part of his brain replied. *And it's only going to get worse from there.*

Beckett's equanimity, already a matter of dubious existence, took another dive when he actually signed the contract. That process took an extra two weeks because of the co-agent mess he'd created by wanting to fire Steve who had also gotten him the damn gig. But it had to be done if he was going to survive this. Or if the contract was going to say all the things he needed it to, not about money, but about his life. The plan was that after he signed, the casting would be announced. Then about a week later, his agency switch would follow.

When Beckett had signed contracts in the past that had happened over the internet, or more occasionally in his agent's office, or even on his first day on set. This time, the studio had let him know that someone would be bringing him papers to sign in person. Beckett figured that made sense — this wasn't the sort of contract you just dropped in the mail or trusted to a shipping service. And you certainly didn't send it over the internet.

But Beckett was not prepared to open his apartment door to find a man built like a linebacker, wearing a suit and carrying a metal briefcase. On the briefcase, a small red light was illuminated, matching the one on what looked like a souped-up, extremely clunky fitness tracker on the guy's wrist.

"Uh. Hi," Beckett said, staring at the matching red lights. It looked like something out of the superhero movie he was about to be in, not anything real.

"Hey there." The dude stepped into Beckett's apartment. He pulled out a pair of keys, one analogue and one electronic.

"Is this...normal?" Beckett asked. "For this kind of thing?"

The man shrugged. "The things with the lights track whether the briefcase and I are in appropriate proximity to each other. Keys do key things, but I gotta tell you, man, I've got no idea what's in here. I just go where they tell me."

"You have a briefcase! Full of very sensitive legal documents I have to sign! Handcuffed to you like an electronic monitoring bracelet as if you'd done some serious type of crime! And you don't know what they are?"

Beckett didn't know if this situation was hilarious or terrifying and wasn't sure he wanted to find out.

"Dude, I'm getting paid, I don't really care." He set the briefcase down on the little round table where Beckett had eaten so many meals — so many of them with Callie.

"That's terrifying!"

The guy just shrugged. "You got a pen? I've got extras if you need 'em."

Beckett took the offered pen, because it was easier and less embarrassing than digging through his drawer of miscellany for one. Before he signed, he paused to look around at his apartment — the random wicker rocking chair he'd read so many script pages in, the couch he'd made out with Callie on, the kitchen where he'd fixed his meals for the last five years. *Remember this moment*, he told himself, and then put pen to paper.

"Do I get a copy?" Beckett asked, capping the pen and handing it back to the guy along with the contract.

"Nope. That would not be maintaining security. You'll get one when it's countersigned and announced," he said, stashing everything in the briefcase and locking it back up.

The next morning at Sweet Claws, Beckett leaned closer to the counter after he'd given his order.

"Hey," he all but whispered, cognizant of the other customers in line behind him and seated at tables.

Callie looked baffled, but leaned forward to meet him. "Yeah?"

"Can I freak out at you sometime? Without an audience?" Beckett asked.

He knew it was anything but an appropriate query to throw at his ex-girlfriend, but their ease of conversation hadn't gone anywhere, and knowing that she knew his secret had been the only part of the process so far that had been easy. So he had to run with the current rapport, even if it was foolish.

Callie blinked at him, and then she laughed, the sound musical and lifting a shadow off Beckett's heart.

"Yeah, sure," she said. "Come by sometime when I'm not busy."

Beckett took Callie up on that offer the first chance he could on the following evening. By six it had been dark for hours, and the lights of the shop glowed golden against the snow as he approached the door.

"So what's up?" Callie asked, once the last group of customers had left. She stood behind the counter, her hands folded in front of her. Her posture wasn't confrontational, but it wasn't the most welcoming either.

Beckett hesitated, his gaze going unconsciously to the door.

Callie gave an exasperated sigh. "I'll close the shades and lock up if you want me to. But there's gonna be even more questions and people wondering things if I keep doing that every time you're in here. And I don't think you need rumors about your love life or anything else right now."

"It also wouldn't be fair to you," he said. That fact was tragic, but he had to at least offer her some reassurance that he was aware of what they were and weren't now — and that he could maintain some semblance of boundaries.

"That is true," Callie said slowly. Her fingers played with the edge of her wrist warmers. They were blue today, with a pattern of white gulls. "Thank you."

He stood across from her at the counter. *So I signed the thing."

"The thing we're not talking about?" she asked. The playfulness was back.

"Yeah, that thing." Beckett was almost relieved that he couldn't name it. Having to talk around the situation was somehow easier than just coming out and saying it all — from the money to the hours to the media frenzy of the thing. It was the difference between being in a tiny photo with his girlfriend on page 37 of *People* and potentially being on its cover.

He was not prepared. No one could ever be prepared for this.

"And you're freaking out?" Callie prompted him.

Beckett snapped back to the current moment. *Focus on the small, absurd stuff. It's much better than trying to understand the whole world,* he reminded himself.

"Callie, the guy had an electronic tracker on his wrist for the briefcase. It looked like more security than they use for the nuclear football."

Callie spread her hands out, palms down, on the counter, like she was steadying herself. "Holy shit."

Beckett reveled in the way she enunciated each syllable. Her reaction confirmed that he was not the crazy one here. Hollywood was.

"I know!" He put his head down on the counter and groaned into his hands.

He felt Callie touch the back of his head gently. A part of him wanted to weep at the pathetic kindness of it all.

"There, there," she said, clearly on the verge of laughter.

"Oh, fuck off," Beckett said, but his heart grew lighter and the panic shrank slightly in response.

Callie had said she wouldn't be his security blanket for this project, and she was right to do that. Beckett needed to do a lot of work with himself, both in general and so that he could successfully meet this change in circumstances as a person and as a performer and, he guessed, as a public figure.

*Am I a public figure now?* he wondered. *Was I one before?*

There were no easy answers to those questions, just as there were no easy answers to whether those questions mattered at all.

But Callie being determined to not take this as seriously as his anxiety demanded he do was, at least, good for his head. No matter what it felt like in his body, there was, at the end of the day, no such thing as an arts emergency.

Callie pet her hand through his hair a few more times.

Beckett's whole body wanted to sink into the sensation and the kindness of it. It was exactly what Marla and the rest of her *Hidden Cove* department already knew: All Beckett wanted was for someone to play with his hair and tell him what to do.

"So, now you've signed it," Callie began, her fingers still doing magic for his nerves. "Does that mean you're moving back to LA? When *Hidden Cove* is over?"

Beckett could hear the tension in her voice, feel it in her fingers even, despite the way she was trying to make a loaded question a casual one. Even though it shouldn't have really mattered to her at all at this point. They were over, Beckett reminded himself. She was, however, also playing with his hair.

*Not good, Beckett. It's your job to keep this from getting messy or at least any messier than it already has been.*

He sat up to look at her directly, and her hand fell away from his head.

"No," he said solemnly. "Except for when I have to, for press or meetings or whatever. And shooting the thing, I guess. But I think a lot of it is going to be on various locations and not out there. Aside from that... the truth is I'm still working out the rest of my life and what happens next."

"Ah." Callie didn't press the question. "We'll put a pin in that one, then."

"Yeah," Beckett agreed. "But, I'm not just going to disappear one day. Assuming you want it, you deserve more warning than that from me."

Callie nodded and bit her lip. "I appreciate that," she said. "I don't know why. But I do. So, thank you. I just want us both to be happy with the very different stuff that we need."

Beckett wasn't sure that what they each needed was all that different in the end, but both his terrible choices at Christmas and the current state of his life made that a hard argument to hypothetically win. Also he was adamantly *not* pursuing Callie. She'd broken up with him, and that was that. If that changed, it was on her to make that change, and he'd deal with it should that happen.

Oh God, he hoped it happened.

Instead of any of that, he said what small relevant thing he could. "I am working on sitting with my discomfort both about things that have gone wrong and things that I want, which is why I'm making a point to only be telling you things I'm sure of and things I have control over."

Callie tilted her head to the side as if she was stretching and scratched the back of her neck. "Can I ask you something where the words mean only exactly what the words mean?"

Beckett's heart gave a little stutter of hope, despite the question including fairly clear instructions not to hope. "Um... I can do my best," he said, like his whole soul wasn't leaping ahead.

"Do you want to grab dinner sometime?" Callie asked. "And talk. About the things we never really told each other and maybe should have?"

"Do I," Beckett said, possibly more eagerly than was seemly. "Um, as friends or —"

Callie gave a nervous laugh and looked down. "As two people who know each other," she said. "No implications. Just two people who are trying to be here now, but aren't really made for that."

Beckett nodded his head and tried not to look too giddy. Because he still loved this woman who had made a project of living the way his job required him to make a project of playing. He had so much to learn from her.

The question of where Beckett planned to live after *Hidden Cove* wasn't looming any smaller, even with the impending big announcement. While the new project meant he could defer his decision for a bit as he lived on location and waited for a bigger payday, he did not want to go into such a radical upheaval without knowing he had a home base waiting somewhere for him. He needed to make decisions while he was still safe from people trying to talk him into buying a glass mansion in the Hollywood Hills.

Once he sat down and put it to himself like that, the answer was obvious: Stay in Maine, just like he had always wanted to do and just like Robert had been telling him to do. He'd always dreaded the day he would have to leave, it had just always seemed impossible to stay.

That was no longer true.

He and Callie drove down to Bar Harbor a few days later. Beckett couldn't help but think of their first date, when they'd come this way for Korean food and Callie had kissed him in an axe-throwing parlor. None of that was going to happen today. Or possibly ever again.

"By the way," Beckett said, as they sat lingering over burgers. The day was cloudy and gray, but a fireplace was crackling merrily on the other side of the restaurant.

Callie looked up at him, clearly braced. "Yeah?"

"So you don't hear about this in a weird small-town or celebrity gossip way later. I'm going to be looking for a house nearby. Not as a place to raise some fantasy family or anything, but because my life is about to get...really, really weird, and I'm going to need a refuge, and I want it to be out here."

"So, like what? A vacation house? For when you're not living — wherever you were living before or wherever movie stars live now?"

Beckett shook his head and resisted the panicked urge to shush her.

"I'm going to shoot this thing wherever I need to shoot this thing. But no. I've lived in Maine for years. I'm going to keep living in Maine. It's just going to be — my house. So if we keep doing..." he gestured between them. "Whatever it is we're doing, you're going to be stuck with me here. And either way I figured you deserved fair warning since I know we're both off the map here and it could look like something other than it is."

He watched as Callie peered at him for a long time, her eyes flickering over his face as if she was trying to judge the truth of him. No pressure. No ulterior motives. Just two people with a connection, some messy shared history, and the same love for a way-too-small town.

Eventually he saw her give the slightest nod. Not for him, but for herself. She probably didn't even know she'd done it.

"I think we'll live," she said.

Internally, Beckett exhaled.

After that, they saw each other regularly. Not just at the shop, where Beckett stopped in dutifully every morning, but for meals and, when the weather was mild enough, hikes. They didn't go to each others' homes, they didn't go to bars and linger flirtatiously over drinks. They didn't hold hands, except for the odd hiking assist. And they didn't kiss, even when Beckett dropped Callie off at the shop at the end of whatever 'dinner with his ex-girlfriend while they talked about their shit' counted as.

And they did talk about their shit. A lot. There was so much they hadn't told each other the first time around in their mutual desperate desire to skip over the stories of what had happened to them to get to the parts about who they were.

Those stories — from Callie's accident and parents to Beckett's genuine frustration at the stifling demands of masculinity his appearance often created — filled in so many gaps. For someone whose job it was to be gazed at while pretending to be other people, Beckett was at times shocked to discover how much he needed to be seen as he truly was, frightening though it could be.

And Callie... Callie needed to be seen, too, in a way that didn't always divide her life into before and after culinary school, or the accident, or him. Where were her trauma points, and what did Beckett need to do to avoid tripping all over them again?

More importantly, what were either of them going to do the next time one of their personal pressure points came into play?

Beckett went house-hunting, sometimes with Robert tagging along, sometimes with his sister on a video call. He didn't want to do this alone; he didn't know how to do this alone! And he needed to not be making decisions that centered what he thought Callie might want in a house or on the potential to raise a family... with her or anyone.

What he needed was a house for who and what he was now and that would help him survive the coming storm. He needed quiet and space for guests. His parents liked to travel, his siblings would appreciate the hospitality, and his niblings were getting old enough that he could have them out in the summertime. He wanted to be able to take the burden of hosting holiday dinners off of Robert now and then, even if he was 'just' cool single Uncle Beckett.

He was beginning to learn — slowly and probably belatedly — that he needed to stop comparing his life to others, for good or for ill. What he thought he wanted, what other people thought he should want — none of that mattered. He just needed to find the things his soul recognized as home and run with that.

That realization, once he reached it, was remarkably freeing.

In the middle of that process, because everything Beckett could possibly have feelings about was destined to happen at the same exact time, he got an invitation in the mail.

Thankfully, it did not come with blinking security bracelets. Nor did it require him to go to LA It was a much simpler matter, at least in some senses.

It was the invitation to Antonia's wedding. While he'd been warned and was happy for her, he felt tension all through his body as he looked at the heavy cream-colored card. Antonia was special to him — when they'd been together and in all the years since when they hadn't been. The thought of anything changing that terrified him and filled him with a completely unfair grief.

"Pull it together, Beckett," he admonished himself at the table of his tiny apartment. "She never belonged to you, and she's certainly not going to belong to someone else just 'cause she's getting married."

He felt a little better for saying that out loud, because Beckett Brown did not have the time to let the patriarchy make him sad about a happy event for one of his dearest friends. He splashed some cold water on his face and then called Antonia right away to RSVP.

"Of course I'll be there," he said as soon as she answered the phone. He was grateful the date was before the superhero thing was scheduled to begin shooting — otherwise, he had no idea what he'd be able to promise.

"That's delightful, Beckett, but you need to fill out the card like everyone else."

"Oh, sorry, right. I got excited. And things here have been...." He searched for the words but couldn't find them. "A lot," he finally settled on. "So much and a lot."

He could picture her face in response to that down the other end of the line.

"Does that mean you will or will not be bringing a plus-one because I, too, saw lobster girl's breakup video?" Antonia asked.

Beckett stammered. He didn't know. And he also didn't know what he thought about Callie being dubbed *lobster girl*. Or how to talk to Antonia about the big, big chaos coming for his life.

"Honestly, I have no idea," he finally said.

"Figure that out before you send in the card, would you," she said drily. "But what's going on?"

"Callie and I...we're kinda dating? Ish? Again? I don't know?"

"How can you not know, Beckett?"

That, honestly, was a very good question. He should know. Time and frequency and the very energy between them all said yes. But they'd been so chaste with each other, despite the obvious chemistry. And while that didn't inherently make or break dating, they had always been very sexual people with each other, so he felt justified in considering the situation unclear.

"We don't touch. We don't kiss," he tried to explain. "We spend a huge amount of time together within the constraints of our schedules —"

"Has it occurred to you," Antonia began, "that you're friends?"

The words hit Beckett like a blow. Not because being friends was a bad thing or lesser, but because he and Antonia were suddenly discussing more than the Callie situation.

"There's a vibe," he offered.

"We have a vibe," she countered.

"That we do," Beckett acknowledged. They hadn't been together in years and years, but it was true the vibe had never really left.

"And we never let it get in the way of us adoring each other in the ways that actually work for each other," Antonia said. "So. Figure out if you're both being rightly cautious —"

"Or figure out if it's something else," Beckett finished for her.

"Exactly that," Antonia said. "And if it turns out you are friends right now, that's a pretty good basis for a romance too, assuming that's what you're both looking for from each other."

As much as Beckett needed to turn these ideas over in his head, he needed to do it on his own, without either Antonia or Callie as an immediate witness to all his feelings.

"There's something else you should know," he blurted out, suddenly changing gears before he had consciously intended to.

Antonia paused for a beat. "...yes?"

"I have recently signed a thing that I cannot talk about," Beckett started. "Sometime in the next few months it is going to be in a press release that actually merits being a press release. And it is not television." That, he hoped, was enough words to give Antonia the scope of the situation.

"Oh!" she said. Then, "Ohhhhhh."

Beckett laughed as the shape of the thing hit her, and she joined in.

"Beckett!" she exclaimed. "Beckett, Beckett, Beckett."

"I know!" he replied. Abruptly, he realized he finally felt giddy about this future instead of being terrified by it.

"At the wedding," Antonia said seriously, "we are going to jump up and down and scream."

On their next mutual day off — Callie was still calibrating the shop schedule to the production schedule — Beckett and Callie went looking once more for Troppy, the wayward tropical bird. And Beckett was also determined to be brave.

"So, I have to ask," Beckett said as they walked along the coastal path. February in Maine was still deep winter, and the sea was gray and cold. But there was a stark beauty to the black rocks and evergreens against the overcast sky he would always love.

"Yeah?" Callie glanced over at him.

*Now or never, Beckett.*

"We keep talking about our stuff and rehashing what happened to...understand what happened? So we can move past it and be friends? To...look forward to...some sort of future with us? Like... this has been profoundly grounding and satisfying, but I have no idea what we're doing, and I thought I should ask instead of making up stories in my head."

Beckett was terrified of her answer. But this inquiry was necessary. Not just because he wanted to know, but because he had learned from the past and was absolutely not going to drift sideways into another disaster.

Callie stopped on the path, her fingers flexing around the hiking stick she had taken to using for their walks.

"I really want to kiss you right now, just so you know," she said. "But I'm not going to do that."

"Is that because we're not dating ever again, or....?" Beckett trailed off, torn between a riot of fear and hope and so deeply mindful of Antonia's advice.

"What?" Callie looked confused. "No, this thing we are doing is definitely dating. I just don't want things to be messy. We know the chemistry works; that's not the thing we need to be exploring here."

"Oh!" Beckett felt staggered. This was not how he would have done things if he had been in the position to be in the driver's seat.

*Which is exactly why you're not in the driver's seat*, his better, self-critical self scolded.

Callie narrowed her eyes at him. "Did you not know that?"

Beckett held up his hands. "I am working on assuming nothing until someone says it out loud." He looked down at the trail beneath their feet for a moment. "I am also working on making sure me and everyone else gets to say what they need to say out loud."

"Oh. Well then," Callie said. "Good job. Consider that point settled."

# CHAPTER 37

44°28'46.3"N 67°30'54.7"W
Temp: 37.9°F
Pressure: 30.22 inHg
Wind: 11.4 mph, S
Visibility: 6.00 mi

ONCE BECKETT HAD ASKED the question of whether they were dating again out loud, it took another three weeks until they finally kissed again and only another eleven minutes after that until Beckett was on his knees in the cabin of the *Lobster Taco* eating Callie out while she leaned against her kitchen counter.

What had suddenly changed things between them? Calie didn't know. But from the moment Beckett had asked for confirmation of what they were doing together this time, it had been obvious to her that a clock was ticking and that it was going to lead, inevitably, to this particular place.

Well, she'd thought she be lying down. But other than that....

They did, actually, eventually make it to her bed, albeit sideways and still not entirely undressed. When Beckett finally slid inside her the chaos of the moment eased suddenly, their eyes locked, and Callie knew, just absolutely knew, they were both remembering the last time they had done this and the absolutely ridiculous thing Beckett had said.

Suddenly she was laughing, which was an extremely strange sensation with Beckett's dick inside her. That he then started laughing too made it all the more absurd.

Callie looked at the ceiling as they tried to get themselves under some vague control, but it was all too funny.

"Chaos sex is the best sex!" she shouted, knowing she'd have to give apology claws to her neighbors on the dock tomorrow. Again.

Beckett grabbed her by the hips and yanked her onto him, but fucking the laughter out of her wasn't going to work.

"Hey," he said, as she stared up at him through her hopefully sexy giggles. "I love you."

With that, Callie subsided and brought her hand to his face, grazing her fingers over his features. The words were so serious and meant so much to her, and the feelings were ones that she deeply, deeply reciprocated. The giddy laughter and the pure comedy of the moment also warmed her heart. This was them without fear, without auditioning for each other, without trying to be perfect or forget past mistakes.

Her fingers fluttered against Beckett's cheek.

"Love you too, baby girl," she said. She had absolutely no idea what had possessed her.

Above her, whatever composure Beckett was trying for shattered and the mutual hilarity started all over again.

"You are a ridiculous human being," he said.

"You definitely started the ridiculousness," Callie countered, shifting her hips.

"I'm not arguing with you about this right now," Beckett said, and crushed his mouth to hers.

After that, they both stopped being verbal for a while.

Just as she and Beckett were really and truly beginning again, *Hidden Cove* was drawing to its inexorable close. All of Fly-Debate was awash in feelings about it. Friendships, businesses, relationships, traffic — all of it would change when the show left town. The drawn-out goodbye leading up to it didn't make that easier for anyone.

There were so many big parties: The start of the last episode, series wrap day for various actors, and the big giant actual end of everything. Robert hosted a lot of them and Callie was invited to almost everything. She even went to some, in between shifts at the shop. This was her community, too, and there was real grief in seeing so many familiar faces for the last time.

Still, some were staying. Robert and his family, of course, and a few others too. Beckett in his own roundabout way. He had been house-hunting she knew, and as curious as Callie was about the process — she loved to scroll through real estate listings as much as anyone — she bit her tongue and determinedly did not ask. That process was about Beckett, not her. Or them.

Maybe if they hadn't started sleeping together again she would have asked. Maybe, too, if he hadn't already started coming and going for his next project and Callie hadn't been wary of looking insecure. But they were and he was, so she didn't. She didn't want to say anything that could be misconstrued or could encourage Beckett or even herself to rush. They could both stand to have their resolve tested.

The announcement that Beckett had been cast in the tights-and-cape movie, as he persisted in calling it, came out a few weeks after *Hidden Cove* had wrapped and the town was helping the last of the stragglers packing up their lives to return to Los Angeles.

Callie watched Beckett brace himself for the world to be strange to him — and it surely would be — but Fly-Debate was just Fly-Debate. People in town were happy for him, of course, but no one really cared in a deeper way than that. Or, if they did, they mostly didn't let it show.

Sydney did, but Sydney was back in New York. And Emma, but that was because she was trying to get Beckett to hook her up with a trainee position in set decoration and design.

Callie, for her part, was relieved. She was no longer holding a terrible and dangerous secret, and Beckett could finally freak out to people other than her. She, after all, had a doughnut shop to run through all this upheaval. Without *Hidden Cove,* her hours would stabilize and there would possibly be a more dramatic shift towards mail order as so many of her regulars left. Finding the new normal was going to be a process.

Because not only was she losing so many of her regulars forever and Beckett for months on end, Emma was leaving too. Beckett's desire to make sure his new gig meant work for the people of Fly-Debate and *Hidden Cove* who wanted it meant that Emma also flying out west, for a six-month production assistant trainee program that would hopefully funnel her into a career in set design. How on earth Callie was going to survive without Emma's combat boots and reality TV wisdom, she had no idea.

Amidst all this upheaval, Callie did not have the monopoly on Beckett's time she might have wished. He spent a lot of time helping friends and coworkers pack, and there was an entire week of madness that involved him closing on a house Callie hadn't seen and that he refused to show her. Apparently it needed major work and contractors were going to do that while he was off playing make-believe. In the meantime he was still living in his little apartment, having taken the lease over from the production. They had talked a bit about him joining her in the *Lobster Taco* until his new place was ready, but beyond cozy overnights, the boat really wasn't big enough for the two of them.

They did, at least, get to have an awesome romantic weekend getaway to New York for Beckett's friend's wedding.

For how busy those months were, Callie also understood them as a calm before a storm none of them really understood. A long-distance relationship. An extremely high profile and physically demanding shoot. A hyper-engaged, decades-old fan base. Neither of them truly knew what they were getting into. And most days that was okay.

In the fall, Beckett began to leave for Vancouver properly. At first it was just for just a few weeks at a time, with long weekends and even whole weeks back in Maine as the engine of pre-production got underway. But when November came, with its short days and fog-swathed nights, Callie dropped him off at the airport one more time and kissed him goodbye for the next six months.

Beckett had warned her he was going to have to lose the long hair and the beard for the role, but she had originally thought he'd do that in Fly-Debate and she'd be able to get used to the new look in person.

"Are you nervous?" she had asked. "About what I'll think?"

"No," he'd said. "Maybe? I just don't want to bring the process of finding this character — or people reacting to it — into our lives here until I have to."

And that had been fair, so she had left it be.

Callie had not expected the aesthetic change to be a livestream event on social media. Beckett, apparently, hadn't expected that either, agreed on the fly, and then texted her in a panic right before it started.

She had no idea what advice or safety she could offer him from afar. But she knew him well enough to know that this was, if he let it, the type of stuff he had nightmares about.

**Callie:** *This is a performance now. So give them that.*

**Beckett:** *Good. Fucking. Plan. Okay. I've got this. Hope you still think I'm hot.*

Callie suspected that, even with his enthusiasm for her pep talk, the whole thing felt like a rite of passage that no one else could comprehend, despite all the people watching it who thought they understood just that.

Selfishly, she was actually a little worried about the change. Would the new look still be her jam? Would he look older? More corporate? Whatever the effect would turn out to be, she knew she'd get over it, but her worries, as she sat on the *Lobster Taco* in front of her little stove and watched the drama unfold on her phone, were unfounded. With the length trimmed away, Beckett's hair showed far more of the stunning silver she had long known was there, and holy shit, his jawline.

*I like it*, she typed in the little comment box, and watched as her comment got dozens of hearts and awwwwws in response.

*So much for keeping that secret.*

For half a second, she worried Beckett would be angry. They hadn't really talked about what to do about the status of their relationship in terms of the general public, other than *no formal announcements*. This wasn't formal, but it sure felt like an announcement.

But then Beckett shouted her name into the phone camera and waved. "Hope you still like it when production dyes most of it black!"

Callie wasn't so sure about that, but it wasn't her hair or her movie. Life would continue on. Tomorrow, if nothing else, she'd have to get up early to deal with a new deluge of doughnut orders.

Not only did Beckett's hours become longer and the work more grueling as the project moved from pre-production to actual shoot, the requirement of secrecy meant calls from set, even in his trailer, weren't really an option. That particular prohibition, plus the time difference and how few non-working hours he was awake each day, so vastly limited Callie's ability to talk to him that they took to having long, involved, and somewhat faux-Victorian email exchanges with each other until the joke stretched so thin that it fell flat. But typing remained a much easier way for them to keep in touch, and allowed them to continue focusing on clear communication, even at such a distance.

Callie missed him, of course, and there was a different rhythm to their life together while they were apart. But she had been so self-sufficient for so long, that she certainly wasn't miserable without him in her life every day.

The same could possibly not be said for Beckett. He struggled, especially at first, and Callie worried from a distance, although she tried not to. This was Beckett's life and career, and while she would support him any way she could, at the end of the day, it was also his responsibility to get himself together. *Even superheroes need therapy* quickly became a mantra they both subscribed to, and while that wasn't a new thing in either of their lives it felt more important now than ever before.

Callie watched as Beckett built a community for himself on his new project, having cast and crew for dinner at his home away from home and leading hiking expeditions on weekends. *Super Beckett* got added to *Saint Beckett*, when people talked about him on the internet.

With Beckett finding his footing, Callie knew it was time to face some of the business conundrums she'd been putting off for some time. The mail order situation was real. And a doughnut empire didn't become an empire on the shoulders of a sole-proprietor shop in the middle of nowhere. If she wanted to expand, now was the time. Should she rent industrial kitchen space? Should she hire employees she didn't see every day or know as she had her first hire?

Callie talked it over with Beckett via email and with Sydney over the phone. She talked it over with her parents, too, when she called to tell them that she and Beckett were back together and finding their way forward again. Her mom was her mom and didn't sound enthused about any of it, but her dad asked her all sorts of business questions about the shop. Ultimately, her parents let her talk and didn't try to dissuade her, which was another entry in the progress column.

In the end, she took the leap, terrifying as it was. She rented a storefront and kitchen space in Bangor, and started her first *Sweet Claws* satellite to serve the, evidently, strong and growing market for celebrity-adjacent mail-order pastry claws. Now she was the one with a commute to and from Bangor half the days in a week.

She quickly understood why Beckett had always chosen to come home to Fly-Debate instead of staying in the city. This tiny town, the rocks, the ocean, even the desolate beach where once had been the fictional village of Hidden Cove...this was home.

44°35'18.8"N 67°25'18.5"W
Temp: 46.9°F
Pressure: 29.60 inHg
Wind: 5.75 mph, S
Visibility: ≥ 10.00 mi

BY THE TIME FILMING WAS over, Beckett felt both stronger and more exhausted than he had ever been in his life, both mentally and physically. He needed to sleep for a year, see just how much permanent damage he'd done to his knees in the course of the shoot, and make some sort of decision about whether he really wanted to continue carrying about this much muscle for the rest of his acting and personal life. On one hand, he sort of liked it. On the other, none of his clothes fit right and maintaining it would require the sort of work he suspected he wasn't really into. Oh well. He'd figure it out eventually.

When he finally got to leave Vancouver for the last time, it was not nearly as wrenching as the end of *Hidden Cove*. How could it be? The difference between a six month shoot in a major city and five years in a small town was significant. Even so, he had a new film family now, and he'd miss them dearly. Of course, eventually the effects would be done, the trailer would be released, and they'd all get to see each other again for the media tour nonsense.

Callie picked him up at the Bangor airport  Beckett nearly collapsed into her with relief, before he picked her up and swung her around with joy.

"Okay, you," Callie said, when he finally set her back on her feet. "Let's get you home."

Beckett nearly dozed off on the drive, kept awake only by Callie's chatter and his own delight in being exactly where he was.

"Hey, do you want to see the house?" he asked.

"Wait what?" Callie said.

Beckett knew she'd given up thinking the house would ever be done and had just decided not to press the issue while he was still away, which he had honestly appreciated. While he was mostly able to be hands off with the contractors, every time the house had demanded his attention during the shoot had been unspeakably stressful.

"They're still doing some stuff, and the next problem is landscaping —"

"Landscaping?" Callie asked, incredulous.

"Don't get excited. Honestly, I'm trying to keep the land as wild as possible, but some of it needs to be cleared and also pollinators need something other than a three-foot high carpet of wild mint."

Callie laughed. The sound was a balm to him after so long of not hearing it in person.

"So the mystery house is still absolutely, completely, totally not ready then?" she asked.

"Nope, but wanna go check it out anyway?"

"You see the GPS, plug in the directions," she said.

Beckett did so eagerly, even as he tried to calm his racing brain. One of the agreements between him and Callie was not getting ahead of where they were at any given moment and he knew he was struggling right now.

He sat up in the passenger seat when Callie pulled down the road his house was on. He hadn't been here since the previous autumn, when the house had been in a startling state of disrepair. Now his entire being exhaled when he saw it sitting on its little rise, with fresh siding and a new roof and surrounded by a carpet of overgrown plant life blooming in the first pale sunlight of spring. This was home.

And God, he could not wait to move in.

Callie parked in front of the house and peered up at it, her forehead doing that thoughtful frown of concentration Beckett had always found so adorable.

"I like it," she finally announced, and whatever tension Beckett was still holding melted from his body. "You make good choices."

Beckett rolled his head sideways to look at her. She was vibrant, glowing with happiness and her own steady, unquenchable sense of self. He was never going to get tired of looking at her.

"Hey," he said. "Wanna get married?"

The words were out of his mouth before he even registered them. And while he should have been panicking, because this question in this moment might definitely be against their rules, all he felt was serene.

Callie stared at him, clearly caught off-guard but smiling. "What the fuck?"

It wasn't the worst reaction she could have had. But Beckett felt maybe less serene now.

"Sorry! Sorry, sorry, sorry." He scrubbed his hands over his face. "I had — I had a plan, but I am so fucking exhausted and I am going to go sleep for a week as soon as I get anywhere that isn't an airport or a construction zone, but I have been thinking about this for months and I have a ring literally burning a hole in my pocket...so...?" He looked around, at the house with the windows that were still empty and dark and that was surrounded by mud rutted with the tires of contractors' trucks. "I did not mean to do this while we're like...sitting in your car in my driveway at a house we can't live in yet. Although, fuck, I mean, that's a whole separate ask."

"Okay, this is very exciting," Callie said slowly. She looked like she was trying not to laugh. "But you're blurting things again. And sometimes that's charming but sometimes —"

"It's disastrous," Beckett finished for her.

"Yes. Definitely. So let's just check a couple of things." She turned in her seat to face him, pulling one knee up to rest her chin on. "Are there any conditions on your offer? Necessary travel? Content of doughnut shop social media posts? Babies?" Her smile was broad, and her tone was teasing.

"God, no." Beckett let his head drop back against the headrest. "Just put up with my shit." He lifted his hand from his knee to gesture vaguely. "Whatever our lives are gonna be, they're gonna be."

"Because I have a huge and very successful business —" Callie continued.

God, he loved her relentlessness. He loved everything about her so much. "I know, and I'm gonna be gone so much for work, it's all good," he said.

"— and a boat that I am very much attached to," Callie continued.

"I'm very attached to her too," Beckett said. "Whatever your answer, don't sell the boat."

"Is this just because you missed me? And think you can't live without me?" Callie asked very seriously, despite the laughter that remained at the edges of her voice.

"No. Although I did miss you. So much. Fuck." As much as he had ultimately survived and even thrived on the shoot, now that he was here with Callie he couldn't bear the idea of being apart from her for that long again. Although there would surely be more separations of the kind. And they would get through them just as well.

"But no," he went on. "This is because we survived the last six months and the social media drama and everything else although — fair warning, that's gonna get even weirder when the movie actually comes out."

"I'm sure you're right, but Beckett, it has already been so fucking weird. I don't think I'd notice another level of it."

"Shhhh, don't tempt the universe," he whispered.

Callie laughed outright. "I'll tempt whatever I damn well want," she said firmly. "Now are you going to show me that ring, or what?"

"You want me to do this here in the car?" Beckett asked. His voice was shaking, he realized. At least it was with pure excitement. "Or do you want me to kneel in the mint forest?"

"You really want to kneel for this thing, huh?" Callie asked, unfastening her seatbelt.

"I do," Beckett said, grabbing her hand and squeezing. "I really do."

"All right," Callie said. "Let's get out there and do this then."

"Is that a yes, then?" Beckett asked.

"Yeah," Callie said. "It is. But I'm not fucking you out here until the landscaping is done, just to be clear."

It was the work of a moment for Beckett to get down on one knee, hold out the ring box and ask the question, but he made sure to steady himself first and think about what he was really asking and why. This wasn't about his dream of getting to propose to someone again — he'd done that clumsily more than once before— and it wasn't about getting or even being married. It was about Callie and partnership and things both too big and too easy for all the labels he'd let himself get obsessed with.

So instead of just asking the question, he told her that. All of it, until she'd said yes and dropped down in the riot of vegetation next to him hidden from the sun and the construction and the public life the both of them each now had.

"So hey, do we have to, like, do a thing, or can we elope?" Callie asked.

"Eloping sounds absolutely great," he said.

Instead of keeping his fantasies about what that would look like in his head, he spun it out for her right then and there.

"So we could go to the courthouse," he suggested, "pay the fee with a couple of rolls of quarters, have complete random strangers as witnesses, and escape up to Canada for a couple of days of honeymoon, and then tell absolutely no one until we both felt ready to deal with it? Maybe have a big party here if we're in the mood?"

Callie looked at him appraisingly. He knew that look. She was weighing his heart again.

"That," she said, "is possibly the best idea you've ever had."

Beckett leaned in to kiss her. He could not have agreed more.

*Fin.*